SEBASTIAN DARKE

Prince of Pirates

Also by Philip Caveney

Sebastian Darke: Prince of Fools

SEBASTIAN DARKE

DARKE

Prince of Pirates

PHILIP CAVENEY

DELACORTE PRESS

Published by Delacorte Press
an imprint of Random House Children's Books
a division of Random House, Inc.
New York

Delacorte Press and colophon are registered trademarks of
Random House, Inc.

Visit us on the Web! www.randomhouse.com/teens

Educators and librarians, for a variety of teaching tools, visit us at
www.randomhouse.com/teachers

Library of Congress Cataloging-in-Publication Data
Caveney, Philip.
Sebastian Darke : prince of pirates / Philip Caveney. — 1st American ed.
p.   cm.
Summary: Having concluded that he will never be a jester, half-elvish
seventeen-year-old Sebastian sets out with his friends to seek buried
pirate treasure but someone—or something—is following them.
ISBN 978-0-385-73468-4 (hardcover) — ISBN 978-0-385-90466-7 (hardcover
library binding) — ISBN 978-0-375-89198-4 (e-book) [1. Adventure and
adventurers—Fiction. 2. Supernatural—Fiction. 3. Witches—Fiction.
4. Buried treasure—Fiction. 5. Humorous stories.] I. Title.
PZ7.C29124Sef 2009
[Fic]—dc22   2008004702

The text of this book is set in 11-point Palatino.

Book design by Kenny Holcomb

Printed in the United States of America

10 9 8 7 6 5 4 3 2 1

First American Edition

For everyone in the Writers' Workshop,
past, present, and future. Thanks for your
good advice and encouragement across the years.
In particular for Terie, who provided a timely
introduction; for Ed, who drives me around and
never complains; and for Eric, who never lived
to see his own words in print.

PART ONE

CHAPTER 1

THE FOREST OF GELTANE

The ancient wooden caravan had been crossing the wide stretch of plain for several days. Pulled by a single buffalope, it was making decidedly slow progress. Now the caravan creaked to a halt a short distance from the edge of a mighty forest.

The owner of the caravan sat perched on the wooden seat, clutching the reins and staring thoughtfully into the trees. He was what many plain-spoken people referred to as a "breed"—the offspring of a human father and an elvish mother. He was not yet out of his teens and his tall lanky frame was loosely draped in the colorful uniform of a jester, one that had clearly been designed to fit a much bigger man. A garish three-pronged hat was perched on his head.

On the sides of his caravan were painted the words SEBASTIAN DARKE, PRINCE OF FOOLS. The word "Sebastian" looked somehow different to the rest. It had been added in a wobbly, amateurish hand, clearly overpainting another name that had been there before.

Alexander, his father, had been a very successful jester. After his untimely death Sebastian had tried to take up where his father left off, but his recent visit to the city of Keladon had taught him one valuable lesson: that whatever skills he possessed, he was not cut out to be a jester. His future lay in a different direction, and this journey, more than anything else, was his attempt to discover what that future might hold for him.

"This looks depressingly familiar," said the buffalope in a slow, gloomy voice. He too was gazing straight ahead into the thick green ranks of the forest, his apprehension fueled by a journey through those self-same woods in the not-too-distant past. "I can't believe we're going through there again."

"What's the problem?" asked a voice to their left, and they both turned to look as a little warrior on a tiny pony came riding abreast of them. Though his voice was deep and sonorous, the face that stared out from under his bronze helmet was smooth and baby-like, completely devoid of hair. His large blue eyes showed not a trace of concern. "Surely, Max, if you've passed through the forest of Geltane once before—"

"It was no picnic," interrupted the buffalope. "There are *things* in there. . . ."

"Things?" The little warrior shrugged. His name was Cornelius; he was a Golmiran and, like most of his proud northern race, he didn't know the meaning of fear. He looked up at Sebastian. "What's he talking about?" he muttered. "What *things*?"

The elfling considered for a moment. "Things that slither," he said at length. "You couldn't see them and yet you knew they were there. You could hear them moving in the trees high above you." He frowned, remembering. "And then there were the lupers, of course. We never encountered any in the woods, but we heard them howling every night."

"We've seen off lupers before now," said Cornelius dismissively. He reached down to rest his hand on the intricately crafted handle of his sword. "Like all creatures, they have a healthy respect for a length of sharpened steel. And they're not so fearsome. Why, even Max managed to fight off two of them."

Max fixed Cornelius with an indignant stare. "What do you mean, *even* Max? I'll have you know, among my own kind I'm considered quite a warrior."

"Quite a worrier, you mean! You haven't stopped complaining. It's one thing after another. Your hooves ache, your shoulders hurt, your snout itches—"

"It's all right for you—you don't have the task of pulling this blooming caravan. I said before we ever left the city that the two of you had packed more equipment than we needed. I understand that we have to bring provisions, but you brought enough to supply an army!"

Sebastian sighed. Cornelius and Max had been bickering like this all the way from the city. It was unbearable, particularly when he was in such low spirits. In leaving Keladon, he had also left Queen Kerin, the woman he loved with all his heart. But she had told him that they simply could not be together. She had said it with tears in her eyes, but she had meant it just the same. And any day now she would be marrying some slope-headed dummy of a prince from the neighboring kingdom, even though she had freely admitted that she did not love him. It would be a marriage of convenience, undertaken for her people, to bring peace and harmony between the kingdoms of Keladon and Bodengen. It made Sebastian's blood boil because he was convinced that, deep down, Queen Kerin loved him back. But he knew that there was nothing he could do. He would simply have to try and forget her.

Meanwhile Max and Cornelius went right on bickering.

"Perhaps if you put more effort into pulling the caravan and less into moaning all the time, we'd be making better progress. We should have reached the forest of Geltane yesterday afternoon!"

"That's easy for you to say, being carried everywhere

by Phantom. I don't see you offering to walk occasionally to give her a rest."

"Perhaps you'd like me to strap the saddle on my back and let her ride me from time to time?"

"Oh, well, now you're just being—"

"Enough!" snapped Sebastian, with such force that both Cornelius and Max turned to look at him. He glared from one to the other, making no attempt to mask his irritation. "Do you think we could journey in silence for a while? Your constant arguing is giving me a headache!"

There was a long pause while his two companions studied him warily. But Max could never stay silent for long.

"Still feeling glum, are we?" he said.

" 'Glum' is not the word I would use," said Sebastian ruefully. " 'Broken-hearted' is closer to it."

"Plenty more fish in the sea," muttered Cornelius.

"Yes, great, if you wish to have a relationship with a *fish*. I, on the other hand, fell in love with a woman—and not just any woman. The most beautiful in all the kingdom."

Max wrinkled his nose. "Hmmph! I didn't think she was that much of a catch," he said.

"Not much of a catch?" Sebastian could scarcely believe his pointed ears. "She was the Princess of Keladon! With our help, she deposed her wicked uncle and became queen. Of *course* she was a catch. If

I'd married her, I'd be minted now. I'd never have to lift a finger ever again."

Cornelius edged Phantom closer and reached up to pat Sebastian's hip. "It was never in the cards, my friend," he said, with what sounded like genuine regret. "I *did* try to warn you. Besides, think about what you're saying. You're not the sort who's happy to sit around in the lap of luxury. You're a man for adventure! Just think, if you'd married *her,* there's no way you'd be out here with us on the trail of pirate treasure."

"No," agreed Sebastian wistfully. "I suppose not."

"Imagine," said Cornelius, warming to his theme. "The treasure of Captain Callinestra, lost for centuries . . . and *we* have the map." He patted his breastplate, beneath which, Sebastian knew, he had a hidden pocket where he kept his most precious belongings. "So come on, I vote we crack on and put some more distance behind us before the sun goes down." He pointed across the plains to where the great golden ball of heat was already beginning its slow climb down to the horizon. "We'll want to find a suitable place to put up for the night, won't we?"

Sebastian nodded and slapped the reins against the buffalope's flanks.

"Was that really necessary?" complained Max. "You could just ask!" But he moved obediently toward the trees.

Sebastian looked left and right, searching for a suitable path into the forest, and after a few moments he spied one, a dark opening beneath low-hanging branches. The earth there was lined and rutted with the imprints of many wheels and countless hooves, so it seemed a likely spot.

Max sniffed at the opening suspiciously. "This is not the path we took last time," he observed.

"I'm sure it doesn't matter," said Sebastian. "It's clearly much used."

Max snorted. "I'd forgotten how dark it is in there," he muttered. "Dark and creepy-looking." But he kept going, and soon the caravan and its occupants were moving into the forest. The sun seemed to go out like a snuffed candle.

It was pretty much as Sebastian remembered it, an eternally twilight world, where countless gnarled limbs rose up sheer on either side of them, to lose themselves in a swaying green canopy far overhead. But something was different. This time he was struck by how silent it was in here. Not a single bird sang, not a pair of wings whirred, and even though the foliage stirred restlessly in the wind, not a rustle did it make. It was as though this part of the forest was quite dead. He remembered how, on their previous journey, it had been rich with the sounds of countless birds; and that when darkness fell, there were other sounds, sinister noises and stirrings aplenty.

"I don't like taking a different path," said Max nervously. "How do we know it will get us to the far side of the forest?"

"They say all routes do that eventually," Sebastian told him.

"Yes, well, I've got a bad feeling about this. Couldn't we just go round it?"

"We'd lose too much time," Cornelius assured him. "Geltane forest is the biggest in the Mid Lands. Only the jungles of Mendip to the south are bigger, and they are reputed to go on forever."

"Nothing goes on forever," said Sebastian. And then he added with the ghost of a smile, "Except possibly Max."

"Oh, don't you worry, young master," said Max, missing the dig completely. "We buffalopes are known for our longevity. I've a good few summers in me yet."

Sebastian and Cornelius exchanged amused glances.

"And a good few complaints, no doubt," murmured Sebastian.

Cornelius chuckled. "Perhaps you are already beginning to heal," he observed.

Sebastian shrugged. "Oh, I don't know," he said.

"Sometimes I forget about her for a while and everything seems fine . . . then, all of a sudden, I see her in my mind's eye and I think how it *could* have been."

Cornelius sighed. "Sebastian, it was never in the cards. A commoner and somebody of royal blood—it just wasn't meant to be. You need to set your sights a bit lower, my friend. There are plenty of girls out there. Ordinary girls, who won't look down their noses at you."

"You say that, and yet Princess Kerin never—
Shush! Listen!"

There was the sound Sebastian remembered with such dread. A dry rustling noise, as if dead leaves were being dragged slowly across tree bark. He looked this way and that, peering into the gloom, but he could detect no trace of movement anywhere around him. He glanced down at Cornelius.

"You hear it?" he whispered.

Cornelius nodded and listened. He looked decidedly unconcerned. "Tree serpents, I suppose," he said at last.

Max jerked his head round to look at the Golmiran. "Tree serpents?" he echoed. "Are you sure?"

"Not positive, but I've heard of such things. Big snakes. They coil themselves in the branches overhead, waiting to drop down on their prey."

Max swallowed loudly. "And . . . what do they eat, these . . . serpents?"

Cornelius considered for a moment. "Oh . . . pretty much anything that's slow-moving," he said. He rode on for a few moments before elaborating. "You see, they hang there, some distance up, and they fix their gaze on whatever's passing below. But if it's moving too quickly, by the time they've fallen from the heights, their prey has passed. Then they have the irksome task of slithering all the way up the tree again on an empty belly. So you see, if you move briskly enough, you have nothing to fear."

"I see . . ." Max actually picked up his pace dramatically for several steps before something dawned on him.

"Just a moment! This is another of your stories, isn't it?" he cried. "Like that yarn you spun me about the grundersnat on the road to Keladon. Just a callous trick to make me hurry!"

Cornelius's baby face split into a huge grin. "You should have seen your face!" he cried. "I've never seen anything so funny in all my life." He threw back his head and laughed heartily.

"Cornelius," said Sebastian, puzzled, "you shouldn't make jokes about things like—"

A sharp cracking sound from under the front wheels of the caravan startled him. He glanced over the side and saw that they had just passed over a scattering of dry white sticks. He looked closer. No, not sticks . . . bones . . .

Cornelius suddenly stopped laughing. Sebastian turned back to look at his friend. The little warrior seemed frozen in his saddle, staring up into the trees in apparent astonishment.

"Cornelius?" said Sebastian. "What's wrong?"

And then, with heart-stopping suddenness, a huge snake came hurtling down from the forest canopy, striking Cornelius and knocking him clean out of his saddle.

CHAPTER 2

COILS OF TERROR

Sebastian sat there, rigid with shock, staring down at the enormous serpent that now had Cornelius gripped in its mighty coils. It was as long as six ponies standing nose to tail, a great green and gray creature with black zigzag markings running the length of its scaly back. Cornelius was struggling desperately to escape but his arms were pinned to his sides and all he could do was lash out frantically with his little legs. Phantom, meanwhile, was lying on her side, snorting and kicking in sheer terror.

Sebastian's mind was a blur and his muscles seemed to have lost all their power. He hated serpents, and this was the biggest he had seen in his entire life.

"Young master!" It was Max's voice that brought him out of his spell. "You must act quickly—he'll be killed!"

Sebastian nodded. Somehow he willed himself into action. He leaped down from the caravan, reaching for his sword as he did so, and ran quickly toward the writhing, twisting coils, his arm raised to strike.

"Stay back!" snarled Cornelius through gritted teeth. "No sense . . . in both of us . . . being killed!"

Sebastian ignored that. He brought the razor-sharp sword down in a hissing arc, thinking it would cleave deep into the serpent's flesh; but the blade just struck sparks off the creature's diamond-hard scales and glanced off. Sebastian stared at the sword stupidly for a moment. Then the serpent's tail came swishing round in a heavy half-circle and struck him hard in the chest, knocking him backward. The forest floor slammed against his shoulders, driving all the air out of him, and an instant later he felt the serpent's pointed tail slide around his middle, gripping him so tightly that he cried out with the pain of it.

Then he was being lifted through the air, and when he opened his eyes, he saw that the serpent was pulling him ever closer to its open jaws. He was afforded a terrifying view of a pink glistening throat and a wriggling forked tongue, fringed by rows of fangs that dripped colorless venom. His arms were free but he had lost his sword and could do nothing but make his hands into fists, and be prepared to go to his doom punching with the last of his strength.

He was dimly aware of a bellowing sound some-where below him and realized that it was Max, making angry buffalope noises, but what good could he do while he was still hitched to the caravan? There was a band of steel tightening around Sebastian's chest; he could no longer get his breath and the ser-pent's huge mouth was opening to receive him.

Is this how it is to end? he thought. *What a stupid way to die!*

Then a feathered stick seemed to sprout magically out of the serpent's eye. A great shudder ran through its body and it thrashed its head wildly, one needle-like fang missing Sebastian's face by the width of a finger. The loop around his chest loosened dramati-cally and he was able to snatch in a gulp of precious air. He caught a glimpse of Cornelius's apparently lifeless body tumbling downward through the crea-ture's winding coils and he opened his mouth to shout. But then he was flung through the air as though he had no more substance than a puppet, and he slammed into something hard, probably the trunk of a tree.

He had no time to dwell on the matter because blackness was overtaking him and he could fight it off no longer. . . .

When he came to his senses, somebody was holding his head and lifting a skin of cool water to his lips. He swallowed gratefully and instantly felt it restore a little of his vitality. He let his eyes focus and saw that a young man was looking down at him, his face expressionless. He had handsome if rather cold features, piercing green eyes, a long aquiline nose and a neatly tended brown beard. His long straight hair hung to his shoulders and he was wearing clothes made of animal hide. Seeing that Sebastian seemed largely uninjured, he allowed himself a thin smile, but there was no real warmth in it.

He helped Sebastian to sit up. Sebastian looked down the track and saw that the mighty serpent was dead, its vast coils motionless. He saw also that the plumed stick protruding from its eye was an arrow. The powerful bow slung across the man's shoulder confirmed that he must have been the archer.

"Cornelius . . . ?" asked Sebastian.

"Your friend is fine," said the young man. "But he is seeing to his pony. She's in a bad way."

Sebastian took in the news, knowing what it must mean; but first he needed to express his gratitude. "It seems we owe you our lives," he said.

The man shrugged. "I have been after that old serpent for an age. When he's up in the trees, I can't get a good enough bead on him. The eye is the one vulnerable spot and your aim has to be perfect."

"I'll try to remember that," Sebastian assured him, "should we encounter more of those beasts."

"You won't see another like him. He was the king of

all the forest serpents and as old as time itself. I dread to think how many unwary travelers have ended their journey in his deadly grip." The young man seemed to remember something. He bowed slightly from the waist. "Forgive me," he said. "I have not introduced myself. I am Adam. I live in this forest with my sister, Leonora."

Sebastian nodded. "And I am Sebastian Darke. My friend is Captain Cornelius Drummel, formerly of the Golmiran army." He heard a cough from across the clearing and saw that Max was looking at him meaningfully. "Oh yes, and that's Max, my"—he hesitated, knowing that he had had problems introducing Max before—"a buffalope," he finished awkwardly.

He got carefully to his feet, assuring himself that there was no permanent damage to his aching ribs. He looked along the trail and saw Cornelius kneeling beside the prone figure of Phantom. "Excuse me a moment," he said, and walked across to stand beside his friend. Cornelius was stroking the pony's head and talking to her in a low voice. He glanced up at Sebastian, who was shocked to see tears trickling down the little warrior's face.

"Is there nothing that can be done?" asked Sebastian quietly.

Cornelius shook his head. "Her leg is broken," he said. "And besides"—he pointed to a pair of livid puncture wounds in Phantom's neck—"the serpent's fangs struck her as it came down. It was trying for me and found her instead."

"I thought you had invented that story about tree serpents," said Sebastian.

"So did I. But there is nothing in this world that you can invent that is not dwelling somewhere in the shadows. If I had been more watchful and not so intent upon scaring Max . . ."

"You can't blame yourself," reasoned Sebastian. "And perhaps the bite's not fatal."

Adam had wandered over to stand with them. He shook his head. "That old monster had enough venom in him to kill a herd of ponies," he said bluntly. "But it's slow-working. She'll be in terrible pain." He reached down and put a hand on Cornelius's shoulder. "If you want, I'll put her out of her misery."

Cornelius shook his head. "No," he said. "She's my responsibility. I'll do what has to be done." He reached into his belt and withdrew a short dagger. "Wait for me by the caravan," he suggested.

They did as they were told. Max was waiting impatiently for some news.

"What's going on over there?" he demanded. "Is Phantom injured?"

Sebastian nodded. "Fatally so, I'm afraid."

"Oh no, tell me that's not so. Not Phantom. She's such a good-natured creature. Isn't there something that can be done for her?"

"Cornelius is attending to it," Sebastian told him.

Max's eyes widened in realization. "But surely—" He broke off at the sound of a brief whinny from Phantom. "Oh dear," he said. "What a pity. She wasn't much of a conversationalist, but she had a very sweet nature. I was only just getting to know her."

There was an uncomfortable silence, which was finally broken by Adam.

"So . . . Mr. Darke, what brings you into the forest of Geltane?"

"Please, call me Sebastian. We . . . we're just passing through. We have business in Ramalat."

"Business?" Adam put his head slightly to one side, a strange gesture which put Sebastian in mind of some kind of alert animal.

"Er . . . yes—just something . . . we have to do . . . at the port." Sebastian didn't want to say too much about the reasons for their journey and he hoped he didn't sound too evasive.

"It's a long path through the forest," observed Adam, "and there's not much light left. I'm heading home now. Perhaps you'd like to camp there for the night? We have fresh water and a good fire—you'd be welcome to join us."

Sebastian opened his mouth to decline the offer, but Max got there before he had a chance to speak.

"It sounds good to me," he said. "It'll be useful to have a skilled archer with us, in case anything else comes visiting in the night."

"Oh, you'll be safe enough in our cave," Adam assured him. "No beasts dare approach it. My sister is a powerful woman."

"Cave?" murmured Max apprehensively. He looked suddenly as though he had made a terrible mistake. "Oh, well . . . I'm not sure we're used to sleeping in *caves*."

Adam laughed. "It is better appointed than most caves you'll encounter. And you needn't worry yourself. As a beast of burden, you'll be sleeping *outside*."

"A beast of . . . ?" Max looked quite affronted and Sebastian sensed that he was about to say something uncomplimentary; but just at that moment Cornelius came trudging toward them, his face grim, his shoulders hunched.

"She's gone," he murmured. "Poor Phantom. I didn't know her long, but she was a fine ally."

"Yes," said Max, trying to be supportive. "And so"—he searched for a suitable recommendation—"polite. You know, at feeding times she always used to stand aside and let me eat first."

Cornelius gave him an accusing look. "Did she have any choice in the matter?" he growled.

Sebastian stepped in to defuse any argument. "Cornelius, Adam here has offered to let us camp the night at his cave. He says there's fresh water there."

Cornelius shrugged, clearly too depressed to consider such an irrelevance. "Whatever," he said. "Just as soon as we've finished burying Phantom."

"Burying her?" Sebastian stared, but Cornelius was already clambering into the back of the caravan. His reply came from amongst the jumble of equipment that was stored haphazardly there.

"Well, you don't expect me to just leave her lying around for the carrion beasts of the forest, do you?"

"Umm . . . no. No, I suppose not." Sebastian turned to look at Adam. "I'm sorry," he said. "We'll be as quick as we can. Is it far to your . . . cave?"

"Not so far," said Adam. "And please don't worry—take as long as you need. I quite understand."

A couple of spades came flying out of the back of the caravan and Sebastian went over to pick them up. He had never dug a grave for a pony before and had no idea how long it would take.

It was early evening when they finally set off. Sebastian found that his arms were aching: it was a long time since he had done that kind of hard manual work and the forest floor had been matted with thick roots and the bones of earlier victims. Cornelius had insisted on digging the grave deep enough to prevent lupers from unearthing the remains, and as they descended through the layers of earth, they continued to find bones, which gave some indication of how long the giant serpent had been preying upon unwary travelers along this trail. Sebastian thought how close he'd come to adding his own remains to the grisly collection and he couldn't suppress a shiver of revulsion.

When they had finished, Cornelius stood at the grave for a long time, his head bowed as if in prayer, though Sebastian was pretty sure he didn't believe in any of the old gods. Then he put Phantom's saddle and bridle into the wagon and they all set off.

Cornelius had opted to ride in the back of the caravan, where he sat hunched and silent throughout the journey. Adam walked alongside, striding at such a speed that Sebastian was obliged to keep slapping the reins against Max's haunches in an attempt to keep pace with him. Max seemed to have slipped into a sad reverie of his own, and for once in his life had absolutely nothing to say. Sebastian occupied himself by throwing a string of questions at Adam.

"May I ask how long you have lived in these woods?"

"Oh, off and on since we were children." Adam kept striding onward as he spoke, moving with an agile grace. "From time to time we have tried other places, but we seem destined to keep returning." He glanced up at Sebastian. "Not far now," he said. "Leonora will have a meal ready for us."

"We have provisions," said Sebastian. "You're welcome to take whatever you want from them."

"No need. The forest provides us with everything."

"Yes, but your sister won't be expecting extra mouths to feed."

Adam smiled strangely. "Of course she will," he said, and walked on.

Sebastian was puzzled by this remark. "But . . . how *could* she know?" he persisted.

"Leonora is special," said Adam. "She has been gifted since birth. She sees and hears things that others cannot see."

"You mean she's a witch?" said Max, speaking for the first time in ages. Sebastian winced and Adam looked far from pleased.

"That is not a word we care for," he said coldly. "But she has special powers. She can look into a man's future and see what awaits him there."

"Sounds exactly like a witch to me," said Max. Sebastian could have slapped him. Had he no gratitude?

"You'll be able to judge for yourself soon enough," said Adam. "The cave is just round this next bend."

CHAPTER 3

LEONORA

The track curved sharply to the left, and they emerged into a small clearing where a cliff of gray rock reared upward from amidst a tumble of vegetation. At one point a constant trickle of water came cascading down and splashed into a shallow pool before overflowing and plunging down a rocky slope beyond. There was a low arched opening in the rocks, and Sebastian could see into the illuminated interior, where the cloaked figure of a woman was sitting in front of a low fire, her face turned away.

"So," she said, in a low, slightly husky voice, "you're here at last."

Adam gestured for Sebastian to climb down from the caravan and led him and Cornelius closer to the mouth of the cave. A delicious meaty smell issued from a black cauldron suspended over the fire.

"Come meet our guests, sister," said Adam.

The woman got up from her seat and turned to face the newcomers. Sebastian snatched in a breath. He couldn't help it. He had expected some grizzled crone like Magda, the sly old harridan he had encountered in Keladon; but this woman was young and quite beautiful. Her most striking feature was a pair of tawny yellow eyes that seemed to appraise Sebastian like a wildcat observing its prey. But her full lips curved into a smile and she said, "You are most welcome, elfling." She nodded to Cornelius. "You too, good sir. I am sorry for your loss."

Cornelius stared at her suspiciously. "What loss?" he growled.

"I'm not sure," she replied evenly. "But I sense that you are grieving for someone . . . or something. . . ." She lifted a hand to her temple for a moment, as though thinking. "I'm getting a word," she said. "A name, perhaps? Ghost . . . Specter, something like . . . no, wait, it's Phantom!"

Cornelius stared at her with open suspicion but Sebastian was simply delighted by her skills.

"How could you possibly know that?" he cried.

"I told you my sister had special talents," said Adam. "We call it the gift of the Inner Eye."

"Still sounds like witchcraft to me," muttered Max.

Sebastian flashed him a disapproving look. "Watch your tongue," he whispered. "We're guests here."

"Please, don't stand outside," said Leonora. "Step

into the cave and warm yourselves at our fire. Supper will be ready presently." She beckoned them inside, and Sebastian and Cornelius did as they were told.

"Hey, what about me?" said Max indignantly. "Would somebody like to unhitch me from this wagon?"

"I don't think the invitation extends to buffalopes," said Sebastian quietly. "You wait here—I'll sort you out later."

"Oh, well, that's lovely, isn't it! You get to warm yourself by the fire and I have to stand out here like . . . like some common animal!"

"I've got news for you," murmured Sebastian. "Despite what you think, you *are* an animal. So please try and behave like one!"

He stepped into the surprisingly warm interior of the cave and took a seat on one of a series of logs covered with animal hides that were arranged in front of the fire. Cornelius and Adam found places opposite him. Sebastian could see that the cave was indeed well appointed, though all the furnishings seemed to have been handmade from branches and logs reclaimed from the forest.

Having ensured that her guests were comfortable, Leonora resumed her own seat. "You have traveled far," she said. Sebastian wasn't sure if it was a question or an observation, so he didn't answer. "But you still have a good distance before you," she continued.

"And you are heading for a world where water is king."

"They're going to the port of Ramalat," said Adam. "Sebastian told me earlier. They have business there."

"Business, indeed! And tell me, brother, did you find our guests where I said they would be?"

"Sure enough. I was just in time too. They were having a slight difference of opinion with a tree serpent. The big one you saw in your dream. I finally managed to put an end to him."

"Ah, good. The forest is well rid of that old rascal. You have tried enough times, brother, to—"

"Just a minute," interrupted Cornelius. He looked at Adam. "Your sister *told* you that we would be there?"

Adam nodded. "She had a dream last night. She saw you entering the forest at that very spot and knew of the danger waiting high above you. She begged me to go there and be ready to help you."

Cornelius looked at Leonora with new respect. "In that case, madam, we are in your debt."

Leonora waved a hand in dismissal. "Do not trouble yourself," she told him. "I only did what I could to help. And besides, I wanted to meet you." She turned her head to look at Sebastian, and he felt the hairs at the back of his neck bristle. There was something about the power of her gaze that made him feel quite uncomfortable.

"Nevertheless, we are grateful," he assured her. "I saw the bones of many travelers who were *not* given help."

"You came from Keladon," she said. "You were loved and valued there, but something made you leave. . . ." She closed her eyes and lifted her hands again, then began making a strange scrabbling motion, as if clawing information out of the very air in front of her. "I see you at the top of a tower," she said. "A very tall tower. And you are fighting an evil man . . . a tyrant." She paused for a moment, as though trying to "see" more. "The tyrant falls!" she exclaimed. "And you are a hero! But . . . something happens and you cannot stay there. You leave because of . . . because of"—she opened her eyes and stared at him with an intensity that made him blush —"a woman," she concluded.

There was a long silence. Then Cornelius spoke.

"Well, she's certainly got you figured," he told Sebastian. He turned to Leonora. "My friend here has a weakness for a pretty face," he said. "One day it's going to land him in real trouble."

"Indeed." Leonora continued to stare at Sebastian, as though trying to puzzle him out. "And I believe that many women will have a weakness for him," she said. "He is fair of face, is he not?"

Cornelius shrugged. "If you say so."

"You were a jester in Keladon," said Leonora.

Again she made the scrabbling motion. "I see you onstage, performing for a noble court . . . but I do not see many people laughing. Why would that be? I wonder."

Max's mournful voice came from outside the cave: "Believe me, you'd understand if you'd seen his act!"

"Go to sleep!" snapped Sebastian. He smiled apologetically at Leonora. "You'll have to excuse him—he has an opinion on everything."

She nodded but did not stop staring at him. "He is the funny one," she said.

There was a long uncomfortable silence while Sebastian thought about that. What exactly was it supposed to mean? Was she proposing that the two of them should team up for some kind of comedy double-act? It was a worrying thought.

Then Leonora said, "The food is ready. Adam, fetch wine for our guests!" She ladled a thick, glutinous-looking stew into earthenware bowls, while Adam fetched a wineskin from the back of the cave and poured red liquid into metal goblets. Leonora passed out the bowls, and as she handed Sebastian his, her fingers brushed against the back of his hand and he felt a shudder pass through him. Startled, he tried to concentrate on his stew, which had a delicious earthy flavor, and the wine, which tasted rich and fruity. Even Cornelius, who was not much given to passing compliments, observed how good it was.

"How do you manage to find supplies in this wild spot?" he asked.

"Oh, everything we need is right here in the forest," said Adam with evident pride. "The stew is made from javralat meat and wild vegetables. The wine comes from a secret grove of blood berries which we harvest every year."

"So why leave?" asked Cornelius.

"I beg your pardon?"

"You told Sebastian that you leave the forest from time to time, but that you keep returning."

Adam nodded. "We leave if there is a strong enough reason to. Perhaps some adventure bids us get up and go . . . or perhaps Leonora has a vision of the future that leads us to something worth investigating."

"Ah yes, her powers of prediction! So far we have seen her speak accurately about that which has already happened. But little about the future. Why is that?"

"It's more difficult," explained Leonora. "The past I can do so easily. But to look into the future, I must be alone with the person who seeks to know what is to come, and they in turn must be ready to accompany me. Then I can give them glimpses of what will be." She smiled at Cornelius. "What about it, little man? Would you like to learn about your future?"

"I would not," said Cornelius without hesitation.

"As far as I'm concerned, that is something that no man should have access to."

"Whyever not?" Sebastian asked him. "Surely it can be helpful to see what lies ahead?"

"I do not doubt it, but for my part I would rather go into the future in blissful ignorance. Too much information can be a dangerous thing, Sebastian—and knowing nothing can mean a happy life."

"Yes, but supposing we'd met with Leonora *before* we entered the forest? She might have warned us against taking that path. And then, who knows, maybe Phantom would still be—"

Cornelius suddenly set down his empty bowl. "I'm tired," he said. "If you'll forgive me, I think I'll turn in." He gave Sebastian a meaningful look. "You could do with an early night too," he added.

"Oh, not yet. I haven't finished eating."

"No. Umm . . . well . . ." Cornelius got to his feet. "See you don't leave it too late—we need an early start in the morning." He bowed respectfully to Leonora. "Madam, good night. I thank you for your hospitality."

"Why don't you use one of the chambers deeper in the cavern?" suggested Leonora. "You'll be warmer and more secure in there."

Cornelius shook his head. "I'm used to sleeping outdoors," he said. "I'm sure I'll be fine." He shot one more meaningful glance at Sebastian and went out into the darkness. Sebastian suddenly felt like a naughty child, determined to stay up past his bedtime. What was Cornelius so worried about anyway?

It was at this point that Adam started yawning. "Do you know, I'm rather tired myself," he announced. "Been quite a day, what with one thing and another." He got up from his seat. "Good night, Sebastian. If I don't see you in the morning, I trust that the rest of your journey will be better than your entry into Geltane Forest." And with that he turned and headed for the stone corridors at the back of the cave. Which left Sebastian and Leonora sitting alone at the fire.

Sebastian was suddenly rather nervous. He glanced up at Leonora and she smiled at him, lifting the wineskin.

"A little more?" she suggested.

"Why not?" he said, almost defiantly. He watched as she filled his goblet to the brim, but in truth he already felt very light-headed. "This stew is delicious," he said, simply to break the silence.

"I'm glad you approve. I like a man who enjoys his food." She was still looking at him intently and he felt decidedly self-conscious. "So, Sebastian," she ventured, "are you a man who is afraid to look into his future?"

Sebastian shrugged. "I'm not afraid of anything," he said. He picked up the goblet and took a big gulp of the warm red wine. "I'll have you know, I'm considered quite a hero in Keladon. It was me who led the army into the city to depose the evil King Septimus. In fact, I single-handedly vanquished him in calmed ombat . . . I mean, armed combat."

"Ah yes, the man I saw on the tower!" She leaned closer. "And what about this woman who caused you to leave it all behind?"

"Princess Kerin. Or rather, Queen Kerin, as she is now. But wasn't then . . . if you see what I mean." Sebastian realized he was rambling and made an effort to pull himself together. "Talk about ingratitude! I was the one who made her queen. Well, not the only one, obviously, but the main one. So I came away to try and forget her. It's like Cornelius says— plenty more sish in the fee!" He glanced suspiciously at the goblet of wine and set it down carefully on the ground.

"But what compels you to go to Ramalat?" persisted Leonora.

"Oh, it's not Ramalat really. That's just the starting point. We're going to—" He caught himself just in time. "I . . . really shouldn't talk about it," he said. "It's a secret: Cornelius says I'm to tell nobody."

"Quite right," she agreed. "You never know who you can trust."

"Oh. I trust *you*!" he protested. "After all, you saved us from that serpent. It's just . . . well, I did promise Cornelius, so . . ."

"I understand. Really. A secret is a secret." She smiled at him. "Well then, Sebastian, do you think you are ready?"

"R-ready?"

"To look into your future."

"Umm. Oh, well . . . I suppose. . . ."

"Good." She leaned closer and extended her hand, one finger pointed toward his face. "I want you to relax," she murmured. "Let every part of your body relax. We're going to take a journey, you and I, into your future. But first . . ." The tip of her finger touched his forehead and a strange warmth flowed out of the end of it. The warmth seemed to travel throughout his body and he was just about to say how strange it all was when he found that he could not even open his mouth. He tried to move but there was no strength in his muscles. The nearly empty bowl of stew slipped from his hand and fell to the floor, where, without a sound, it broke into several pieces. Sebastian registered this even as a black hole seemed to open at the back of his skull and spread outward like a growing stain, until it had claimed him completely.

He knew nothing else for quite some time. . . .

CHAPTER 4

THIEVES IN THE NIGHT

When he woke, he was still slumped in front of the fire; or rather, what was left of it. The wood had long since burned away and all that remained was a heap of cold gray ash.

The broken bowl still lay scattered at his feet and the half-empty goblet of wine stood beside it. He felt terribly groggy, as though he'd drunk much more than he actually had, and when he got unsteadily to his feet, he realized that his shoulders and knees were aching from having slept in such an unnatural position.

He gazed blearily around the interior of the cave, but there was nobody else about and he could only surmise that Leonora had left him asleep and gone to her own bed. He imagined himself dozing off in front of her and felt mortified. What if he'd been snoring? Or, worse still, drooling like an imbecile? Clearly he had been more tired than he thought. He had the distinct impression that he'd missed something very important but couldn't for the life of him think what it might be.

He turned and stumbled toward the cave mouth. Stepping out into the night, he took a much-needed breath of fresh air and looked around. Max was slumped on the ground beside the caravan, fast asleep and snoring at an incredible volume. Presumably Cornelius had unshackled him before turning in for the night. Sebastian felt vaguely guilty since that was usually *his* task. Cornelius himself, as was his usual custom, was lying under the caravan, all bundled up in his bedroll. Sebastian fumbled around in the back of the caravan, found his own blankets and, wrapping himself up in them, lay down beside Cornelius and fell swiftly and deeply asleep.

He dreamed he was back in the cave, sitting with Leonora beside the blazing fire. She was talking to him in a low, hypnotic tone but he couldn't make out what she was saying; the words seemed to fragment around him like a blizzard of falling snow, and he was really only aware of her big, tawny eyes staring at him, seeming almost to devour him with their intensity. It occurred to him that she was even more beautiful than he had first thought and he just sat there, gazing at her in helpless devotion.

Suddenly she reached out to him and opened her hand to reveal something set into her palm—a strange oval of smooth, raised flesh. As Sebastian stared at it, a layer of skin slid back, revealing an eye gazing steadfastly up at him, the same tawny color as the ones on Leonora's face.

Sebastian woke abruptly to the sound of Cornelius bellowing beside him. He sat up quickly and banged his head on the underside of the wagon. Turning to his left, he saw two dark shapes struggling beside him. Cornelius, lying on his back, was wrestling with a tall figure kneeling over him. A shaft of moonlight filtering through the spokes of a wheel revealed the man's face. It was Adam. In the same glance Sebastian saw that one of Adam's hands was trapped inside Cornelius's breastplate. The little warrior had both his hands gripped tightly around Adam's wrist and was attempting to pull him to the ground.

"Try to rob me, would you?" he roared. "You two-faced lizard—I thought there was something about you that couldn't be trusted!"

In reply, Adam simply pulled back his other arm and struck Cornelius hard across the chin, making him relinquish his grip. Adam scrambled out from under the caravan and ran back toward the cave entrance, where, Sebastian could see, Leonora was waiting for him.

"After them!" growled Cornelius. "Come on, man, don't just lie there!"

Cornelius moved off in hot pursuit and Sebastian followed, still trying to get his thoughts in some kind of order. As he passed Max, he saw to his amazement that the buffalope was still sound asleep and snoring contentedly.

Adam and Leonora ran into the cave and Cornelius followed close on their heels, reaching for his sword as he did so. Sebastian experienced a powerful jolt of dread at the sight. He didn't want any harm to befall Leonora, and he quickened his pace to try and intercept the little warrior.

"Cornelius!" he yelled. "Wait, don't do anything rash!"

Adam and Leonora raced straight through the main part of the cave and into the gloomy tunnel beyond. After running a short distance, they ducked to their left, through a small opening. The cavern beyond appeared to be in total darkness, so Cornelius pointed to a burning lantern on the wall, which was out of his reach.

"Pass me that light!" he growled.

Sebastian did as he was told and took the opportunity to speak. "Cornelius, calm down a moment," he said.

"Calm down be blowed! That rascal was trying to get the treasure map out of my pocket."

Sebastian stared at him. "But . . . how would he know about it?"

Cornelius gave him an accusing look. "A very good question. Come on, bring that light!"

They stepped through the opening and found themselves in a small circular cavern. No other exits appeared to lead off from it and yet there wasn't a sign of Adam or Leonora.

"What witchcraft is this?" cried Cornelius in disbelief. "I saw them come in here with my own eyes."

"There *is* a way out," said Sebastian, raising the lantern. "Look—there!" He indicated a small opening a few hands' height from the floor. Beyond it, when they stooped to look, they could see a narrow trail leading into the forest undergrowth. Items of clothing were scattered in front of the opening and Sebastian recognized the cloak that Leonora had been wearing.

"It's too small for them to fit through," protested Cornelius. "Even *I* would have a tough time getting out."

"Well, where else could they be?" said Sebastian. "We both saw them come in here. And why did they leave their clothes behind?"

Cornelius frowned and turned away. "I can only surmise that their wizardry is more powerful than we imagined." He glared at Sebastian again. "What happened after I went to bed?"

"Nothing! Well, not very much. We just sat around and . . . talked."

"And I suppose you told her all about the map."

"Of course not!" Sebastian was indignant. "You must think I'm stupid! I never breathed a word about it."

Cornelius was evidently far from convinced. "Oh, so Adam just *guessed* that I had something worth stealing, did he?"

Sebastian shrugged. "He must have. Anyway, he wasn't around; he went off to bed and left me alone with Leonora. So . . ." He noticed the despairing look on Cornelius's face and spread his arms in a gesture of helplessness. "What?" he cried.

"You amaze me," said Cornelius. "Do you know that? One moment you're being all lovesick and pathetic about Queen Kerin, and then you're bewitched by the very first woman you clap eyes on!"

"Nonsense! I'm not bewitched. I just . . . We had a pleasant conversation, nothing more."

"Oh yes. And what did you talk about exactly?"

"Umm . . . well, we . . . we . . ." Sebastian frowned. Now that he thought about it, he couldn't remember a single thing they'd talked about. "It's all a bit fuzzy," he admitted. "Probably the wine—"

"Wine, my backside!" growled Cornelius. "Obviously she put some kind of enchantment on you. You probably told her everything. That's exactly why I didn't want you lingering in that cave." He turned and strode toward the doorway.

Sebastian followed with the lantern. "Well, it's not so bad, is it?" he reasoned. "He didn't get the map."

"No, he didn't. But if that witch knows about the treasure—"

"Don't call her that!" snapped Sebastian. He stared at his friend in dismay. He had no idea why he'd leaped to her defense.

"You see," said Cornelius. "She has quite obviously bewitched you." He shook his head. "I don't know. All it takes is a skirt, a pretty face and you're putty in their hands." They entered the main cave and moved toward the exit. "Well, one thing is for certain. We dare not sleep any more tonight in case they come sneaking back for another try. We'll take turns standing guard until daybreak and then we'll be on our way."

They emerged from the cave and walked across the clearing to the caravan. Max was still sound asleep and snoring.

"Look at him!" exclaimed Cornelius. "Oblivious! We could have been murdered in our sleep and he'd still know nothing about it. It would be different if we'd started cooking some food though, wouldn't it?"

As if by magic, Max stopped snoring. He opened

his eyes and lifted his head to look at his two companions. "Did somebody mention food?" he asked
innocently. "A couple of those fresh pommers would
go down rather well."

Cornelius's face was a picture. He stormed off to
gather some kindling for the campfire. Sebastian
offered to take first watch but Cornelius didn't feel
much like sleeping either, so they built up the fire to
a cheery blaze and then sat close to it, talking in
hushed voices and waiting for the approach of dawn.

CHAPTER 5

HASTY DEPARTURE

At the first blush of light on the horizon, they were packed up and ready to leave—though unsurprisingly, Max took some persuading.

"I haven't eaten breakfast yet!" he complained bitterly as Sebastian strapped him into his harness. "What's the big hurry?"

Sebastian explained what had happened the night before and Max couldn't resist commenting.

"I'm not at all surprised," he said with a sniff. "Perhaps this will teach you to take more notice of me in future. I said right from the moment I clapped eyes on her, that witch was not to be trusted—"

"Don't call her a witch!" shouted Sebastian; and once again he was astonished by his own reaction. It was as though he simply couldn't stop himself from springing to her defense.

Max gave him a knowing look. "Well, she's obviously made a big impression on you," he observed.

"That's what Cornelius said. But I just . . . don't think it's fair to call her . . ."

"A witch! That's exactly what she is."

"No. She . . . she's just . . . I don't think she had anything to do with that attempted robbery. Adam was probably acting on impulse . . . and she . . ."

"Didn't you say you saw her standing by the cave?"

"Umm . . . yes . . . I expect she was trying to stop him."

"But they ran off together!"

"Of course! Blood's thicker than water—she probably *had* to help her brother. He probably *made* her do it."

Cornelius strolled past, shaking his head. "Forget it, Max—the poor lad's under an enchantment. He'd argue that black was white if Leonora wanted him to."

Max looked quite shocked. "But what of your true love, Queen Kerin?"

Sebastian felt a jolt of irritation. "She's hardly my true love," he argued. "However I feel about her and however she feels about me, it's a love that can never be. So I'm perfectly free to look elsewhere."

"Yes, but not at an old witch!"

"She's not a witch! And she's not old!"

"She *could* be for all you know," argued Max. "She could be a wizened old hag who uses black magic to make herself look reasonable. Underneath that pretty veneer could be a hideous, wart-ridden old harridan with white hair and rotten teeth."

"Whatever she is," interjected Cornelius, "my suggestion is that we put as much distance between her and us as is humanly possible. Come on, let's make tracks."

Sebastian clambered into the driver's seat and Cornelius climbed up beside him. Sebastian saw that he was carrying his handmade crossbow, the one that slotted together from a set of beautifully engineered metal pieces. This was the same weapon that had proved so useful on their recent visit to Brigandia.

"What's that for?" asked Sebastian anxiously.

"In case," Cornelius told him, but didn't go into any more detail.

Sebastian flicked the reins and Max started forward, grumbling every step of the way.

"Oh really, this is too much! I'm expected to pull this heavy caravan when not a scrap of food or water has passed my lips. My old master never treated me in such slipshod fashion, I can tell you!"

Sebastian sighed. Max was very fond of singing the praises of Alexander, Sebastian's father. But Max was remembering him as he was at the height of his fame, when everything was going well. Later, when he lost favor with the king and fell on hard times, the picture was not quite so rosy. There were several occasions when Max had gone without food or water because Alexander was so preoccupied with his plans for a "comeback." But Max didn't choose to remember them.

They traveled in silence for several hours, and at first there were no real problems. The morning mists had soon dispersed and the forest rapidly filled with the joyful sounds of birdsong, the first they had heard since entering this place. Sebastian realized that it must have been the presence of the huge tree serpent that had driven other creatures from that part of the woods and he said as much to Cornelius; but he noticed as he did so how the little warrior's eyes kept moving back and forth to survey the trees all around them.

"What are you worried about?" he asked nervously.

Cornelius shrugged. "I'll just be glad when we're out of these trees and onto open ground," he said.

Sebastian could understand what he meant. Even on a bright, sunny day like this one, the surrounding trees provided plenty of cover for anybody who might choose to follow them, and wherever he looked, he was aware of leaves and bushes stirring, as unseen creatures slunk deeper into the shadows. As the three friends traveled onward, it was hard to shake off the notion that they were being watched; but by whom or by what it was impossible to say.

They were moving through a particularly dense area of forest when it happened. Once again, as if by magic, the birds all stopped singing and the only sound was the restless rustling of the forest canopy high above their heads. Sebastian and Cornelius gazed around, feeling distinctly anxious.

"I don't care much for this," muttered Sebastian fearfully. "Do you think it's more tree serpents?"

"Who can say?" said Cornelius. "But clearly something has changed. Perhaps we should try and—"

But he didn't finish the sentence. He snapped round in his seat and lifted the crossbow, ready for use. There had been a sudden movement in the branches of the trees away to his left.

"What was that?" asked Sebastian.

"I don't know. It was moving too quickly. Try and get that fleabag of a buffalope going a bit faster."

"I heard that!" said Max. "There's really no need to—"

"Shhh!" Sebastian flicked the reins and Max dutifully picked up the pace a little, but it was hard to get up much speed on these rough woodland tracks, and Max, hungry as he was, clearly wasn't inclined to hurry.

Sebastian was suddenly aware of another movement

in the branches of a tree away to his right. He caught a glimpse of a long, muscular body, tawny in color, moving through the patches of green foliage.

"See that?" hissed Cornelius.

Sebastian nodded. "What was it?" he whispered.

"Some kind of panther, I think. . . . Oh, there's another one!"

A second lithe creature had just run along a branch to their left. Cornelius raised the crossbow but was unable to draw a bead on the big cat.

"Maybe they're friendly," suggested Sebastian.

"I very much doubt it—we need to get moving!" Cornelius turned to shout at Max's swaying backside. "Do you think you could put a bit more effort into it?" he pleaded.

"Hmmph! You should have thought about that before we set off. A little breakfast would have helped me focus."

"There wasn't time to eat! Now, I would suggest that you hurry."

"Give me one good reason why I should."

"I'll give you two. There are a couple of panthers following the caravan. Judging by the size of them, I'd say that they could drag you down and polish you off before you even knew what was happening."

"If this is another of your tricks . . . ," began Max. "I just want to say—" But he was cut short by a low, rumbling growl issuing from the undergrowth. He swallowed noisily. "Yes, well, perhaps it wouldn't harm to stretch my legs a bit—"

Immediately he broke into a trot and the caravan bounced forward on its heavy wheels. Sebastian slapped the reins against the buffalope's haunches and Max put his head down and picked up the pace, moving rapidly into a canter, and then a full gallop. It wasn't a great idea on this rough dirt track. The caravan bucked and shuddered across the uneven ground and Sebastian and Cornelius had to hang on for dear life. But at last they were covering the ground at a good speed.

"How much further before we're out of these ruddy woods?" shouted Max.

"Your guess is as good as mine," Sebastian yelled back.

The caravan thundered down an incline and then hit a level stretch. Sebastian told himself that they should be all right, just so long as the ancient caravan didn't shake itself to pieces. He glanced at Cornelius, but the little warrior was peering back down the trail, and the expression on his face suggested that he didn't much like what he saw there.

CHAPTER 6

THE CHASE

"They're still following!" yelled Cornelius.

Sebastian risked taking his eyes off the track and ducked his head round the side of the caravan to look behind. As he watched, one of the big cats leaped down out of a tree. It didn't hesitate but came loping after the caravan in a fluid, seemingly effortless motion, its long tail stretched out behind it, its massive paws eerily silent on the forest floor.

"It's gaining on us!" shouted Sebastian.

"I noticed." Cornelius gripped the side of his seat and swung himself out to take aim, one-handed, with the miniature crossbow; but the caravan was shuddering and bouncing so much, it was impossible to get in a decent shot. Moreover, the cat seemed to realize what was happening, because it immediately swung to Sebastian's side of the wagon, shielding itself from Cornelius's view.

"Drat the thing!" Cornelius abandoned that idea and started to clamber up onto the roof.

"What are you doing?" yelled Sebastian. A low-hanging bush swept at him and he was obliged to duck beneath it. It glanced off the back of Cornelius's helmet, almost knocking him from his perch. He shrugged his shoulders and continued to pull himself up.

"I'm trying to . . . get a better view," he said, gasping. He was just easing one knee up onto the flat roof when a front wheel thudded into a pothole and the caravan bucked wildly. Cornelius lost his grip and started to slide. Sebastian reached out and grabbed his friend's sword belt just as he was about to fall. He hung in midair for a moment, his little legs kicking, but he refused to let go of the crossbow. After a few moments he managed to pull himself, one-handed, back onto the seat.

"You all right?" asked Sebastian.

"I'm fine but—"

They heard a crash from the back of the caravan as something thudded heavily into the jumble of equipment. Sebastian and Cornelius exchanged horrified looks, realizing what must have happened. The panther had somehow managed to scramble up the steps at the back and get in through the open window. It was in there now, crashing around the crowded interior.

"Right," said Cornelius. "I'll settle this." He started

to pull back the heavy drape that covered the doorway behind them, but as he did so, something came leaping out from within, tearing down the curtain and smashing headlong into Cornelius, tipping him backward. The crossbow went spinning out of his grasp and he fell, crashing onto Max's swaying rump. The panther, still entangled in the curtain, came down on top of him with a terrible roar. Sebastian looked down helplessly. He desperately tried to pull Max to a halt but the buffalope was so terrified by the sensation of two figures fighting on his back, he wouldn't slow his pace, and the caravan raced on along the narrow track.

Cornelius was in danger of slipping sideways off Max and being trampled by the wheels, but he managed to cling on somehow, gripping the harness while using his feet to try to fend off the cat, which was still struggling to escape from the curtain, its claws shredding the heavy fabric.

At first Sebastian sat there in a sheer funk, not knowing what to do. Then, realizing he had to do something, he abandoned the reins and clambered through the doorway into the swaying, rattling interior of the caravan. He started searching frantically for a weapon.

He saw a longbow hanging on the wall but realized that he couldn't use that for fear of hitting Cornelius or Max. Then his gaze fell on a long coil of rope and, unwilling to waste any more time, he grabbed it and clumsily fashioned the end into a noose. He stumbled back through the doorway and saw that Cornelius was still spread-eagled across Max's back. The panther was virtually free of the curtain now, and the Golmiran was desperately trying to fend off its teeth and claws which, had it not been for the protection of his breastplate and chain-mail jerkin, would have ripped into his flesh by now.

Sebastian started twirling the rope above his head to try and generate some momentum. "Get its head up!" he yelled, and Cornelius must have heard him, because he did his best to comply. He got his little legs in under the cat's chest and began to push with all his strength, raising the beast's torso and great snarling head. Sebastian flung the rope and, more by good fortune than good aim, the noose dropped around the panther's neck.

Now Sebastian braced himself and pulled with all his might. The cat's guttural sounds turned abruptly to a shriek of alarm as it was yanked backward, and it began to lose its grip. It made a desperate attempt to bury its claws in Max's haunches, causing bellows of pain from the buffalope. Sebastian jerked with all his strength, and the big cat slipped and fell, tumbling under the caravan. There was a terrible crunch as the wheels passed over its body, and then it was gone in a flurry of dust, the rope paying out behind it. At the last moment Sebastian remembered to let go.

He looked toward Cornelius and was rewarded with a grim thumbs-up from the little warrior. Reassured, he took up the reins again and began to heave on them. This time, freed from the terror of having a cat's claws locked into his flesh, Max reacted and began to slow his pace. He dropped back to a canter, a trot, a walk, and then finally came to a halt, his great head lowered, his breath snorting from his nostrils in loud gasps.

Sebastian jumped down from the caravan and ran to Cornelius, who was scratched and bloodied but seemed to have escaped serious injury.

"Are you all right?" Sebastian asked him.

Cornelius grimaced. "I lost my crossbow back there," he complained.

"Never mind about that. The main thing is that you're not badly hurt. Max, what about you?"

Max was still fighting to recover his breath. "For somebody . . . who's just had a panther . . . and a Golmiran . . . fighting to the death on his backside . . . I'm in surprisingly good shape," he panted.

Cornelius jumped down off Max's haunches. "What about the other cat?" he demanded. He and Sebastian walked round the side of the wagon to look back along the trail. A crumpled shape was lying in the dust a good distance away, but from where they were standing it didn't look anything like a panther.

"Shadlog's beard!" muttered Cornelius. He drew his sword from its scabbard and began to walk back along the trail. Sebastian followed, drawing his own sword. First they came to the end of the long length of rope; they followed it to find that the noose was looped around the neck of a dead man. He lay face-down, naked and bloodied. Cornelius knelt beside the body and turned the head round to reveal the face.

"Adam!" whispered Sebastian. "But . . . how can that be? It was a panther I roped—we both saw it."

"A changeling," said Cornelius. "A shape-shifter. I've heard people speak of their existence but I've never seen one till now." He thought for a moment. "That's how they were able to escape through that narrow gap in the cave!"

"*They?* You mean—"

A deep rumbling growl snapped Sebastian's gaze back up to the tree line. The second panther, a female, was crouching there, staring at him intently with her malevolent yellow eyes. Oddly familiar eyes, Sebastian thought, and a cold chill ran through him. As he watched, the panther began to change her shape. Her body reared upward, her fur receded, her paws melted and elongated into fingers, and almost faster than his eye could follow, the cat was a naked woman and it was Leonora who stood there, glaring at him with cold hatred in her eyes.

"You killed my brother," she snarled.

"It . . . it was an accident," said Sebastian. "Well, no, it wasn't an accident, obviously, but I thought he was a panther. Well, he *was* a panther! And he was attacking my friend! Er . . . look, do you know you haven't got any clothes on?"

She said nothing for a moment, just stood there glowering at him in silent accusation. Then she raised an arm to point a finger at him. "I curse you, Sebastian Darke," she said.

"Oh no, don't do that! There's really no need to—"

"I curse you and your friends. You will find what you seek but it shall never be yours. Never! And you shall see me again. This I swear!"

"Look, can't we just talk about this?" Sebastian spread his arms in a gesture of helplessness. "Adam shouldn't have attacked us like that. We—"

But now Leonora was muttering some strange, incomprehensible language and waving her hands in front of her, as though plucking invisible objects out of the air.

"Right," said Cornelius. "I've had about enough of this."

He leaped to his feet and, lifting his sword above his head, raced toward Leonora, bellowing as he ran.

But as he brought back his sword to strike her, there was a sudden flash of brilliant light, so intense that he and Sebastian had to cover their eyes with their hands. And when they could see again, Leonora was gone. She seemed to have vanished.

Sebastian stared at Cornelius. "What happened to her?" he gasped.

"Who cares?" said the little warrior. "Let's get out of here."

Sebastian pointed to Adam's body. "What about him?"

"Leave him here. Let *her* take care of him, since she's so upset." Cornelius saw the look of dismay on Sebastian's face and slapped him on the hip. "Don't torment yourself, lad—you were only doing what any of us would have done. You didn't know it was him."

"What about the curse?" said Sebastian as they walked back to the caravan. "You heard what she said."

"Pah! I don't give any credence to that sort of codswallop." Cornelius clambered up onto the seat of the caravan.

"Yes, but I bet until today you wouldn't have believed that a man could turn into a panther," argued Sebastian, climbing up beside him.

Max looked back over his shoulder. "A man turned into a panther?" he echoed.

"Yes, Max," said Cornelius. "It was Adam, Leonora's brother. And she can do it too. They're shape-shifters!"

"I knew there was something funny about that witch," said Max.

"Don't call her that!" Sebastian slapped a hand over his mouth. Even the ordeal he had just endured hadn't cured him of his instinctive need to defend her. "Sorry, but . . . well, you're not being fair."

"Fair?" cried Cornelius. "Not fair? Let me see now: first they put you under an enchantment. Then they try to steal our treasure map. Then they turn into bloody great panthers and try to kill us—"

"Yes, but it was Adam who did all the bad stuff. Leonora probably did her best to talk him out of it."

"Oh yes? And who do you suppose found out about our mission in the first place? Who was it who sent Adam out to collect us and bring us back to the cave?"

Sebastian looked at him blankly. "But . . . she just wanted to help us, didn't she?"

Cornelius made a gesture of exasperation. "Come on, let's just leave. The sooner we're out of this infernal forest, the better."

"Hang on a moment!" complained Max. "I've got great big claw marks on my bottom, my lungs are about to burst, my legs are aching and you two won't give me any time to rest!"

Cornelius shrugged. "Take as long as you like," he said. "But I should perhaps mention that Leonora is still out there: she can still change into a ravening beast and she blames us for the death of her brother."

Max frowned. He considered for a moment, then shrugged his massive shoulders. "Perhaps I'll have a rest later," he said.

And without further argument he set off along the track.

CHAPTER 7

A FOLLOWER

After the excitement of the morning, the rest of the day's journey was mercifully uneventful. The well-traveled track led onward across rolling stretches of moor, rising occasionally to ridges and falling down again into shallow valleys. Occasionally large flocks of black birds traversed the unbroken blue vista of sky but otherwise they saw no signs of life.

"Would somebody mind telling me what actually happened back there?" asked Max eventually.

Cornelius glared at him. "Which bit did you not understand?" he growled. "We stayed the night with a pair of shape-shifters, one of them put an enchantment on Sebastian, and then they turned into panthers and we killed one of them. Simple, really. Oh yes—and the female one put a curse on us. Mustn't forget that bit. Not that I believe in any such mumbojumbo."

"Well, I hope you're right," said Max. "We've had

enough bad luck on this trip; a curse would be the last straw. Shape-shifters, you say! Mind you, I can't say I'm surprised. I knew there was something funny about that Adam the minute I saw him. His eyes were too close together."

"Hmm . . . funny you didn't mention it at the time," muttered Sebastian.

"Well, I could hardly say anything with him standing there, could I? I could hardly say, 'Ooer, look at him, don't you think his eyes are too close together?' That would have gone down very well, wouldn't it? But I knew he was a wrongun. And as for Leonora . . . well!" He rolled his eyes. "You wouldn't want to trust her any further than you could butt her." He glanced slyly at Sebastian who, for the moment at least, wasn't going to be drawn on the subject.

They moved on in silence for a while and then Max lifted his head, looked around and made a big show of sniffing the air.

"You know, this landscape is beginning to look vaguely familiar," he said. "We can't be all that far from the Darke homestead. Maybe we should make a little detour—drop by and see if your mother's all right. We could spend a night or two resting up before we continued on our—"

"Mother will be fine," Sebastian assured him. "She'll have received those gold crowns by now, so she'll be living in the lap of luxury."

"Yes, well, I wouldn't mind experiencing a bit of that myself," said Max wistfully. "There've been very few luxuries on this trip. When I think of that lovely warm stall in the stables of Keladon—"

"What's the matter, shaggy?" asked Cornelius. "Getting too old to rough it, are we?"

"It's nothing to do with age! It would just be polite to drop round and make sure everything is all right. Not that a Golmiran would know anything about manners."

"At least I know that passing wind in front of others is rude," snapped Cornelius.

"In Golmiran society, perhaps," said Max. "But in buffalope society it's considered the height of good manners to let out the occasional trump. Why, back on the plains of Neruvia there was one buffalope who—"

"—could play tunes!" finished Cornelius. "Yes, we've heard about him, time and time again, and I'm sure he was a very talented fellow. But rude or not, the fact remains that we're not going to call in at Sebastian's place." He glanced at Sebastian. "Unless, of course, you really *want* to."

Sebastian shook his head. "A detour would cost us a couple of extra days' travel," he said.

Max snorted. "So what's the big hurry?" he wanted to know. "If this blooming treasure has been lying around for so long, a few more days isn't going to make a lot of difference, is it?"

"Maybe we'll visit on the way back," said Sebastian; and the tone of his voice made it clear that as far as he was concerned, that was the end of the matter. He wasn't sure why he was so reluctant to visit the home where he'd grown up. Perhaps it was that he'd only been gone a relatively short while. Or perhaps it was simply that he didn't want to have to go through the ordeal of leaving his mother a second time.

The truth was, he was feeling decidedly strange. Ever since leaving the forest he had been experiencing a powerful aching sensation deep inside; and whenever he closed his eyes, his head filled with the vision of a pair of tawny eyes gazing intently at him. He realized that he was still under Leonora's spell, but try as he might, he could not seem to shake off the longing that filled his heart and soul.

Max, meanwhile, was incapable of remaining silent for long. "So we're really going through with this madcap idea?" he said.

Cornelius smiled. "It would appear so," he said calmly.

"And you actually think that this treasure—the treasure of Captain Aspidistra—is genuine?"

"That's Captain *Callinestra*," Cornelius corrected

him. "And of course I don't know for sure. But that's the gamble we're taking; that's the excitement of the thing!"

"Huh!" Max shook his huge head. "You'll forgive me if I don't get too excited. The only thing that would fire me up right now is a barrel of fresh pommers. And to be honest, it sounds like a load of old mulch to me. I've never heard of this legendary Captain Alan Extra."

"*Callinestra!*" barked Cornelius. "And his exploits are legendary. Why, my father used to tell me tales of his adventures when I was only little."

"So quite recently then," said Max.

"You watch it, shaggy—there's a limit to my patience!"

"My father told me the same stories," said Sebastian, making an effort to join in the conversation. "When I was disobedient, I was told that if I didn't shape up, the ghost of Captain Callinestra would come sneaking up in the night and take me off to work as a slave aboard his pirate ship. I tell you, I soon got my act together once I'd been threatened with that."

"Yes, but you see, they're only fanciful stories," argued Max. "He's like the Snipper, something made up to keep youngsters in line."

Sebastian and Cornelius were looking baffled.

"The Snipper?" echoed Sebastian.

"Yes, a legendary beast supposed to haunt the plains of Neruvia. If a young buffalope had been misbehaving, the Snipper would come in the night, lop off his tail and take it home to use as a skipping rope."

Sebastian and Cornelius exchanged amused glances.

"Well, point taken," said Cornelius. "But stories about the good captain are told everywhere. Anything that well known must have some foundation in fact. Why, it is said that his treasure hoard has been looted from the merchant ships of the known world and that it is hidden in some remote spot, where only the bravest dare venture. Now, Nathaniel told me—"

"Hold on a moment!" said Max. "Who's Nathaniel?"

"The chap in the hospital. The one I got the map from."

"Ah yes—carry on."

"He told me that the last time he tried to mount an expedition, he found the island exactly where the map said it would be. He and his men landed in rowing boats and started off into the jungle, heading for the peak of a high mountain. Then . . . something happened and they had to make a run back for the beach."

"Needed the loo, did they?" asked Max.

"No, it wasn't that! He said there was something

waiting for them out there . . . something . . . horrible . . . it was—"

"What?" cried Max impatiently. "What horrible thing was waiting for them? A monster? A demon? A bowl of lumpy porridge?"

Cornelius sighed. "I don't know," he said. "Nathaniel was just telling me about it when he . . . you know . . . popped off."

"Popped off?" Max looked back over his shoulder with a puzzled expression. "What does that mean?"

"He *died*, you idiot," snapped Sebastian.

"Oh, I see!" Max snuffled. "Bit inconvenient, I must say. Popping off before he'd told you exactly what was waiting for you."

"Yes, well, he didn't have a lot of say in the matter, did he?" growled Cornelius.

"No, but still . . . he could have tried to hang on a bit longer."

"Max, please shut up!" said Sebastian.

"Oh, well, that's charming," observed Max. "I was only trying to make some pleasant conversation."

"If that's pleasant, I wouldn't like to hear you being *un*pleasant," said Sebastian. "Now please, give it a rest and let me think."

He lapsed into a moody silence and remained that way for much of the day's journey, only venturing to ask a question when they were reaching the top of a ridge and he noticed that Cornelius was leaning out to look back down the incline.

"What's wrong with you?" Sebastian muttered.

Cornelius frowned. "Stop for a moment," he said.

Sebastian did as he was told, reining Max to a halt. Cornelius pulled a battered old spyglass from his belt. He stood up on his seat and extended the device to peer back down the trail. He sat still for several moments, squinting into the eyepiece.

"What are you looking for?" demanded Sebastian irritably.

"Not quite sure," said Cornelius. "But I have a sneaking suspicion that— Aha! Just as I thought."

He handed the spyglass to Sebastian and pointed down the trail. Sebastian got to his feet and lifted the device to his eye.

"What exactly am I supposed to be looking for?"

"Just keep watching," Cornelius told him.

Sebastian moved the focus of the telescope impatiently back and forth before he picked up a distant cloud of dust. He homed in on it and, after squinting for a while longer, was able to discern a cloaked figure mounted on an equine and riding slowly toward them. At first he was unable to make out much detail, but then he realized that it was a woman.

"It would seem that your shape-shifting friend is not quite finished with us yet," observed Cornelius.

"Leonora?" Sebastian couldn't help it: at the very mention of her something in his heart seemed to leap in exultation. "I . . . I wonder what she wants?"

"What do you *think* she wants?" retorted Cornelius. "Revenge for her brother, no doubt. Not to mention the treasure."

"Oh no, I don't think she'd be interested in that. No, it's probably just a coincidence that she's heading this way."

"Oh dear," observed Max. "He *has* got it bad. Isn't there anything we can do for him, Cornelius?"

"What would you suggest? I'm no magician." Cornelius looked thoughtful for a moment. "Perhaps if I waited here behind a rock and cut off Leonora's head as she rode by, that might lift the enchantment."

"You'll do no such thing!" protested Sebastian. "She has a lovely head and it will look a lot better left on her shoulders."

"Yes, but, Sebastian, think about it! If we don't stop her now, she's liable to follow us all the way to the treasure. And who knows what dark arts she might practice on us along the way? I'm afraid of no mortal man or creature . . . but an evil witch like her makes me very nervous indeed."

"I don't know why you keep calling her that," protested Sebastian. "I mean . . . if it wasn't for her, that snake would have eaten the pair of us."

"Oh yes, she arranged our rescue, I'll grant you

that. But only because she suspected we might be of value to her. And once she had a sniff of our reason for making this journey, she and her brother came sneaking like thieves in the night, as you well know."

"I still think that could have been a misunderstanding."

"Oh really! And what about when they turned themselves into panthers and tried to kill us? That would be a misunderstanding too, I suppose?"

"Umm . . . well, you see, I've been thinking about that. I believe that when they change into cats, their animal instincts probably get the better of them. They can't actually help themselves."

"The young master is addled in the head," observed Max glumly. "We'd do better to take him to a doctor."

"There's no doctor who can prescribe a cure for what he's got," muttered Cornelius. "Come on, let's get moving before she starts to catch up with us!"

Sebastian found himself wanting to linger so that he could speak to her again; but Cornelius was giving him a certain look and he knew that there was little point in arguing. So he slapped the reins against Max's shaggy flanks and they went on their way and began to descend the ridge into the valley below.

CHAPTER 8

ALL CHANGE

They made camp for the night and kindled a fire. Sebastian and Cornelius dined well on a javralat that the Golmiran had killed, back along the trail. Afterward they laid out their bedrolls, but the little warrior kept gazing off into the darkness, and after a while he was able to point out the distant twinkle of a campfire.

"There she is," he muttered. "Looks like she's gained some ground on us too. An equine travels faster than an old buffalope and a caravan."

"Oh, don't mind my feelings," grunted Max, who was browsing the grass a short distance away. "Talk about me as if I'm not here."

"It's not a criticism," said Cornelius. "I'm just stating a fact." He stared moodily toward the distant light. "I could easily go out there, you know. We

Golmirans are renowned for our stealth. I could wait till she's asleep, creep up on her with my sword and—"

"Nobody's creeping up on anybody!" Sebastian assured him. "My goodness, earlier today you were criticizing her for doing the very same thing. Let's just get some sleep." He made a point of waiting until Cornelius had climbed into his bedroll before following suit. He lay there for a while, thinking about Leonora sleeping only a short distance away, and part of him wanted to go to her, just to look into those beautiful tawny eyes again. Yes, he knew it was madness; he understood that after what he'd done to her brother, she would most likely try to kill him; and yet whatever it was she had planted in his unconscious mind, it had a powerful hold on him. It would not allow him to rest; he could feel it tugging at him, nagging at him like some strange malady.

Finally he managed to shrug off the notion and pulled his blanket tighter around him, because it was cold out here at night. He listened for a while but there was just the sound of the restless wind whistling across the wide stretches of grassland. But the day's journey had tired him, and he finally fell into a deep and dreamless sleep.

* * *

He woke suddenly with a rising sense of apprehension. He wasn't sure what had woken him, but now that it had, he was strangely anxious and sleep seemed a million miles away.

It was late and the moon was full, spreading a pale glow across the plains. He rolled over to say something to Cornelius and was shocked to see that his friend's bedroll was empty. He snapped upright, blinked away the last threads of sleep and gazed around nervously. The moonlight gave good visibility for quite some distance. He saw Max, huddled down in the shelter of the caravan, fast asleep, his huge shoulders rising and falling. But there was no sign of Cornelius anywhere.

With a mounting sense of panic, Sebastian realized what must have happened. He struggled out of his bedroll, strapped on his sword and started off in the direction of the distant campfire, walking at first but then breaking into a run, heedless of the noise he was making—he didn't know how much of a start Cornelius had on him.

The twinkling light of the campfire grew rapidly closer but he didn't slow his pace. He kept thinking about what Cornelius had said to him just before they'd settled down for the night. He must have gone to kill Leonora, and Sebastian knew that he could not allow that to happen.

He was still some distance away when he spotted Cornelius, moving stealthily toward a sleeping figure that lay stretched out on the ground beside the low, flickering fire. There was a glitter of steel and Sebastian could see that his friend was holding out his sword. He was close now, so very close. Sebastian redoubled his efforts, pumping his arms and legs desperately, but now Cornelius was stepping up to the bedroll; he was raising his sword high and—

"No!" yelled Sebastian. He flung himself forward, his arms outstretched to grab the little warrior, but he was an instant too late. Cornelius's arm came down in a swift, brutal arc and the blade bit deep into the blankets and cut through to the ground beneath. An instant later Sebastian slammed into him and sent him sprawling to the ground.

They rolled over in the dust. Cornelius came swiftly back to his feet and adopted a fighting stance, his weapon raised to defend himself; and Sebastian couldn't stop himself from drawing his own sword and moving forward to meet him. Suddenly Cornelius realized who it was and lowered his weapon, but Sebastian felt no compulsion to do likewise. A terrible rage was burning in his chest.

"Sebastian, what are you doing?" growled Cornelius, but then had to duck beneath a savage swing from Sebastian's sword that would surely have taken his little head clean off his shoulders. "What's got into you, man?" he cried. He took a couple of steps back but Sebastian kept coming at him, anger pulsing within him like a living thing.

"You killed her!" he screamed. "After everything I said, you killed Leonora!"

"I killed nobody," said Cornelius flatly.

"Yes you did, I saw you! Don't lie to me!" Sebastian ran forward again, his sword ready to strike his friend, and Cornelius gave a tut of irritation. He intercepted the blow with his own blade, flicked the weapon expertly aside, then launched himself upward in an almost leisurely somersault. Sebastian saw it coming and tried to step out of the way, but he was too slow. Cornelius's boots connected with his chin and he went down in an ungainly sprawl, dropping his sword. He lay there, stunned, the moonlit plain seesawing crazily around him. He saw Cornelius walk up to the pile of blankets, reach out with his sword and flip them open to reveal another roll of blankets inside the outer ones.

"Not here," said Cornelius regretfully. "She must have known what I was planning."

"Thank goodness," whispered Sebastian. "I thought—"

He broke off at the sound of a distant bellow—the sound of a terrified animal.

"Max?" Sebastian whipped round to look back the way he had come, and suddenly he could see everything with startling clarity: the light of his own campfire back there and, a short distance from it, another fire—a much bigger one—blazing up under the night sky.

"Shadlog's beard," snarled Cornelius. "The caravan!" He began to sprint back the way he had come and, after a brief hesitation, Sebastian scrambled to his feet, grabbed his sword and followed him. They ran side by side in silence, neither of them wanting to believe what was happening. But they only had to travel a short distance to confirm their worst fears. The caravan was burning. Everything they owned was going up in flames.

When they finally reached the blazing shell, it was too late to save anything. The flames were too powerful, leaping up as though trying to claw at the sky. They found Max wandering agitatedly round the fire, shaking his head and apologizing to anyone who would listen.

"I'm so sorry," he said. "It's not my fault. I was having a wonderful dream in which I was eating my way through an entire field of sweet berries, and then I woke up and the caravan was already burning. I couldn't find you two and I had no way of putting it out. I tried weeing on it, but I couldn't produce enough. Oh dear! What's going to happen to us now?" He thought of something. "Oh no! The barrels of pommers—I was looking forward to those!"

Sebastian couldn't find the words to reply. He stood there watching in disbelief as a large part of his young life was destroyed. It wasn't just the food and supplies they'd brought for the expedition, though that was bad enough. All his father's props and costumes had been in the caravan; his journals, his boxes of souvenirs and mementos from the glory days when he was jester to the king's court. Such treasures had little material value but were irreplaceable.

Cornelius made a sound of disgust and spat onto the earth at his feet. "Still think so highly of your precious Leonora now?" he growled. Lit by the glow of the fire, his face looked positively diabolical. "She's been creeping around in the dark again."

"Just as *you* were," snapped Sebastian. "Only you had cold-blooded murder on your mind. She merely wanted to deprive us of our comfort."

"Think so? For all she knew we could have been sleeping in there."

Sebastian sighed and shook his head, realizing that it was pointless to stand there debating the matter. He glanced at Max, who was still pacing anxiously up and down.

"Well, one thing's for certain," he said. "For some time now I've been talking about the possibility of

making a career change. Looks like I no longer have any choice in the matter." He took off his jester's hat and threw it into the blaze. The fabric caught fire immediately and went up in a flash of sparks.

The three of them stood there in silence and watched the burning caravan. It went on blazing all through the night.

CHAPTER 9

ON FOOT

When the wooden embers of the caravan were finally reduced to a pile of gray ash and blackened timber, they set about rescuing whatever they could. It was precious little. A few metal tools and knife blades had survived, along with a handful of coins and a couple of stone pots, but everything else had perished. Refusing to be downcast, Cornelius set about making backpacks out of the bedrolls, telling the others that maybe it was all for the best.

"That old caravan was only slowing us up," he said as he stowed his few remaining belongings in his pack. "It's better this way: we'll travel faster and we can easily buy more provisions when we get to Ramalat. I'm told that the markets there are the finest in the known world. Luckily the treasure map was here at my breast the whole time. If that had been in the caravan, then we really would have been in trouble. So things aren't as bad as they may seem."

"You are the eternal optimist," observed Sebastian. "If somebody had cut off our legs in the night, you'd say it was all the better for us to walk on our hands."

"Oh, it's not so bad. What was in that caravan anyway?"

"Well, let me see now. Tools, cooking implements, weapons—"

"That's not what I meant. I'll tell you what was in there—a bunch of old memories, tying you to the past. Now you are free to concentrate on the future."

Max looked particularly unconvinced by this. "But what am I going to do?" he complained. "Pulling that caravan was my job. Now I'll only be able to amble about without purpose."

"Not much change there then," murmured Cornelius.

Sebastian stroked the buffalope fondly on his great horned head. "Why don't you find your way back to Mother's?" he suggested. "You said yourself it's not all that far from here. Cornelius and I can carry on alone; you may as well be back there in a nice comfortable stable."

Max thought about it for a moment, then snorted and shook his head. "No fear," he said. "For one thing, that wicked witch is lurking out there somewhere. . . . And yes, young master, I know you'll immediately jump to her defense and say that she's not as bad as all that, but I would rather not risk it. For another thing, I do not relish the prospect of returning to my mistress to tell her that all her late husband's belongings have been destroyed in a fire."

Sebastian scowled. "It was everything we had of him," he murmured. "All my mother's memories, gone up in smoke. She'll be mortified when she finds out."

Max shook his head. "She'll be sad, of course. But though I hate to agree with Cornelius, for once he was right. They were only possessions, young master. Memories—true memories—are what we carry in our hearts. No flame could ever destroy them."

Cornelius smiled. "You know, Max, for a simple buffalope you can sometimes be quite eloquent," he said. He lifted his improvised pack and tested its weight. "Anyway, I for one am glad to have you along with us."

"Really?" said Max, surprised.

"Yes. It means you'll be able to carry our packs for us." He took hold of Sebastian's pack and set about fixing the two of them together to form a pair of makeshift saddlebags.

"Oh, well, that's marvelous, isn't it," said Max mournfully. "So nice to know I can still be of service!" He glanced warily at Sebastian. "Are you sure about this business of abandoning your career? You know, your poor late father wanted nothing more than for you to follow in his footsteps."

"I realize that. But I may as well face the fact that I have no talent for telling jokes and riddles. I think that much was proved back in Keladon."

"Hmm. Problem is, young master, what *do* you have a talent for?"

Sebastian shrugged. "Perhaps we'll find out somewhere on our travels," he said.

"Here, Sebastian," said Cornelius. "Help me tie these packs. We'd best be getting on our way if we ever want to reach Ramalat."

They tied the packs securely across Max's shaggy back and set off, leaving the great pile of smoldering ash behind them.

Cornelius had been right about one thing: losing the caravan had freed them up considerably. They were able to move off the beaten track and take short cuts, which sped up their progress. When they rested, Cornelius used the time constructively. He cut lengths of supple wood and made himself a primitive bow and some arrows, which he used to hunt their food.

The landscape had begun to change again, and they found the route winding back and forth up steep, wooded hillsides, which Sebastian observed would have been very hard to negotiate with the caravan in tow. They were taking a break around midday when they looked up and saw a mounted figure observing them from a distant hillside. Despite everything that had happened, Sebastian felt the usual flutter in his chest, while Cornelius could only lament that Leonora was out of range of his new bow.

"Why hasn't she galloped on ahead of us?" muttered Max. "If she knows where the treasure is, she could be there before us and have it all plundered by the time we arrive."

Cornelius scratched his chin thoughtfully. "Perhaps she *doesn't* know exactly," he reasoned. "I've been thinking about this." He settled himself cross-legged on the ground. "My theory is that she reads people's minds—that's how she finds out all their secrets. But the treasure map is complex: I certainly couldn't picture its exact contents."

"No, and besides, it's Sebastian's mind that she's looked into," Max reminded him. "I doubt that she'd find very much in there."

Sebastian gave him a look of annoyance.

"What?" said Max innocently. "Well, be fair, young master—could you picture the treasure map in your mind's eye?"

Sebastian shook his head. "I don't remember much about it," he admitted.

"Well, then that must be it," said Max. "She knows only the approximate whereabouts of the treasure . . . and she needs us to lead her to it."

Cornelius looked determined. "There's a long way to go yet," he said. "We'll find a way to shake her off or my middle name isn't Algernon."

Sebastian and Max stared at him in surprise.

"*Is* your middle name Algernon?" asked Max.

Cornelius gave him a disgusted look. "Of course not," he said. "Don't be ridiculous." He stood up and started walking.

After looking at each other in puzzled silence for a few moments, Sebastian and Max followed. But glancing across to the far hillside, Sebastian saw that Leonora was on the move again, guiding her equine along the wooded track at a leisurely pace, taking her own sweet time, clearly in no great hurry to catch up with them.

They camped that night in a copse and roasted a haunch of velderbrox over the campfire. Cornelius had stumbled across the beast earlier in the day, an elderly male with a broken leg, which had become separated from the rest of the herd. Cornelius had reacted instinctively and felled it with a single arrow through the heart. It had been much too big to carry so they had trimmed off the best parts to take with them. Max had been rather upset by the whole business, pointing out that a velderbrox wasn't that far removed from a buffalope and that technically he'd been an accomplice to murder. But even he had to admit that the smell of roasting meat was very appetizing.

"I wonder if that's what I would have smelled like," he mused, "if King Septimus had succeeded in having me barbecued."

"I imagine you would have," said Cornelius gleefully. "Actually, I haven't told you this before, but I have dined on roast buffalope in Golmira."

"Really?" Max looked shocked. "What did it taste like?"

"Somewhere between a javralat and a velderbrox. Quite succulent. Of course, that was a young beast, not a dried-out, stringy old devil like yourself."

Max looked positively insulted. "How dare you! I'm in my prime," he said. "I've no doubt I would taste delicious. What do you say, young master?"

Sebastian smiled. "I think I'll stick to velderbrox, thank you. Anyway, *you* can't talk, Max. I seem to remember that on the journey to Keladon, a certain hungry buffalope partook of javralat meat—"

"I was *starving!*" protested Max, glancing around anxiously. "And please keep your voice down. I'm not proud of what I did!"

"You ate some gallock eggs too," Cornelius reminded him. "Hardly a usual meal for a buffalope. Are you sure I can't tempt you with a little morsel of velderbrox?"

Max turned away and began to chomp on the surrounding vegetation with exaggerated fervor.

As Sebastian and Cornelius settled down to eat, the

little warrior noticed the twinkling light of another campfire off in the distance.

"She's still with us then," he observed, "your friend Leonora." He studied Sebastian as he spoke.

"She's no friend of mine," said Sebastian unconvincingly.

"You say that, and yet you nearly took my head off when you thought I'd killed her."

"It's the strangest feeling," admitted Sebastian. "I know it's wrong and yet I can't stop myself from trying to defend her. Do you suppose I'll ever be free of the enchantment?"

"Probably only when she's dead," said Cornelius. "But don't worry, I shan't be going after her again. I've learned my lesson. Maybe we'll be able to throw her off the trail in Ramalat. It's only a few more days from here."

"Ah yes, Ramalat," said Max mournfully, lifting his head from the undergrowth. "I've heard it said that it's a terrible place, packed full of pirates, Brigands and cutthroats."

"You shouldn't believe everything you hear," Cornelius told him. "Besides, it's merely a stopping-off place for us. Somewhere to hire a ship that will take us to our true destination . . . and the pirate king's treasure."

CHAPTER 10

THE PORT OF RAMALAT

Two days later, a little after midday, they climbed to the top of a ridge and unexpectedly found themselves gazing down on a long stretch of coastline. Immediately below them lay a huge bay, where countless wooden ships of all sizes rode at anchor; and in the curve of that bay, nestled against the hillside, was the port of Ramalat, a large cluster of timber and rough plaster houses, rising steeply from the water's edge and so tightly packed together that they seemed to be piled one on top of the other.

But it was the sea itself that caught Sebastian's attention. He had never actually seen it before—only heard about it—and he was stunned by its apparent endlessness; the way it stretched to the horizon from east to west. He remembered Cornelius's wild tales of how he had traveled upon the oceans of the world and his claim that if a man sailed far enough across those waters, he would eventually arrive back at the place from which he had departed. It had all seemed incredibly far-fetched, but looking at the vastness of the sea now, Sebastian thought that anything seemed possible.

"It's quite a sight, isn't it?" murmured Cornelius. "I know the first time I saw it, as a young lad, it quite amazed me."

"My father spoke of the sea many times," said Sebastian. "I swam in a big lake once and thought I had the measure of what the sea must be like, but now that it's before me . . . well, it's extraordinary."

"And just breathe in that air! You know, people say that sea air has special healing qualities. Why, I once—"

"It looks deep," interrupted Max apprehensively. "How deep do you suppose it is?"

Cornelius laughed. "What's the matter, old shaggy? Can't you swim?"

"I can swim very well," Max assured him. "It's just that I'd rather not if I don't have to. So I ask again, how deep is it? Is it shallow enough to paddle?"

Now Cornelius roared with laughter. "Paddle? Why, it's deep enough out there to cover the peak of the highest mountains!"

Max looked uneasy. "Well then, when we hire a ship, we'd better make sure we get one that's not likely to sink. One with no holes in it."

Cornelius shook his head. "I'll make especially sure of that," he said. "If there's one thing I can't stand, it's a ship with holes in it." He turned and led the way onward. "Come on. We're to look for a place called the Spyglass Inn. Apparently that's where all the ships' captains do their drinking."

The ridge sloped rapidly down out of the woodland and curved round to join a cobbled road that led them through the city gates, where they joined a milling throng of tradesmen, sailors, merchants and nobles moving to and fro along the street. A couple of uniformed soldiers lolled beside a gatehouse but took no notice of who was coming and going.

As the three friends strolled through the gates and along the main street of the city, a little weasel-faced man with a shaggy beard sidled up to Sebastian and pointed at Max.

"Is that your buffalope?" he asked.

Max looked at the man indignantly. "I'm not anybody's buffalope," he retorted. "I am my own free agent."

The man stared at Max. "A talker, eh? I've been told that some of them can talk." He looked slyly at Sebastian. "I'll give you three gold crowns for him," he said. "He's a bit old, but I can always use a big lad like him."

Sebastian shook his head. "He's not for sale," he said.

"Not at that price, anyway," added Cornelius.

"Not at *any* price!" added Max.

"Oh, come along, gentlemen, this is Ramalat. Everything has a price here." The man rubbed his beard for a moment. "All right, I'll go to five crowns, but that's my final offer."

Cornelius grinned up at Sebastian. "Five crowns," he said. "That's not bad—I think we should consider it."

Sebastian tried not to smile. "I don't know, Cornelius. I think he's worth a bit more to me than that."

"Quite right, young master!" Max looked horrified. "Five crowns, why it's an absolute insult! A buffalope of my experience . . . If I was for sale—and I assure you I'm not—I would think a reasonable starting price would be twenty, twenty-five crowns."

The bearded man looked alarmed. "Twenty-five! You are joking, I trust! I could get a lusty young fellow for less than that."

Max shook his huge head. "Age is not the issue. Look at my physique. You can see I've worked hard all my life. Any man who was lucky enough to purchase me would be buying the most hardworking buffalope ever."

The man snorted. "I'm not bothered about work. Meat's all I care about. I supply rations to the army and a beast like that would feed a squad of soldiers for a month."

"Oh well, don't mind my feelings!" said Max. "Just act as though I'm not here!"

"Six crowns!" said the bearded man. "My final offer. Take it or leave it."

"Leave it," said Sebastian, and the man shrugged and disappeared into the crowd. Sebastian and Cornelius laughed at Max's outraged expression.

"The cheek of the man!" he stormed. "No respect at all. He didn't even take you to one side and have the discussion out of my hearing."

"Yes, well, you'd better be careful," Cornelius warned him. "If we run short of money for this expedition, we'll know exactly where to get six crowns."

"It's typical, isn't it? Somebody wants to buy me, but it's not for my strength, my wit, my intelligence. Oh no, he just wants to braise me over a fire and serve me up on a plate to a bunch of squaddies! I'm not at all sure I approve of this place!"

The street inclined gently down to the harbor now, and they saw that a fishing boat was moored at the jetty. A couple of muscular, barechested fishermen were unloading barrels packed to the brim with little silvery fish. People were crowding round the dock, clamoring to buy them, and there was a tumult of good-natured shoves and loud banter. Sebastian had never tasted sea fish and would have been interested to try some, but Cornelius firmly led the way on along the quayside. At the end they found the place they were looking for.

The Spyglass Inn was a great big timber-and-daub building, several floors high. Smoke belched from its many chimneys and the crudely painted inn sign depicted a piratical-looking sailor peering into an ancient telescope. Menu boards chalked up outside advertised the fact that food was available and that there were rooms for hire on the top floor. OUR BEDS ARE BUG-FREE, announced one sign proudly.

"Right," said Cornelius, rubbing his hands. "I'm about ready for a tankard of strong Ramalatian ale. We'll go straight in and see if we can scare up a captain and crew."

Sebastian nodded and told Max to wait for them outside.

"Are you sure that's a good idea?" asked the buffalope, glancing about nervously. "Everybody in this place seems to want to eat me!"

"Hardly everybody," Sebastian corrected him. "Only one man. But if you have any problems, just give us a shout." He indicated an open window, then patted Max on the head and followed Cornelius in through the ancient wooden door. He found himself in the main room, which was dim and smoky and crowded with drinkers. The air was thick with pipe smoke and the buzz of scores of jumbled conversations. Somewhere, somebody was playing a wheezy-sounding instrument, though the noise it produced could hardly be described as musical. The roof was low, only a few inches above Sebastian's head. He followed Cornelius to the bar. The Golmiran was obliged to scramble up onto a high stool at the counter to make himself seen by the landlord, a big, bald brute of a man with a dark leathery face covered with intricate tattoos. When he grinned, he displayed a set of badly fitting false teeth fashioned from some kind of highly polished shell. Cornelius ordered a couple of tankards of the local ale and immediately engaged the landlord in conversation.

"You seem to be busy today."

"We're always busy here!" said the landlord. "Traders from all over the known world come to Ramalat to sell their goods." He filled two tankards from a huge barrel and set them before his new customers. "That'll be two croats," he said. Cornelius found his moneybag and handed over the coins, which the landlord tested between his strange teeth before dropping them into his purse.

"New in town?" he asked.

"Yes," said Cornelius. "We've traveled here from Keladon."

The man's eyebrows raised slightly. "Keladon! That's quite a distance. I heard there's been a big ruckus over there. Some kind of uprising against the king."

"Yes," said Sebastian. "We were the ones who—" He broke off as Cornelius elbowed him in the ribs.

"—saw some of it," continued his friend. "I understand it was quite a nasty business. But they say the new queen is well loved by her people." He gave Sebastian a sly look, warning him not to say anything further on the matter.

"So what brings you gentlemen here?" asked the landlord.

"My friend and I have need of a ship and a captain," said Cornelius. "We'd be willing to pay handsomely for the right one." He leaned over the bar and adopted a conspiratorial air. "I don't suppose you could recommend somebody reliable?"

The big man thought for a moment. His expression remained blank until Cornelius reached once again into his moneybag and placed an extra croat on the counter.

"Well, sir, I will tell you this," he said. "The captain and the crew of the *Sea Witch* are in today. You'll find them in the snug." He indicated a small room at the other end of the bar. "They've been sitting around for quite a few days now with time on their hands. They often undertake work for various people and I understand they are honest which, believe me, is a pretty rare thing among seafaring folk."

Cornelius nodded and placed another coin on the bar. "Thanks for the tip," he said. "And have a couple of drinks on us."

The landlord gave his shell-encrusted grin and once again tested each coin with his teeth before slipping them into his purse.

Sebastian and Cornelius took their tankards and pushed their way through the crowds toward the snug.

"Why did you stop me telling him that we led the uprising in Keladon?" asked Sebastian.

"I didn't think it was a good idea to go advertising the fact. This is supposed to be a low-key operation—the last thing we want to do is draw attention to ourselves."

Sebastian nodded. He could see the sense in that.

In the snug they found a motley collection of some ten or so sailors slumped around a huge oak table, nursing drinks and looking distinctly bored. Sebastian realized that it was one of the sailors who was making the "music," alternately opening and closing a strange box that rested on his lap. None of the other men were giving him any encouragement to continue but he was going at it anyway, his craggy, weather-beaten face a picture of concentration. One tall character, wearing the flamboyant three-cornered hat of a sea captain, was facing away from Sebastian and Cornelius, staring out of the open window.

Cornelius stepped up to the table and cleared his throat. "Good day to you!" he said. "Do I have the honor of addressing the captain of the *Sea Witch*?"

The figure nodded but didn't turn.

"Excellent," he went on. "I am here, sir, to see if you would be willing to hire out your ship and crew to me and my friend. We wish to make an expedition and need the services of somebody reliable. I can assure you that you would be handsomely rewarded for your work."

The figure turned, and Sebastian was shocked to see that the captain was a young woman, dressed in the frock coat and breeches of a man. Though a tangle of long red curls spilled out from beneath her hat and over her shoulders, she had an evil-looking cutlass strapped around her slender waist, and the confident look in her deep-brown eyes announced to the world that she was not to be underestimated. She studied the two of them for a moment and then smiled.

"Come, sit at the table, gentlemen," she said. "We'll have a drink together and see if we can come to some arrangement."

CHAPTER 11

JENNA SWIFT

Sebastian found a seat beside the captain and Cornelius was able to locate a high stool which, when customized by the addition of several cushions, brought him up to the level of the other drinkers. Sebastian settled himself in his chair and then allowed himself a quick glance around the table.

The crew of the *Sea Witch* were a fearsome-looking bunch and no mistake; and they were all regarding him with flat, unflinching gazes, as though challenging his very right to be sitting at this table. Sebastian had never seen such a collection of strangely shaped noses, rotten teeth and missing limbs in his entire life. The man who had been playing the musical instrument grinned at Sebastian, revealing teeth that were made not of shell like the landlord's, but predominantly of what looked like pure gold. He had an ancient leather patch over one eye and huge silver hoops through his earlobes.

"Welcome, lads," he said, extending a filthy hand to shake. "I'm Lemuel, the captain's first mate. Everyone calls me Lem."

Sebastian took Lemuel's hand and nearly had his fingers crushed to a pulp by the man's powerful grip. He was glad to turn his attention to the captain, who was a lot better-looking than Lemuel but had just as firm a grip. As he shook her hand, trying not to wince with the pain of it, Sebastian saw that she was still appraising him, a curious half-smile on her lips.

"I'm Captain Jenna Swift," she said in a deep, slightly husky voice. "Who do I have the pleasure of addressing?"

"Ermm . . . Sebastian Darke. I'm—"

"—former Prince of Fools and jester to the court of King Septimus of Keladon," finished Cornelius. Sebastian glanced at him, surprised.

"A jester, eh?" Jenna seemed pleased to hear this news. "We could do with a few laughs around here, couldn't we, lads?" There were general yells, grunts and curses of agreement.

She looked at Sebastian thoughtfully, appraising his tattered-looking outfit. "Where's your hat?" she asked him. "Jesters wear special hats, do they not?"

"I'm not Prince of Fools anymore," protested Sebastian. "I've given it all up. Now I'm . . . I'm . . ."

"Prince of Pirates!" announced Cornelius dramatically.

Jenna looked none too impressed by this. "We're not too keen on pirates at this table," she said coldly.

"Of course not!" said Cornelius without hesitation. "The title does not suggest that he *is* a pirate, but that he is a vanquisher of them."

Lemuel's bristly jaw dropped several notches. "What, him?" he growled. "He don't look capable of vanquishing a rice pudding."

"Ah, don't let his slender appearance deceive you," insisted Cornelius. "Why, this young lad has taken on the roughest, scurviest of adversaries and, by the power of his mighty sword, tossed them into the ocean like chaff. Like chaff, I say!"

There was an incredulous silence after this.

"Thanks a bundle," muttered Sebastian, already wishing that Cornelius had kept his mouth shut. "I thought you said we were going to keep a low profile." He decided that the very least he could do was return the favor: "May I in turn introduce Captain Cornelius Drummel, late of the Golmiran army, and former member of the Crimson Cloak. Killer of Brigands, hero of one thousand battles to the death, feared exponent of the Golmiran death leap and heroic slaughterer of man-eating lupers."

There was another silence while everyone considered this information and then looked disbelievingly at the tiny figure seated on cushions before them.

Cornelius gave a weak smile. "All true," he said. "But my friend did exaggerate about the one thousand battles to the death. It's more like . . . ooh, nine hundred and twenty."

Captain Swift laughed at that. "It's an honor to be in such distinguished company," she said. She waved an arm toward the bar. "Jacob, let's have another round over here. My new friends will pay."

Sebastian opened his mouth to protest but was beaten to it by an unexpected voice from behind him.

"While you're at it, bring a drink for me! I'm dying of thirst out here!"

Sebastian turned in surprise to see that Max had stuck his big shaggy head in through the open window. "Max, I thought I told you to wait outside!"

"I *am* outside! At least, most of me is. But if you think I'm going to wait here without something to wet my whistle while you're inside knocking back the ale, you've another thing coming."

"But you don't even drink ale!"

"I'm quite prepared to give it a try. My mother always told me that I should take every opportunity to try new experiences."

Captain Swift seemed delighted by this new arrival

and there was much laughter amongst her crew. "Who is this impudent fellow?" she asked.

Sebastian felt obliged to explain. "He's . . . he's Max. My buffalope. Well, not mine exactly. He . . . he's the third partner in this expedition." There were some raised eyebrows at this. Presumably the sailors weren't used to seeing a beast of burden elevated to such a position of authority.

"You 'ave a buffalope for a partner?" said Lemuel incredulously.

"Er . . . yes. He . . . You see, Captain Swift, he—"

"Jenna! Call me Jenna."

"Er . . . yes, well, Jenna, Max has been in my family for a long time and—"

"What my young master doesn't want to say," said Max, "is that as well as being the muscle in this operation, I also provide the brains."

This remark was greeted by a chorus of raucous laughter from the sailors.

Max looked rather dismayed at the reaction. "Well, I hardly think it's a matter for jocularity," he protested. "I'm merely stating my position as clearly as possible!"

"Jacob!" yelled Jenna. "Bring over a bucket of ale for this funny talking beast."

"Funny talking beast?" cried Max. "Well, really!"

He would probably have had more to say on the

matter, but at that point the landlord set down a great foaming bucket on the wide windowsill and Max greedily plunged his snout into the contents, which caused even more hilarity. Tankards were raised in exaggerated toasts to Max's health, but he was too busy drinking to take much notice.

"So," said Jenna, after the laughter had subsided and everybody had taken a long gulp from their own tankards, "you wish to hire the *Sea Witch*. What would be our destination?"

Cornelius frowned. This bit was going to be tricky. "I cannot tell you exactly . . . at least, not yet. Our destination is a small island due south of the pirate stronghold of Lemora. I have a map . . . but you will not be able to study it in detail until we are out of the harbor. At that point I will be prepared to share the information."

"And when will you be ready to leave for this . . . mysterious destination?"

"At your earliest convenience."

Jenna considered this for a moment. Then she seemed to come to a decision. She clapped her hands together. "All right, lads," she said. "Finish up your drinks and get back to your homes. I'll want you at the jetty tomorrow morning at first light."

There were grunts and nods and a general move to do her bidding. All but for one man, a big dark-skinned fellow with tribal scars cut into his face and a shock of black hair in a series of tightly coiled dreadlocks.

"We still have some business to attend to, Captain," he growled. And he stepped forward and slapped a bag of coins down onto the table.

Jenna regarded it for a moment and sighed. "Can't this wait, Cassius?" she asked.

"With respect, Captain, I think it needs to be settled, once and for all."

She sighed. "Very well. But let's make it quick." She glanced up at Sebastian and Cornelius. "Excuse me for a moment, gentlemen. This shouldn't take long. Mr. Darke, if you would humor me by leaving your seat for a moment?"

Sebastian did as she asked and she ushered Cassius into the seat beside her. Then she took up a stance with the elbow of her right arm on the tabletop, her hand open. Cassius took up a similar position with his right arm extended and the two of them clasped hands. The remaining sailors gathered eagerly around the table to watch. "Right then, Lem," said Jenna. "Count us in."

Grinning, Lemuel did as he was told. "One . . . two . . . three!" he growled. And the two contestants took up the strain and began pushing for all they were worth.

Sebastian stared in amazement. He wouldn't have

given a croat for Jenna's chances against somebody as powerful as Cassius, but it quickly became apparent that she was holding her own against him; more than that, in fact. For while he was straining and sweating to make any impression on her, she looked perfectly relaxed, even breaking off at one point to lift her tankard with her free hand and take a sip from it. The surrounding crew shouted advice and encouragement to Cassius, but try as he might, he could not seem to better her. After a few moments of this, during which their entwined hands wavered slightly to one side or the other, Jenna began to apply steady pressure; and though Cassius struggled valiantly to resist, she began to force his hand steadily downward until it was pinned tight against the tabletop.

Cassius got up, shaking his head in disgust, while his shipmates slapped him on the back, enjoying his dismay. It was evident this was not the first time it had happened.

"Keep trying, Cassius," Jenna told him. "You're definitely improving." She gazed around the table at them. "And, lads, one more thing: tell nobody of our movements tomorrow. If anybody asks, we're taking a cargo of cloth round the coast to the Southlands. Is that understood?"

Again there were nods and grunts of agreement. Though they were evidently a rough bunch, it was clear that Captain Jenna Swift commanded their respect. The only one who made no move to leave was Lemuel, but Sebastian supposed that was only natural, if he was her right-hand man. The remaining crewmen left the room and Sebastian was able to resume his seat. Jenna slipped Cassius's purse into the pocket of her waistcoat.

"Some people never learn," she said with a smile. "Cassius challenges me again and again, and every time I take his money from him. But his male pride just won't let him stop making the challenge."

Cornelius leaned forward to fix Jenna with a hard stare. "You are powerful, Captain Swift. You must allow me to challenge you some time."

"You, Golmiran? Are you adept at arm wrestling?"

"I was considered a champion in my homeland. But that's for another time." He made a dismissive gesture. "I must say you were very prompt in dismissing your men. We have not yet agreed payment for the trip."

"No, we haven't," she admitted. "But let's see . . ." She settled back in her seat. "I'm a reasonable woman. And I'd be prepared to settle for . . . a one-third share of the treasure."

Cornelius and Sebastian rocked back in their chairs as if they had been punched, and even Max was disconcerted enough to leave off swigging from his bucket for a moment. He stared at Jenna, oblivious to the fact that he had a great white beard of foam hanging from his snout.

"Who said anything about treasure?" cried Sebastian. Then, glancing around, fearful that he'd spoken too loudly, he continued in a hushed tone. "Nobody even mentioned it, so why—?"

"Nobody needed to," said Jenna, laughing at his discomfort. "Of course there's treasure—why else would you be so secretive? And if it's somewhere due south of Lemora, then it can be only one treasure: that of Captain Callinestra."

Lemuel's one good eye seemed to twinkle at this news. "Of course!" he whispered. "People have spoken about its existence for centuries but there's never been a map . . . at least, not a real one. Plenty of fakes around, of course, but—"

"This map is no fake," Cornelius assured them, and Sebastian wondered how he could be so confident. "Of course, there's no guarantee that somebody hasn't been there before us. It might be a safer bet to take a standard wage for the trip. Otherwise you risk coming back empty-handed."

Jenna smiled. "It's a risk I'm prepared to take," she said, "because I *could* come back rich beyond my wildest dreams. Which is frankly too good a prospect to ignore."

"She's got a point," said Max, and hiccuped loudly.

Cornelius gave him an irritated look. "Stay out of this," he said.

"What? I was only shaying! There's no need to look at me like I'm a bad muffalope . . . I mean, a mad buffalope!" He lifted his head and stared toward the bar. "Landlord! Another belping of heer, if you please! I'm starting to get a taste for this stuff!"

Sebastian grimaced. That was all they needed right now. A drunk Max.

"Well, gentlemen, you're not saying much, are you?" observed Jenna. "Do we have a deal or not?"

"Well, for a start," interrupted Max, "you've got your figursh wrong, young lady. It would be a one *quarter* share of the treasure, because there are four of us, not three!"

Jenna looked at him for a moment and then turned to Sebastian. "You're not seriously giving a share to *him*?" she cried.

Sebastian winced. "Well, we've never formally discussed it," he admitted, "but—"

"Thersh no need for discussion," insisted Max. "We are partners. We share *everything*. So it's a one-quarter share, or you can go and take a junning rump into the ocean, young lady."

"But . . . what would a buffalope do with treasure?" Jenna wanted to know.

"I would give some to my mistress and . . . the rest

I would shpend on pommers to eat and beer to drink." Max became aware of Sebastian glaring at him and blew him a fruity raspberry. "Oh, loosen up!" he said. "Landlord, what are you doing with that ale, screwing it from bratch? I mean, brewing it from scratch?"

Jenna shrugged. She turned back to the table. "Very well," she said. "It sounds like madness to me, but a one-quarter share for me and my crew." She looked from Sebastian to Cornelius and back again. "You may as well accept my terms, gentlemen, because let me assure you, if you choose to go with another captain, you'll have the *Sea Witch* on your tail the moment you leave the quayside. And then we'd be rivals, not allies."

"And you wouldn't want us as rivals," Lemuel assured them. "Oh no, you would most definitely not want that."

Another bucket of ale arrived and Max set to with a vengeance, his loud slurps rudely breaking the silence.

Sebastian and Cornelius exchanged worried glances. Clearly Jenna Swift was as sharp as a cut-throat razor. Finally Cornelius sighed and spread his hands in a gesture of defeat.

"Very well. I suppose there's nothing else we can do. But listen well to these words. I don't want this matter to go any further. If any of your friends or relatives start following us to our destination, all deals are off. And you'll answer to my sword."

Jenna grinned, as though she liked the sound of this. "So, you're a swordsman as well as an arm wrestler! I'm no mean fighter myself," she told him. "Perhaps we can put it to the test someday." There was a short silence while the two of them appraised each other. "But yes," continued Jenna, "I agree that total secrecy should be the order of the day. Don't worry, I've no wish to share my cut of the spoils with anyone else. Or do you perhaps have a pet boobah hiding in the woodwork who wants to claim *his* share?"

"Very funny," said Sebastian.

Jenna bowed slightly. "I'll take that as a compliment from a professional joke-teller," she said.

"I already told you, I'm not in that line of work anymore," he said.

"Oh, that's right," she said, her eyes mocking him. "You're a pirate-killer now. I'd quite forgotten." She shrugged. "Well, I hope it's no idle boast, Mr. Darke. The waters we'll be sailing are infested with pirates—there's every chance we might see some action."

Cornelius grinned. "We're not afraid of a bit of action," he assured her. "You might say it's what we're used to." He raised his tankard in a toast. "So," he said. "To a successful trip."

"To success," said Jenna; and she and Lemuel raised their own tankards and drank deeply.

And then Max started singing. Well, not singing so much as bellowing.

> *"Out on the wild and rolling plain,*
> *I met a buffalope!*
> *His eyes were filled with tears of woe,*
> *It seemed he'd lost all hope.*
> *When suddenly he heard a sound,*
> *A voice that called his name*
> *And from that day that buffalope*
> *Would never be the same!*

> *"The voice of Colin, Colin, a buffalope so true . . .*
> *Colin, Colin, he's calling out to you!*
> *Colin, Colin, the king of all the beasts*
> *Colin, Colin, he calls you to the feast!"*

Heads appeared in the doorway from the other room. Some of the drinkers appeared to like the song, and were raising their tankards to the performer, but the landlord with the shell teeth didn't seem quite as impressed.

"Who owns that great noisy brute?" he bellowed.

"Time's moving on," said Cornelius hastily. "I think we should leave."

"Er . . . yes," said Sebastian. "I'm feeling pretty tired too."

They finished their drinks as quickly as they could

and virtually ran from the room, telling Jenna that they would see her the following morning. Once outside, they ran round the side of the building and did their best to drag Max away from the window, but having found an appreciative audience, he was somewhat reluctant to pack it in.

Eventually they managed to prise him away. As they moved off, Sebastian glanced through the open window and saw Jenna watching the incident with some amusement, her dark eyes flashing with mischief.

He waved to her, and then he and Cornelius led a very unsteady buffalope away in search of somewhere to spend the night.

CHAPTER 12

EVE OF DEPARTURE

After finally locating the only stable in Ramalat that was prepared to put up with the raucous din made by a singing buffalope, Sebastian and Cornelius trudged back to the Spyglass Inn and took a room for the night on the top floor.

Through the open window they had a magnificent view of the moonlit rooftops of Ramalat, sloping steeply down the hillside to meet the restless ocean, which rushed to and fro beneath the mantle of myriad glittering stars.

Sebastian stood looking out across the water with a strange mixture of feelings within him. There was excitement, yes, because this trip across water would be a totally new experience for him. But there was apprehension too. He remembered how Cornelius had said that the ocean was deep enough to cover the peaks of the highest mountains and the thought of going down into those terrible depths filled him with an unspeakable dread. There was one other thing. Try as he might, he couldn't rid himself of the image of Leonora's face.

Cornelius sat at a rough-hewn table, counting up his remaining coins. "We should be all right," he said. "In a way, Jenna's decision will work in our favor. If she'd asked for a straight fee, we'd have had trouble scraping it together."

"I suppose we could go to a moneylender," said Sebastian.

Cornelius scowled. "I wouldn't give those grasping scum the business," he said. "They'd only add on huge amounts of interest, and besides, we'd have to tell them what we wanted the money for. Even if we were vague about where we were actually going, they'd soon put two and two together, and before you know it, everybody in Ramalat would find out what we were up to." He placed his last coin on the small pile. "We can't even afford to replace all the equipment we lost in the fire," he said. "We'll just have to make do with very little until we find the treasure."

"And if there *is* no treasure?"

"We'll cross that bridge if and when we get to it," he said. "Jenna has agreed to a cut of whatever we find. If we find nothing, she gets a cut of nothing.

That's the way it works. But as for me, I trust the man who sold me that map."

Sebastian turned back from the window in surprise. "What?" he cried. "I thought . . . I thought you said you were *given* it. Somebody at the hospital in Keladon, you said. A man on his deathbed!"

"Well . . . he was dying, yes, but he . . . he didn't exactly *give* me the map. He sold it to me."

Sebastian could hardly believe his ears. "But why would anyone do that? I mean, what use was money to him if he was dying?"

"He had nothing left in the world," explained Cornelius. "The money was to pay for a decent burial. What's your problem?"

Sebastian shrugged. "Well . . . call me stupid if you like, but I don't feel inclined to trust a man whose last act on leaving this world is to get a few more croats in his pocket."

"More like five gold crowns," said Cornelius quietly.

"Good grief." Sebastian thought for a moment. "He must have been buried in real style for that, with a fine coffin and a site in the poshest graveyard in Keladon. Still . . . I suppose you took the money back once he was dead," he ventured.

"Absolutely not! I do have some principles, you know."

"Well, it's good to see that *somebody* does." Sebastian turned back to look out of the window. "So, we're five crowns down before we even start."

"No, *I'm* five crowns down. I'm the one who paid the money, remember. And it's not as if—" Cornelius broke off. "Why are you gazing out of the window like that?"

"Hmm? Oh, I was just wondering . . . do you suppose Leonora will be able to follow us across water?"

"Shadlog's beard, what are you blathering about?"

"Leonora. I was just wondering if I would ever see her again."

Cornelius stared at him for a moment. "You are a hopeless case, do you know that? Don't you realize that woman wants nothing more than to see us both die a horrible death?"

"I suppose . . . and yet, I can't stop myself from worrying about her."

"That's rich. The only worries she has about you are that you might go on living a bit longer. For my part, I hope we never lay eyes on her again, but something tells me that we won't be that lucky. And you'd better watch out, my lad. As if things aren't complicated enough, I'd say you have a new admirer."

"Really? Who would that be?"

"Jenna Swift, of course! She has her beady eyes on you."

"Me?" Sebastian stared at him. "Oh, I don't think so."

"Believe it! I know when a woman is making moon eyes at a fellow, and she was certainly doing that this evening."

Sebastian frowned. "Hmm, well, if that's really true, she needs to understand that there's only one woman in the world for me."

"Ah yes, of course. Queen Kerin. Still carrying a torch for her, eh?"

Sebastian looked at him blankly. "Who?" he said.

Cornelius slammed a hand down on the tabletop with a force that caused the piles of coins to go flying in all directions. "I don't believe it!" he cried. "You are the absolute end!"

"What have I done now?" cried Sebastian.

"You've only gone and forgotten the name of the woman who you claimed you'd love till the end of time!"

"Did I say that?"

"Yes, you did. And then you wandered about saying that your heart was broken and that there would never be another woman who could measure up to your beloved Queen Kerin. . . ."

"Well, yes, but—"

"And then, practically the next day, you set eyes upon that hideous scheming witch, Leonora—"

"I've warned you, don't call her that!"

"And suddenly you're completely besotted with *her*, a woman who would happily slice your head from your shoulders if she could only get within striking distance. A fine sweetheart she makes!"

"I appreciate she's not perfect, but—"

"And finally, to cap it all, you've got what must be the only female captain in Ramalat going all weak at the knees over you. I suppose it's only a matter of time before you fall for *her* charms!"

"That's nonsense. Me and Jenna Swift? I can't think of a more unlikely partnership. I mean, she wears men's clothes, for goodness' sake! All right, she's quite good-looking, I suppose. . . ."

Cornelius shook his head and buried his face in his hands. "We are most definitely in trouble," he concluded. "If you've noticed that much about her, the rest is sure to follow."

"No, I assure you, the only woman who occupies my mind is Leonora."

Cornelius groaned. "Perfect," he said. "The one who wants you dead is the one you'd give your heart to. Sebastian, you are the absolute limit!"

"Oh, now, don't be like that." Sebastian left his place at the window and went to sit at the table opposite his friend. "Come on, Cornelius, you must have been through similar times yourself."

"You are joking. When it comes to matters of the

heart, nobody in the world has had similar times to you. You're a . . . serial romancer!"

"I'll take that as a compliment. But . . . there must have been young ladies in Golmira when you were a young man. *Little* ladies. You're not telling me you didn't fall for any of them?"

Cornelius sat up straight in his seat and smiled wistfully. "There were plenty of young ladies in Golmira. It's famed for the beauty of its women. But there was only one who I ever really cared about."

"Aha!" Sebastian clapped his hands triumphantly. "And what happened to her?"

Cornelius's smile faded. "She married somebody else. A rich merchant, if you must know. So I enlisted in the army and since then I haven't so much as looked at another woman. And do you know what, Sebastian? I've been happy. Romance is an unnecessary complication. You're better off without it."

Sebastian thought about that for a moment. "Perhaps you're right," he said. "But what can I do? I'm under an enchantment. And until I find a way to shrug it off, I must accept what my heart tells me is true."

Cornelius gave a loud tut of annoyance and went back to counting his coins. "You're a hopeless case," he said.

"Maybe," admitted Sebastian. He got up and

walked back to the window, where he stood gazing out over the great restless sweep of the ocean, shimmering like a carpet of precious jewels in the moonlight. Amidst the other points of light, two glittering jewels seemed to stand out from the rest, burning with a powerful tawny glow.

PART TWO

CHAPTER 13

THE SEA WITCH

Sebastian and Cornelius were at the quayside as the first light of morning began to color the eastern horizon. They were leading a very sorry-looking Max, who had quite clearly endured a restless night.

"My poor head!" he groaned. "Which one of you insisted on me drinking that second bucket of ale?"

"Neither of us," said Sebastian, not without a certain sense of satisfaction. "That was all your idea."

"I'm nauseous, I tell you! I've spent the entire night groaning in my stall. And that ostler wasn't very sympathetic either. Kept telling me to belt up!"

Cornelius gave Max a suspicious look. "I hope you didn't tell him anything you shouldn't have," he growled.

"Of course not! I was too sick to form actual words. Fine friends you two turned out to be, allowing me to get into such a state!"

"You're an adult," Sebastian reminded him. "It's up to you to exercise control. You've never drunk ale before and do you take it easy? Oh no. You drink two bucketfuls!" He glanced at Cornelius. "I suppose we should have warned him that Ramalatian ale is the most powerful gut-rot known to man."

"Oh, stop fussing!" said Cornelius. "So he's got a bit of a headache. I'm sure he'll survive. Ah, that must be the *Sea Witch*!"

Sure enough, the ship was moored at the jetty and her crew were busy preparing her for sea, swarming up rope ladders and edging out along yardarms to unfurl the great canvas sails. Sebastian and Cornelius were able to study the ship in detail, noting that she gave the impression of a once-proud vessel that had seen better days. Here and there she had been roughly repaired, and Sebastian noticed that the carved figurehead of a strange, witchlike woman that hung from the prow had suffered an accident at some point: her nose had been sliced off and one cheek flattened. But he would have been the first to admit that he knew nothing about ships, and Cornelius, when pressed, had to confess that he was no great expert either.

"The only ships I've been on were troop-carriers," he said. "Great slow hulks with massive holds for carrying hundreds of men. This one looks a sleeker, faster kind of beast in my estimation."

"Oh, she's fast, all right," said a gruff voice, and they turned to see Lemuel shuffling down the gang-plank. "Don't be fooled by the few bumps and scratches we've suffered. There's not a faster ship in Ramalat."

Cornelius smiled. "I'm glad to hear it," he said.

"So, have you bonny lads been to sea before?" asked Lem slyly.

"I've done some sailing," said Cornelius. "But as for my friends here . . ."

Lemuel looked at Sebastian. "Oh, so you've yet to get your sea legs?"

"Sea legs?" echoed Sebastian. "What exactly are—?"

"You'll discover soon enough," Lem assured him. "When you get out on that deck and it starts going up and down, up and down, up and down—"

"Do you have to say things like that?" groaned Max. "I'm feeling a tad sensitive this morning."

Lem grinned. "I shouldn't worry," he said. "You'll be all right, great big rough lad like you." He glanced at Sebastian. "It's the more sensitive ones that usually have a problem." He glanced up at the sound of boots on wood. "Ah, here comes the captain!" he said.

And indeed, Jenna was approaching, striding along the quayside, a wide grin on her face as though she couldn't wait to be off. Sebastian watched her and had to admit grudgingly to himself that she *was* a fine-looking young woman. Not a patch on Leonora, of course, but still . . .

"Good morning!" she said as she approached. "Mr. Darke. Mr. Drummel. I trust both of you had a restful night." She looked cautiously at Max. "And . . . you . . ." She looked thoughtful for a minute, then took Sebastian's arm and led him a short distance away from the others. "Do you really think it's wise to bring the buffalope with us? I mean, wouldn't he be more comfortable staying in a stable until we return? I don't wish to seem awkward, but it's hardly the right place for a beast of burden, is it? He isn't going to like the motion of the sea one little bit."

Sebastian frowned. He was going to have to disappoint her in this matter. "To tell you the absolute truth, Captain Swift . . . er, Jenna . . . I'm afraid he simply wouldn't stand for it. You see, when I left home, my mother instructed him to look after me and he's stuck to that order ever since. I'm afraid he's as stubborn as a . . . well, as a buffalope."

Jenna looked slightly irritated at this news. "So you're telling me that the beast is some kind of . . . nursemaid to you?"

"Yes . . . er, no! No, it's not like that at all! But you see, he's more than just a buffalope. He's my . . . well, I suppose he's my friend."

"I see." Jenna seemed dismayed by this news. But after a few moments she shrugged. "Oh, well, you're the customer, you call the tune." She gestured to a couple of men up on the deck, who were operating a simple hoist with a heavy counterweight that they were using to lift provisions onto the ship. "Get the buffalope strapped up and swung aboard," she yelled.

The men looked at her incredulously. "On the deck?" one of them shouted down to her.

She shook her head. "In the hold," she shouted back. "I'm not having him trotting around pooping all over my ship!"

"Not even on the poop deck?" murmured Cornelius slyly, but she either didn't hear the comment or chose to ignore it. Max, of course, was offended by her remark.

"I'll have you know I'm perfectly able to control my bodily functions," he said. "Anyone would think you were talking about some common animal."

"Oh, do pardon me, Mr. Buffalope," said Jenna, giving him a mocking bow. "I was forgetting myself for a moment." She gestured to a couple of men on the dockside who were unbuckling a strong leather harness. "Strap this brute up and get him aboard," she said.

"Now look here," began Max. "I don't think there's any need to use that tone of voice. I was just—"

Before he could get any further, the two men had hurried over and were looping straps around his body.

"Here, go easy!" protested Max. "That's chafing me!"

One of the men snapped a metal catch into position and gave a thumbs-up to the sailors on the deck.

"Wait just a minute!" said Max. "I'm not—Aaaaarghhhh!" And his huge body was lifted up off the ground as though it weighed no more than a sack of vegetables. Sebastian raised a hand to shield his eyes as Max went flying across the skyline like some mythological beast. "This is not a good idea," he roared. "I have a very delicate stomach this morning. I'm not used to—Uuuurp!" There was a sudden belching noise and a great stream of vomit came hurtling down onto the quayside, obliging sailors to scatter out of the way.

Jenna gave a look of disgust. "If he's like that now, how will he be when we get under sail? Honestly!" She gestured for Sebastian and Cornelius to follow her. "This way," she said. She led them up the gangplank. As they climbed, Sebastian caught a glimpse of Max, still vomiting as he was lowered into the hold. From the cavernous interior of the ship, the sound of him being ill took on quite terrifying proportions. It sounded like he was shouting out the names of major cities. *Ramalat! Keladon! Jerabim!*

"I'll pop down and visit him later," said Sebastian.

Jenna looked at him and smiled. "You're devoted to that beast, aren't you?" she observed.

"He's been around for as long as I can remember," he said. "Of course I care about him."

"And tell me, Mr. Darke, is it true what they say about you elvish people?" she asked him. "That you can look at a person for the first time and see everything there is to know about them?"

Sebastian shrugged. "My father was human," he said, "so I suppose I only picked up some of the skills. But I like to think I'm a good judge of character. . . ."

Cornelius stifled a snort of laughter and Sebastian glared at him; but Jenna seemed not to have noticed.

"So what did you think when you first saw me?" she asked.

"Er . . ." Sebastian didn't want to admit to her that he hadn't thought of anything when he'd met her; that his head had been so full of images of Leonora that he'd been fairly indifferent to her. "I thought that you seemed a trustworthy person and a . . . very accomplished sea captain."

"Really? Well then, I'll know who to ask if I ever need a job reference!"

Jenna laughed and strode across the deck of her ship, her silver-buckled boots clumping on the scrubbed

planks. She led them up a short flight of wooden steps
to a high deck at the stern of the ship. From here, she
took a long slow look around the *Sea Witch*, checking
that everything was to her satisfaction. Then she nodded to Lemuel, who stood at the tiller.

"Take her out, Lem," she said. "Head due east until
I tell you different."

"Aye, aye, Captain," he said. "Cast off!" he roared.

Eager sailors ran to carry out the orders. The gangplank was pulled up, the hatches swung into position
and locked. Muscled arms pulled on ropes and the
yardarms swiveled; the sails billowed as they filled
with wind. More crewmen ran to cast off the great
mooring ropes and winch up the anchor—and the
ship began to move, gently at first, but gradually
gathering speed. After a short distance she began to
rise and fall on the restless waves. Sebastian and
Cornelius moved to the port side to watch the quay
slipping away from them. Cornelius was obliged to
clamber up onto a barrel to get a good view.

"Always a strange time, this," he observed, resting
his elbows on the wooden rail. "That moment when
you move away from land and set off into the great
vastness of the sea."

Sebastian didn't say anything. He was suddenly
filled with a terrible sense of apprehension. The
dockside was dwindling in size at a surprisingly

rapid rate, and after what seemed like only a few moments it had the dimensions of a child's toy. Then he was horribly aware of the way the deck planks were lifting and falling beneath his feet. He kept thinking that his unease would pass after a little while, but as they moved further and further away from land, so the motion grew more pronounced. Down in the hold, he could still hear Max roaring and groaning.

"I . . . I suppose you get used to the . . . the rhythm," he said quietly.

"Yes. Eventually." Cornelius studied his friend with some amusement. "But it's like I told you this morning, the best thing you can do in this situation is get a decent breakfast inside you. I noticed you didn't eat very much, did you?"

"I . . . wasn't really hungry," said Sebastian, who was finding it very difficult to take his eyes off the horizon. "Too excited, I suppose."

"Well, that's where you went wrong," said Cornelius, smiling gleefully. "Now, me, I had a hearty breakfast."

"Did you?" whispered Sebastian, not really wanting to hear about it.

"Oh yes. Three fried gallock eggs—you know, the really tasty green ones—several rashers of javralat meat with all the fat left on them . . . some taties fried in the meat juices . . ."

"Could we talk about something else?" said Sebastian, who could actually feel the color draining from his face. He looked hopefully back toward the shore and was shocked to find that it had become nothing more than a faint brownish streak on the horizon.

"And then I mopped the whole thing up with a big slice of—"

Cornelius stopped talking suddenly. His eyes widened and he looked as though he had just come to a terrible realization.

"What's wrong?" asked Sebastian. "Did you forget to bring something?"

Cornelius shook his head. "No. It's odd but . . . I do believe . . . I do believe I feel a little bit . . ." All the color suddenly left his face, and he abandoned the idea of talking and threw himself across the rail. He began to vomit, long and loud, into the sea.

"Aha!" cried Sebastian jubilantly. "That'll teach you! All that talk about greasy breakfasts—you were trying to set me off . . . but it backfired!" He started to dance a little jig, but had trouble placing his feet on the seesawing planks and quickly abandoned the idea. He put a hand on the rail to steady himself and then felt a dry belch rise up in his throat.

"I'm not going to be sick," he said aloud, though he wasn't sure who he was supposed to be talking to. "I . . . I most definitely am *not* going to be—"

And then he gave up trying to talk himself out of it and made for the rail alongside Cornelius.

The pair of them looked as though they were leaning out to shout insults at the land they had left behind.

Jenna breezed past them, not even bothering to stop and see if they were all right. "Gentlemen," she said, "when you've quite finished, I'd like you to join me in my cabin. I'm dying to have a look at that treasure map."

And she moved on without even slowing her pace.

CHAPTER 14

THE CAPTAIN'S TABLE

It was quite some time before they managed to prise themselves away from the ship's rail and venture down the swaying stairs that led to the captain's cabin. The first time they tried it, they both had to dash back up on the deck for another bout of coughing and retching, but eventually, when there was nothing left in them to bring up, they found themselves sitting, pale-faced and weary, at the round table down in Jenna's cabin, Cornelius perched on his usual stack of cushions to bring him up to the right height.

Behind them, the windows in the ship's stern afforded a fine view of the churning wake flowing out behind the ship but, for the moment at least, they didn't have much inclination to look out.

Jenna was eating a ripe red pommer. She was either oblivious to their delicate condition, or determined to make them feel even worse. Lemuel entered the cabin, carrying a large wooden bucket. He closed the door behind him, set the bucket down between Sebastian and Cornelius and took a vacant seat at the table.

Jenna smiled at them. "You two quite finished?" she asked them. They both nodded, but without much enthusiasm. It was evident that either of them might succumb to further bouts of sickness at any moment. Jenna pointed to the bucket. "Use it if you have to," she told them. "And ensure a good aim—I like to keep a tidy ship."

They nodded at her, their faces two pictures of misery.

"Now," she said expectantly, "if we are ready . . . ?"

"Hmm?" grunted Sebastian.

"The map!" she said.

"Oh yes." Cornelius nodded. He reached beneath his breastplate, pulled out the ancient sheet of paper and unfolded it across the table.

Jenna pulled it closer and examined it carefully in absolute silence. Then she lifted her head to look at them. "It certainly looks authentic," she said. "This is undoubtedly very old parchment, and there are proper coordinates written here." She indicated a near-indecipherable scrawl, inked in blood on one corner of the page.

"It's somewhere south of Lemora," muttered

Sebastian, who still wasn't convinced he'd finished vomiting. "Do you need to know any more than that?"

"Of course," said Jenna. "That's not enough information to find an island. It's a very big ocean. It would be like looking for a tiny seed thrown onto a massive blanket. If we don't plot our course perfectly, we could easily sail right past it. One thing's for sure: whoever put this map together knew a thing or two about sailing."

Cornelius struck Sebastian on the elbow. "What did I tell you?" he said excitedly.

Now Jenna and Lemuel busied themselves with their charts, consulting the scribbled notes from time to time.

"There are lines of latitude and longitude here," continued Jenna, "so plotting a course shouldn't be that difficult. We'll take readings at noon and midnight."

"Where did you learn to do that?" Sebastian asked her, not really that interested but wanting to give the impression that he was.

She glanced up at him. "From my father, of course. He's sailed these waters all his life, and that was in the days before we had the quarterstaff."

Sebastian frowned. "What's a quarterstaff?" he asked Cornelius, but the little warrior just shrugged.

"It's a wooden instrument that helps us find our way across the ocean," explained Jenna. "We use it to take readings from the sun and stars." She indicated the charts spread out before her. "These were my father's," she said. "He drew them up himself, every last one of them. And when I was a little girl, he taught me how to use them."

Cornelius forced a smile. "Unusual for a young lady to move into such a profession," he said.

Jenna shrugged. "I think it's no secret that he would have preferred a boy. But my mother could never give him one, and I suppose I showed no interest in the fripperies that most girls care about—dolls, dresses, that kind of thing. So he got a tomboy instead and had to make the best of it."

"So . . . what happened to your father?" asked Sebastian.

"Oh, he's still around," said Jenna. "But he's not able to captain the ship anymore." She looked sad. "He was on a voyage down to the Southlands four summers ago when a man fell overboard. My father went over the side to try and help him and . . . there were kelfers in the water."

"Kelfers?" Sebastian was mystified. "What are kelfers?"

"Hideous sea creatures," said Lemuel. "The deadliest, fastest beasts in the ocean. One of them took the captain's legs before we could haul him back aboard. Took 'em both off with one snap of its jaws."

Sebastian blanched and felt his face drain of color once again. "How . . . terrible," he said.

"Aye, it was that." Lemuel shook his head and his one good eye looked misty, as though he was reliving the incident. "It's a miracle he didn't bleed to death, but we had a good ship's surgeon and he managed to staunch the blood with boiling tar."

Sebastian winced, imagining the agony it must have caused.

"When we got back to Ramalat, I was faced with a difficult decision," said Jenna. "My father had survived, but it was obvious he could never captain the *Sea Witch* again. He gave me a simple choice. I could sell the ship or I could take his place. And I knew that selling her would break his heart, particularly as he hated the man who wanted to buy it." She extended her hands in a pantomime of helplessness. "It was no choice at all, really. It was difficult at first. There were many of the crew who felt that I couldn't handle it. . . ." She glanced accusingly at Lemuel and he held up his hands in playful surrender.

"Not me, missy! I always knew you could do it."

She smiled. "True enough, not Lem. But many of the others took some persuading. Luckily my father had taught me everything he knew. He still *is* teaching me, and I've added a few ideas of my own." She smiled proudly. "I've been running the ship for three summers. I don't think any of the crew have a problem with me now."

"Apart from the fellow we saw you arm wrestling," said Cornelius. "How did a slight thing like yourself become so strong?"

"Oh, it's a tough life aboard a ship. Muscles become powerful. But I'll let you into a secret about Cassius. He's much stronger than I am. And he could beat me at arm wrestling, there's no doubt of that."

Sebastian was puzzled. "Then how . . . ?"

"He's sweet on me, of course. He thinks that constantly losing to me will make me feel the same affection for him. But of course, the effect is quite the opposite. No woman wants that which she can have too easily."

"I . . . don't understand," said Sebastian.

"She's talking about playing hard to get," Cornelius told him. "The more a man shows disdain for a woman, the more she wants to win his heart. Everyone knows that."

Sebastian frowned. He still wasn't quite getting this. "So the way to win a woman's heart is to be . . . horrible to her?"

Jenna grinned. "Not too horrible," she said. "Just disdainful enough to make her work harder." She laughed and Cornelius laughed with her, as though the two of them were sharing some kind of private joke. Sebastian looked from one to the other and wondered what they found so funny; he was way out of his depth here. Jenna looked at Lemuel, who was still fussing with the charts, making measurements with a metal compass.

"Looks like we'll be heading out over the Angel's Lair," he told her.

"What's that?" asked Sebastian.

"Oh, that's something you'll need to see for yourself," said Jenna. "I'll give you a call when we come to the place. Should be sometime tomorrow. People who've never seen it before are usually astonished by it. We'll also be passing very close to the pirate stronghold of Lemora," she added. "Hopefully, if we keep our sails full and our heads down, it won't bother us too much."

"We've fought off enough pirates in our time," said Lemuel fiercely. "They should have learned by now to give us a wide berth."

"Perhaps," she said. "But some of them take a lot of convincing." She threw another mocking look at Sebastian. "Mind you, why should we worry? We have the Prince of Pirates with us. I'm sure he'll protect us!"

But Sebastian hardly noticed the jibe. "You know," he said thoughtfully, "you've succeeded where I've failed."

Jenna looked puzzled. "What do you mean?"

"Your father wanted you to captain his ship and you've done that—very successfully by the look of it." He sighed. "My father wanted nothing more than for me to succeed in the role of jester. I tried after he passed away, but sadly I had no talent for it. I failed him."

"But I thought you said you were Court Jester to King Septimus?"

"I was, but only for a day. Then I was sentenced to death."

"Goodness me, you *must* have been bad!"

"Oh no, that's not why! It was a little matter of the disappearance of the king's niece, which he thought I had a hand in. But, if I'm honest about it, I *was* pretty dreadful."

"I think you're being a bit hard on yourself," said Cornelius. "You weren't *that* bad."

"How do you know? You weren't even there—you were fighting fifteen Brigands in a barn at the time." Sebastian looked at Jenna. "That's why I'm on this ridiculous expedition. Trying to discover what I *am* good at."

Jenna put a hand on his and he almost flinched away in surprise. "I'm sure you'll find something," she assured him.

"That's easy for you to say," he muttered. "You're a sea captain. And Cornelius here, he's just about the finest warrior that I've ever seen. All I've managed to do on this trip so far is throw up and have an enchantment put on me."

"An enchantment?" Jenna was intrigued.

"Yes," said Cornelius. "That was courtesy of a shape-shifting witch back in the forest of Geltane—"

"I keep warning you—stop calling her a witch!" yelled Sebastian.

"You see?" Cornelius spread his hands. "He can't help himself. She's put some kind of love spell on him and he can't shake it off."

"A love spell?" Jenna's lips curved into a smile. "And what's it like, Sebastian, being enchanted by a strange woman?"

He gazed back at her across the round table. "It's . . . weird," he admitted. "I don't know why, but whenever she's mentioned I want to . . . protect her . . . *be* with her."

Jenna was still holding his hand. She squeezed it gently. "You poor thing," she said. "We must see what we can do to distract you."

CHAPTER *15*

THE ANGEL'S LAIR

Sebastian and Cornelius spent a fitful night in their cramped cabin, but at least the sickness seemed to have left them, and by the following morning they felt recovered enough to stomach a little breakfast. But the bowl of thick salty porridge, served up by the ship's cook, Thaddeus, down in the stinking, damp confines of the galley, did little to encourage them to eat.

Afterward they made their way up on deck to discover that it was a fine sunny morning and the ship was moving across a stretch of calm blue water. There was no sight of land in any direction, an occurrence which made Sebastian feel vaguely anxious; but on such a beautiful day he could not allow himself to be in low spirits for long. Then Jenna came striding across the deck toward him, a welcoming smile on her face. He noticed that she was carrying a three-cornered hat much like her own, as well as a pile of clothes.

"Ah, gentlemen, just in time," she said. "We're approaching the Angel's Lair—I thought you'd like to take a look at it."

"This is the place you mentioned yesterday?" said Sebastian, intrigued. "But what is it, exactly?"

"You'll see soon enough," she assured him. "I don't want to spoil the surprise." She lifted the hat and clothes she was carrying and handed them to Sebastian. "I found these down in my cabin. I thought they might be more appropriate and since you no longer have your jester's hat, you might like to wear a tricorn instead."

"Why . . . thank you." Sebastian took the clothes and lifted the hat and placed it carefully on his head. It felt strange, quite unlike the soft, three-pronged hat he had worn for so long. He looked doubtfully at the others. "What do you think?" he asked.

Cornelius shrugged. "Not bad," he said.

"Oh, better than that," said Jenna. "The perfect headgear for a vanquisher of pirates." And she gave Sebastian that mocking smile. "How many is it you've killed, Mr. Darke?"

"Erm . . ." Sebastian shrugged. "I haven't really kept count," he said.

"Not since he polished off the first fifty," added Cornelius, and Sebastian glared at him, wondering why his friend couldn't seem to stop exaggerating his prowess. True, Sebastian had finished off the odd Brigand and had even engineered the death of a king back in Keladon, but he had never so much as seen a pirate, let alone killed one.

"Now," said Jenna brightly, "the wonders are about to unfold." She took Sebastian's arm and led him over to the port side of the ship. "We'll have a good vantage point here," she said. "Captain Drummel, if you cannot see over the rail, you could always perch yourself on that barrel."

Cornelius did as she suggested. "You're being very mysterious," he said.

"Not really. It's just that the Angel's Lair is one of the most astonishing sights in all the known world. Everybody who sees it is amazed. I'm sure even two men of your experience will be suitably entertained." Sebastian noticed that the crew were all pausing in their duties and moving to positions where they could see over the side. Jenna pointed at the water a short distance from the ship's hull, beyond the churning wake made by its passage. "Keep looking down there," she said, "and soon enough you will start to see its secrets."

The water was unusually clear here and Sebastian noticed that the rays of sunlight seemed to penetrate to the lowest depths. In fact, in certain places he could actually see the ocean floor, a carpet of swaying grasses, illuminated here and there by rays of flickering light.

"It's not very deep," he observed, and Jenna nodded.

"We have to be careful. There's many a ship that's come to grief in the Angel's Lair. But I know this place as well as any sailor; I must have passed over it a hundred times. And if memory serves me correctly, the wonders start . . . just about . . . here!" She pointed again, and Sebastian looked down in the direction she had indicated. At first he saw nothing and he started to think that she had been pulling his leg; but then something came into view, something he at first took to be a series of large, straight-sided, rectangular rocks. But then he realized what he was looking at and he couldn't hold back a gasp of astonishment.

It was a house. He was gazing down on the roof of a house that somebody had built on the ocean floor. It was encrusted with coral and clumps of vegetation, so that it looked as though it had been carved from a block of half-melted, multicolored candle wax, but it was a house nonetheless. He was about to say something, but at that moment more houses came into view and he realized that he was looking at a whole series of dwellings, with what looked like roads in between. And they weren't like any houses he had ever seen before; they were neat, oblong shapes and there were rows and rows of them, laid out like a patchwork quilt below him. Here and there, some buildings had collapsed in on themselves, but many were intact. Sebastian could even make out the shapes of doors and windows beneath the covering of coral.

"I . . . don't understand," he said. "Who could possibly live down there?"

Jenna laughed. "Nobody!" she said. "But obviously they must have done, once. Before the waters covered them."

"You mean . . . ?"

"I mean, at one time this was dry land. And this city was built on its highest point. But for reasons we can only guess at, the waters swept in and engulfed it. Now . . . look there!"

Another building had come into view. It too was partially collapsed and encrusted with a multitude of sea creatures, but it was like some great palace, set much higher than the surrounding buildings. It was decorated with strange carvings and details, and at one end rose sheer up to a tower, which extended almost to the surface of the ocean. Sebastian could see that the top of the tower was broken off in a ragged point.

"There used to be a big metal pole on the top of that thing," Jenna told him. "Came up to just below the surface. But a clumsy sea captain ran his ship across it last winter and broke the pole off. Made a big hole in the bottom of his ship too—he was lucky to get back to port without sinking!"

"But what kind of a building *is* that?" asked Sebastian.

"Must have been the palace of a mighty king," mused Cornelius. "I've never seen anything like it. Such craftsmanship! It puts even the palace of Queen Kerin of Keladon to shame."

"Keep watching, Golmiran," said Jenna. "The best is yet to come."

Sure enough, as the ship plowed onward, she passed over a whole series of incredible details—so many that Sebastian was quite overwhelmed and afterward could only recall a succession of brief images.

There were gigantic flat-roofed buildings, long raised roadways into which countless arches had been cut, a whole series of tall stone chimneys, bigger than any that Sebastian had ever seen. There were row upon row of buildings all packed tightly against each other and forming intricate geometric designs. There was even what looked to Sebastian like the curving, twisting line of a river bed that had been swamped by a much bigger mass of water; and, most amazing of all, a tower with a mighty metal bell hanging in it. As the *Sea Witch* passed over, unseen currents made the bell swing back and forth, and Sebastian could actually hear its muffled peal rising up from deep below the waves.

"That's a good omen," Jenna told him. "When you hear the Angel's Bell, you usually have a good voyage!"

Finally the ocean floor seemed to drop rapidly back into the depths. For a while there was still the occasional glimpse of half-seen things down there, but then it became too deep to discern anything much and Jenna clapped her hands with a sense of finality.

"The show's over," she announced, not without a trace of regret. "But I expect we'll return this way and see it again."

"Why's it called the Angel's Lair?" asked Sebastian. "And what exactly is an angel? I've heard the word but I don't really know what it means."

"I have some notion that it's a man with wings like a bird," said Jenna. "There are old stories that speak of them."

"And do people really believe that such creatures lived down there?"

Jenna shrugged. "It's what the old sailors call it, and if you ask them, they say they learned the name from their fathers and their fathers learned it from their fathers before them, and so on. I suppose it must have meant something once."

"And have any of the old sailors heard of a time

when there was no ocean in these parts?" asked Cornelius.

She shook her head. "Whenever this happened, it must have been in ancient times," she said.

"But who could build like that in those days?" asked Sebastian. "We can barely do it now. That great palace we saw . . ." He shook his head. "It was out of this world. Like something a god would create."

Cornelius looked thoughtful. He stared down into the water as though looking for clues. "I do not know of any race of people that can build the kinds of things we just saw in those depths." He lifted his eyes back to Sebastian. "Perhaps our world is much older than we imagine. Perhaps people have been here before us . . . great empires that have risen and fallen away into ruin."

Sebastian followed Cornelius's gaze and was about to put forward some speculations of his own but was distracted by a big, streamlined shape moving through the water. He was looking at a long supple sea creature with massive jaws and distinctive dark stripes across its back. It was the length of two ponies standing end to end and it was skimming along at incredible speed just below the surface. A tall curved fin jutted up from its back, leaving a V-shaped wedge of foam in its wake. Now Sebastian could see that other, smaller fish were leaping out of the water in their haste to get out of its way.

"What's that?" he whispered.

"A kelfer," said Jenna, putting a whole wealth of loathing into the word. "I hate them." She stepped quickly away from the rail, shouting to Lemuel to fetch her a bow. As Sebastian gazed down, more kelfers began to appear, moving to join the first creature as though hunting in a pack.

"It was a kelfer that took her father's legs," Cornelius reminded Sebastian. "Little wonder she hates them."

"I've never seen anything like it," admitted Sebastian. "Look at the speed of that thing!"

No sooner had he said this than Jenna appeared at the rail clutching a powerful longbow and carrying a quiver full of arrows on her back. She pulled out an arrow, nocked it and took careful aim at the nearest of the kelfers, the one at the tail of the pack. She pulled the bowstring as far back as her strength would allow her, and took a moment to steady her aim, murmuring to herself as she did so, "Now, you evil filth, let's see how you like the taste of this." She released the arrow. It flew, straight and sure, into the creature's striped flank, burying itself deep. A ribbon of bright red trailed back into the water.

"An arrow isn't going to do *him* much harm," observed Sebastian.

"It doesn't have to," Jenna assured him. "There are others that will do that." She gave him a sly wink.

Sebastian looked back at the kelfers and saw that another two had suddenly appeared behind the wounded one. They began to close in on it and it quickly became apparent that they'd been attracted by the blood in the water. They overhauled the wounded kelfer and then, with two swift, terrible lunges, slammed into it, their great mouths open, their razor-sharp teeth ready to go to work. The kelfers in front, alerted by the struggles of the stricken beast, turned as one and came racing back into the fray. There was an incredible commotion in the water as the twisting, lunging bodies smashed the waves into a foaming cauldron. So frenzied was the action that the kelfers started attacking each other and the water turned bright red as more and more blood began to flow. Sebastian had to look away from the carnage, and he was relieved when the ship moved on and left the creatures to their senseless slaughter.

"That's a kelfer for you," said Jenna with quiet satisfaction. "If they see so much as a drop of the red stuff, they go mad for it. I've seen one going round and round in circles, tearing at its own tail. So the best advice I can give you, elfling, is never go swimming with them."

Sebastian nodded. He had no intention of doing so. Ever.

"Sail ho!" cried a voice from up in the rigging.

Jenna tilted her head to peer up into the crow's nest at the top of the mainmast. "Where away?" she called.

"Hard astern, Captain!"

Jenna walked to the stern of the boat. Sebastian and Cornelius followed her. She lifted a hand to shield her eyes from the sun, while Cornelius took his battered old spyglass from his belt and climbed to a position where he could use it. Sure enough, Sebastian could see the distant white smudge of a sail on the horizon.

"I thought you assured me that nobody would know of our expedition," growled Cornelius.

Jenna took out her own spyglass and studied the ship for a moment. "It's the *Marauder,*" she muttered. "Captain Trencherman's ship." The contempt in her voice was evident.

"Who's he?" asked Sebastian.

"Another captain out of Ramalat," she told him. "My biggest rival, and one of the richest men in the port. He seems to have made it his personal quest to acquire as many ships as possible. Owns a whole fleet of them."

"There's no crime in being prosperous," observed Cornelius.

"No. But nobody seems to know where his riches have come from and he isn't too fussy about how he acquires ships or who he steps on in the process. When my father lost his legs, Trencherman did everything he could to persuade me to sell the *Sea Witch* to him. But my father always hated him, and I was determined to chance my hand at being captain. Since then he's done everything he can to hinder me." She lowered the spyglass. "But I'm puzzled as to how he found out about this trip. There's not a man in my crew who would betray a word about our purpose to that old villain."

"Perhaps they didn't have to," snarled Cornelius. He gave Sebastian an accusing look. "Perhaps somebody has simply hired the captain's ship and crew, just as we have yours."

Sebastian stared at him, not understanding at first. And then it dawned on him. "Not Leonora!" he groaned.

"Yes, of course Leonora. Who else?"

Jenna looked at Sebastian with interest. "I doubt that Captain Trencherman would be interested in hiring out his ship. It's not as if he needs the money."

"Yes, but I'm sure Leonora would have no problem persuading him. She's an enchantress."

"Oh, the woman you spoke of? She's still following you?"

Sebastian spread his arms in a gesture of helplessness. "It would seem so," he admitted.

Cornelius stroked his chin with one hand. "Captain Jenna, what would it cost for you to turn round and give the *Marauder* a broadside with your cannons? Perhaps we could send that witch to the bottom of the ocean. Even *she'd* have trouble weaving her web of intrigue and devilment down there."

But Jenna was shaking her head. "I couldn't do that for any price," she said. "Captain Trencherman may be a spineless, lying jellyfish but he's just doing his job. I cannot simply attack him for no reason other than that I do not like him."

"Hmm. Pity. Can he catch up with us?"

"Not if I order full sails and tell the crew to push her to the limit."

"Let's do that then," concluded Cornelius. "And in the meantime we'll set our minds to thinking of some way we can get that woman off our tail once and for all."

"Perhaps Sebastian does not want that," said Jenna. She gave him a sly look. "Perhaps he would rather slow down so that he might speak to the woman who has enchanted him."

"That's ridiculous," said Sebastian; but in his heart he was experiencing a curious mixture of emotions. Unable to hide them, he turned on his heel and started walking away.

"Where are you going?" Cornelius shouted after him.

"To check on Max," he replied. "I've been too ill to even think of him since we left shore." He tried to keep his expression blank, but in his chest his heart was banging like a war drum. Leonora was coming after him. Perhaps, before much longer, he would see her again. . . .

CHAPTER 16

DOWN IN THE DUMPS

Sebastian clambered down the wooden rungs of the ladder into the cargo hold. He paused halfway down to scan the various crates, boxes and piles of equipment, but for the moment at least he could detect no sign of the buffalope, other than a certain unpleasant smell that drifted up to him, a pungent mingling of dung and vomit.

Sebastian remembered that Max had been spectacularly unwell when he was being lifted aboard. He had promised to visit him but had been so caught up with his own sickness he'd simply not been up to the task of tending to his faithful buffalope. He frowned. Max would doubtless have something to say on the matter.

Sebastian's feet touched down on the rough boards of the hold and he turned to look about him.

"Max?" he ventured. "Are you down here?"

The only reply was a pitiful moan that seemed to come from behind a huge stack of barrels. Sebastian approached and peered round them cautiously. There was Max, slumped in a corner, lying on a patch of hay that somebody must have thrown down for him. He was clearly not at all well. His eyes were rimmed with red and his beard was matted with dried vomit. He looked very, very unhappy.

"Oh, so you've finally bothered to make an appearance, have you?" he said, in a voice as cold as a Golmiran ice field. "I thought perhaps you'd abandoned ship and swum back to Ramalat."

Sebastian tried his best to ignore the jibe. He unhitched a gourd of fresh water from over his shoulder. "I thought you might like a drink," he said meekly.

"How very thoughtful. The fact that I've lain here all night, parched to the point of unconsciousness, never occurred to you, I suppose."

"I've been rather ill myself," Sebastian assured him.

"Ill? *You've* been ill?" Max tossed his head toward the far corner of the hold, where a pool of something horrible was slowly congealing. "That's what you call ill," he said. "I must have coughed up three times my own weight over there. At one point during the night I thought I was dying. Actually dying! No doubt you were up in your cabin drinking wine and eating a slap-up meal."

"Not at all! I just told you, Cornelius and I were as sick as a pair of mutts. It's only this morning that we've felt strong enough to even walk." He unstoppered the water and held it out to Max. "Here, have some of this and then we'll get you cleaned up a bit."

"Hmph!" grunted Max. But he dutifully opened his mouth and accepted the stream of water flowing from the neck of the gourd. He drank greedily, gulping down mouthful after mouthful, before he nodded that he'd had enough. Sebastian pulled a piece of rag from his pocket, soaked it in water and began to clean up the buffalope's face.

Max regarded him the while with mournful brown eyes. "I *hate* it down here," he said. "It's boring. I don't even have a view."

"I appreciate that. But this is where Jenna said you had to go. She won't allow you up on deck."

Max's expression became even more disgruntled. "You mean I'm stuck down here for the entire trip? That can't be right. Surely there must be laws about this kind of thing. Cruelty to buffalopes, that's what it is! I wouldn't leave an *animal* in conditions like this!"

"Max, you *are* an animal. You keep forgetting that."

"When I say 'animal,' I mean something thick and primitive, not a sophisticated creature like myself. I need stimulation of some kind. Music, perhaps, or an adventure story."

"I wasn't aware that you liked music," said Sebastian.

"It would be something to pass the time," moaned Max. "The way things are down here, even some of your abysmal jokes would be welcome."

"Well, thanks very much," said Sebastian. "It's good to know that you'll turn to me as a last resort."

"Don't be so touchy! You've said yourself that you were never cut out to be a jester. And you needn't think wearing a different hat is going to turn you into a sailor overnight."

"Do you like it?" Sebastian tilted the tricorn to a rakish angle. "Jenna gave it to me."

Max made a face. "Oh, did she now? I'm not sure I approve of that one, marching around, shouting orders. 'Stick that buffalope in the hold!' How'd she like it if somebody trussed her up in a harness and dumped her down here in the dark?"

"Max, she *is* the captain, and on a ship the captain's word is law."

"I might have known I'd get no sympathy from you." Max snorted and shook his head. "Well," he said, "what's been happening? If I can't be up there, you'll have to be my eyes and ears."

So Sebastian settled himself down and recounted everything he could remember. He told Max about Captain Jenna and what had happened to her father. He told him about the strange sunken city of the

Angel's Lair and he described the horrible bloody attack of the kelfers. Finally he mentioned that Captain Trencherman's ship was following them and that it was almost certainly carrying Leonora.

"Not her again!" growled Max. "She's like a bad smell, that one. Follows you everywhere."

"Tell me about it." Sebastian sighed. "She is a bit of a nuisance."

Max stared at him in disbelief. "I'd say she's considerably more than that. Hideous, rotten old witch . . ."

Sebastian was aware that Max was watching him slyly, waiting for some kind of outburst at this description; and though he felt like objecting, he somehow managed to rein himself back. Max wasn't fooled though. "So you've still got her stuck into you like a thorn," he observed. "We have got to do something about that enchantment. Otherwise who knows where it might lead us? Cornelius and I will simply not be able to trust you."

"That's ridiculous!" cried Sebastian. But even as he said it, he knew in his heart that Max had a point. He no longer felt as though he had any free will of his own. But what was he to do? He was a prisoner of her witchcraft and sometimes, it had to be said, a most willing one—

Sebastian started as a sound came to him from above, a deep, distant, booming noise.

"What's that?" gasped Max.

"I'm not sure," said Sebastian; but he had an idea that it was the sound of gunfire. He had thought that the *Sea Witch* was out of range of the *Marauder*'s cannons, but even so, he knew that this needed to be investigated. He got to his feet and hurried toward the ladder.

"Wait! Where are you going?" protested Max. "You can't just leave me down here!"

"What do you want me to do?" countered Sebastian. "Carry you?"

Max considered this for a moment. "No offense, young master, but I don't think you're up to it. Perhaps if you were to bring down some sailors . . ."

But Sebastian had already started to climb.

Clambering out onto the deck, he saw what looked like the entire crew gathered at the stern of the ship and looking back toward the *Marauder*. Sebastian shouldered his way through the crowd until he found Cornelius, standing on the lid of a barrel and studying the scene through his spyglass.

"What's going on?" he asked.

"Looks like somebody is doing our dirty work for us," said Cornelius, not without a certain smug satisfaction. He handed the spyglass to Sebastian, who lifted it to his eye. Now he could see that a third ship had appeared on the horizon and was sailing alongside the *Marauder*, only a short distance off her port side. As Sebastian watched, tiny puffs of smoke belched from the hull of the new ship, and corresponding explosions rippled across the deck of the *Marauder*. From this distance it seemed almost polite, but after a few moments the sound of the guns came rolling like thunder across the surface of the water and there was no disguising the power of them.

"Somebody's attacking the *Marauder*," gasped Sebastian. He realized he was stating the obvious, but he didn't know what else to say, and all he could think of was that Leonora was aboard and might be badly injured, even killed.

"They've caught them napping," said Cornelius. "Trencherman's crew haven't managed to fire a single shot in retaliation. Must have been too intent on watching us."

"The other ship's flying the skull and crossbones," observed Jenna, who was standing nearby, peering through her own spyglass. "Looks like Captain Kid's schooner, the *Black Hand*. That makes sense. Trencherman has attacked the Kid's ship time and again. Seems to have a personal grudge against him."

"Captain Kid?" Sebastian stared at her, aghast. "The pirate?" He licked his lips anxiously. "Well, we . . . we have to do something. We can't let the *Marauder* be attacked without trying to help."

"Nonsense!" roared Cornelius. "Let them send that evil witch to the bottom of the sea. Then you'll be free of the enchantment and we'll not have to risk sharing the treasure with others."

"I've asked you before not to call her a witch," snarled Sebastian. "And we cannot leave the ship's crew to such a fate, just because you want to be rid of Leonora."

"He's right," admitted Captain Jenna. "We'll have to go back and help."

Now it was Cornelius's turn to stare. "Have you taken leave of your senses? Why would you help this Captain Trencherman? You said yourself he was your greatest rival."

Jenna nodded. "I *did* say that. But there is a thing called the Code of the Sea, and it is considered unthinkable to leave your fellow sailors to the mercy of pirates, no matter how much you despise them. I would have thought, Captain Drummel, that men of the Golmiran army operated by a similar code."

Cornelius glowered but his expression was somewhat sheepish. In the end he could only give a reluctant nod. "I suppose you're right," he admitted. He glanced at Sebastian. "But let me warn you now, if Leonora comes within range of my sword, she'll need all her witch's arts to survive."

"You'd use your sword on a defenseless woman?" asked Jenna, raising her eyebrows.

"You've never met her," said Cornelius darkly. "*Defenseless* is the last word I'd use to describe her."

Jenna moved to the center of the deck and waved an arm at Lemuel, who stood at the tiller. "Turn us round, Lem," she cried. "A good wide turn. We'll drop astern of those sea rats and come up on their port side."

"Aye, aye, Captain." Lemuel swung the tiller with practiced ease, and crewmen ran to realign the sails.

"With any luck they'll be too busy with the *Marauder* to notice us," said Jenna. She gazed around at her crew. "Lads, make preparations to engage an enemy ship. Hurry now, there's not much time! Prime the cannons! Prepare grappling irons! Let's show them that it's the seamen of Ramalat who rule these waves!"

The well-drilled crew scurried to their positions, their bare feet thudding on the wooden boards. Jenna threw a sidelong glance at Sebastian and Cornelius.

"You gentlemen may want to take cover below," she said. "It's going to get quite nasty up here."

Cornelius grinned. "That's just how we like it," he said. "Isn't it, Sebastian?"

"Huh?" Sebastian stared at him. Once again he was experiencing a strange conflict of emotions. Part of him wanted to be rid of Leonora and her mysterious hold on him . . . but another part was quite ready to give his life in order to protect her.

"What's the matter with you?" Cornelius asked him. Sebastian shook his head and tried to get a grip on

his emotions. "Nothing," he said. "I'm . . . I'm fine."
But he was far from fine. There was a thick film of
sweat on his face and his heart seemed to be racing
at twice its normal speed. Leonora was somewhere
on that ship, the one being smashed to pieces by
enemy fire. Soon he would be able to see her, speak to
her. . . .

Max's voice came bellowing up through the open
hatch. "Yoo-hoo! Hello? What's going on up there?"

Jenna grimaced and snapped a command at a couple of sailors. "Batten down that hatch!" she yelled. "I
don't want that loudmouthed beast alerting the
pirates to our presence." The men moved to obey her,
swinging down and bolting the heavy wooden doors.
Max's shouts were immediately muted. Jenna moved
to the rail and stared at the two ships, which were
now just a short distance off to port. "OK, Lem, that's
far enough. Let's turn her round."

Those crewmen who were not manning the guns
below deck ranged themselves along the starboard
rail, grappling irons and ropes at the ready. The *Sea
Witch* was closing in now, Lemuel swinging the ship
round in a great arc so that she could come up on the
Black Hand's port side and move into position alongside her. Sebastian could feel the impact of the pirate
ship's cannon as they roared in unison, again and
again. The shots were pulverizing the *Marauder*'s
hull, smashing great ragged holes in her port side

and sending lethal fragments of wood flying in all directions. Captain Trencherman's crew had managed to get their gun hatches open and were struggling to bring the cannons to bear on their attacker, but they had paid a high price for being so unprepared and already looked to be in very bad shape.

Meanwhile Jenna's plan seemed to be working like a dream. The pirate crew were so intent on their attack, they had not even noticed the *Sea Witch* sliding into position, hatches open, cannons ready to fire.

"Here we go," said Cornelius with grim good humor. He pulled his sword from its scabbard and winked at Sebastian, who unsheathed his own sword, though the last thing he felt like doing now was engaging in hand-to-hand combat.

Jenna was armed with her longbow and she raised it so every member of the crew could see. "Right, lads," she said. "Let's show them how we deal with pirates on these waters." Then she took a deep breath to yell at the top of her voice, *"Fire!"*

And the battle began.

CHAPTER 17

THE BIG BRAWL

The impact of the big guns discharging below them seemed to make the deck leap beneath Sebastian's feet. Clouds of smoke billowed up from the open gun hatches, and through the haze he saw the pirate ship's hull being blasted open by a series of impacts.

The pirate crew reeled in shocked surprise as they realized that the tables had unexpectedly been turned: now it was the *Black Hand* that was under attack. They hadn't even opened the gun hatches on their port side. One man ran toward the shattered rails and Jenna sent an arrow flying across the intervening space, straight into his chest, dropping his lifeless body onto the deck.

"Fire at will!" roared Jenna.

"Which one's Will?" asked Sebastian, peering at the pirates on the other ship. Cornelius opened his mouth to say something, but then another volley blasted out, the shots shredding the *Black Hand*'s rails and bringing the foremast crashing down onto the deck, scattering crewmen in all directions and in some cases burying them under piles of heavy canvas.

"Cease firing!" yelled Jenna. "Grappling irons ready . . ." The crew took up their positions, arms lifted, ready to throw. *"Now!"* she screamed, and the heavy irons were flung in a series of arcs, trailing lengths of rope behind them, to thud down behind the ruined rails of the *Black Hand*. "Take up the slack," commanded Jenna; and for a moment Sebastian forgot about his apprehension and watched her in admiration: she really was rather magnificent in the heat of battle. "Now *heave!*" she cried; and muscular arms began to pull on the ropes, drawing the two ships closer and closer together.

Some of the pirate crew saw what was happening and, snatching up axes, ran to the port rail to try to sever the ropes, but Jenna's arrows dropped three of them in their tracks before they ever reached the side. As the ships drew closer, a couple of hatches on the *Black Hand* opened. There was a muffled roar of cannon fire and thick clouds of smoke billowed up from the gap.

Then there was a heavy impact as the *Sea Witch*'s

hull thudded against that of the *Black Hand* and, exchanging her bow for a sword, Jenna raised the weapon high and waved her crew forward. She was the first to leap across the rails, through the clouds of smoke and onto the pirate ship. Sebastian was instantly scrambling after her, and then he had little time to see what was going on around him because he was too busy trying to stay alive.

He came through the thick, choking smoke and dropped onto the deck. Immediately a huge, shaven-headed pirate came lunging at him with a heavy broadsword, unleashing a powerful swing that was designed to take Sebastian's head clean off his shoulders. He ducked and was horribly aware of the mighty blade scything a chunk of material from the top of his tricorn. There was no time for hesitation. He immediately struck, slashing his own curved blade across the pirate's chest. The man cried out and spun sideways, rolling over and over on the deck.

Sebastian was just telling himself that now he really was a vanquisher of pirates when two other men immediately took his first opponent's place, dirty bearded fellows, one tall and thin, the other short and squat. They advanced on Sebastian, swords raised, and he squared up to them, unsure which of them to take on first. The squat man lunged, aiming a straight stabbing thrust at Sebastian's chest. He tried to retreat, tripped over a prone figure behind him and fell backward. The little man was unbalanced too and couldn't stop himself from falling forward with the impetus of his blow. Sebastian grabbed his wrist, pulled him forward and whipped his own blade up into the man's stomach, impaling him as he fell; but the man's body was heavy and Sebastian realized that he was trapped, his sword stuck.

The thin man was still coming at him, a gleeful expression on his smoke-blackened face. Sebastian started to grope frantically around for another weapon but found nothing. The thin man lifted his sword to strike but then his expression changed to one of pain. He stood there for a moment, mouth open, eyes staring straight ahead; and then he dropped to his knees, revealing Jenna standing behind him, a bloodied sword in her hand. She stepped over the fallen man, pulled the dead pirate off Sebastian and helped him to his feet.

"Come along, jester," she said. "This is no time to take a nap."

"I wasn't napping!" protested Sebastian. "And I already told you, I'm not a jester anymore, I'm a—"

He broke off in alarm as yet another pirate came leaping at them. Jenna calmly parried the man's blade with her sword, then ducked under his guard and punched him in the face with her free hand. The man went flailing backward, hit the shattered rail

and tipped over the edge out of sight. An instant later there was the sound of a body splashing into the water.

"Some people," muttered Jenna, looking ruefully at her knuckles. "Any excuse to go for a swim." She and Sebastian exchanged grins and then Sebastian retrieved his sword and the two of them looked quickly around the crowded deck. It was apparent at a glance that the pirates were already as good as beaten. The crew of the *Sea Witch* were now streaming onto the deck, and sailors from the *Marauder* had taken the opportunity to start boarding from the starboard side. The pirates simply didn't know which way to turn. Everywhere, they were throwing down their weapons and lifting their arms in surrender. But in the far corner of the main deck one battle still raged in earnest.

Sebastian was astonished to see a small figure, dressed in the flamboyant hat, waistcoat and boots of a sea captain. He was fighting like a wildcat, even though he was surrounded by armed men. He carried a sword that looked several sizes too big for him and was whirling it round in a deadly arc every time somebody attempted to step closer to him.

"Come on then!" he yelled. "Who's next to feel the edge of my blade, eh? Who wants to be next to die?"

"Who on earth is that?" asked Sebastian, amazed.

"It's Captain Kid, of course," said Jenna.

"But . . . he can't be the captain. He couldn't be any more than . . . fourteen summers old!"

"That's right. How do you suppose he got the name?"

"I . . . I assumed he was a grown man who was nicknamed Kid."

"No. His father was Captain Jack Donovan, a very successful pirate. But he died a couple of years ago and the Kid took his place." She smiled. "It would seem we've both got something in common with him. Come on, let's sort him out. I've no wish to see such a plucky lad killed." She led Sebastian through the ranks of surrendering pirates to where the Kid stood at bay, shouting defiance at the men who surrounded him.

"Well, come on!" he roared. "Don't any of you want to fight me?"

"Throw down your weapons, Captain," shouted Jenna. "You are surrounded: you cannot hope to win."

"Can too!" retorted Captain Kid.

"No, really, you haven't a hope."

"Have so!" The captain stamped one tiny booted foot on the deck in a fit of anger. "Come on, I'll take you all on, one by one." He stepped toward the big dreadlocked sailor, Cassius. "What about you? You want to try your luck?"

Cassius grinned but shook his head. "I would rather fight someone my own size," he said.

"So would I!" snapped the Kid. "But there isn't anyone my size, is there?"

There was the sound of somebody clearing his throat and Cornelius stepped forward. "What about me?" he suggested.

Captain Kid looked at Cornelius in amazement. "But . . . you're tiny!" he exclaimed. "You're even smaller than me. A midgeling!"

"Actually, I'm a Golmiran," Cornelius assured him. "And though I am small in stature, I do not much care for the term 'midgeling.' However, as you are still a child, I'll simply assume you know no better." He took up a fighting stance and beckoned to the boy with the crook of one finger. "Well, come on, Captain. Let's see what you're made of."

"Cornelius, take it easy on him," said Sebastian. "He's just a boy."

"Yes, I *had* noticed," Cornelius assured him. "And don't worry, I have no intention of—" He broke off in surprise as the Kid came running at him, his sword swinging furiously. Cornelius managed to block the first blow and push it aside, but an instant later, another came at him, then another and another, the blows falling with such dizzying speed that for a moment the arms of the two fighters were little more than blurs. They whirled up and down the deck, dealing blow and counterblow, the blades striking

sparks and neither opponent showing any domi-
nance over the other.

"You're good," observed Cornelius. "But I'm better."

"Says you!" retorted the Kid. "Take that! And that!"
He started lashing out at Cornelius with renewed
vigor, and Sebastian was amazed to notice that the
Golmiran's confident smile had faded somewhat and
that he was having to work really hard to parry the
blows. Finally even his endurance seemed to be failing
and he had to resort to sleight of hand. He performed a
lightning-fast flick of the wrist and the Kid's sword
went flying from his grip, the point of the blade
thudding deep into the mizzenmast and then
shuddering from the impact. The Kid stared in amazement at his empty hand as though he couldn't believe
what had just happened.

"You . . . ," he said. "You . . ." Then he descended
into what could only be described as a tantrum. "It's
not fair!" he cried, stamping around the deck in disgust. "You cheated!"

"I certainly did not," Cornelius told him. "I used a
perfectly acceptable maneuver to disarm you."

"No way!" screamed the Kid. "You're a big cheat!"

Cornelius gave him a rather puzzled smile. "I can
assure you, Captain, that I beat you fair and square,"
he said. "And I must now ask you formally to surrender your vessel to us."

"Will not!" bellowed the Kid. "Not going to surrender to a rotten cheat!"

Cornelius looked at Jenna in exasperation and shrugged, as if asking her what he should do next. But she was prevented from offering her opinion by the arrival of a deputation from the *Marauder*. This comprised a tall, dour-looking man with a disapproving face and a haughty way of walking that suggested he thought he was pretty fantastic. This had to be Captain Trencherman, Sebastian told himself.

He was accompanied by what must have been his first mate, a big, powerful-looking man with a strangely flattened nose and a mouthful of yellowed, misshapen teeth. Trailing just behind them was a beautiful woman who Sebastian recognized only too well.

She stood there, smiling dangerously, her big yellow eyes regarding Sebastian as though she could see into the very heart of him.

CHAPTER 18

THE CODE OF THE SEA

It was Captain Trencherman who spoke first. "Captain Swift," he said. "It would seem I am in your debt." He had a cold, expressionless voice, which Sebastian disliked immediately but which seemed a perfect match for his slate-gray eyes and disapproving expression.

"Do not trouble yourself," Jenna assured him, her voice polite but distant, making no attempt to hide her contempt for the man. "I was merely following the Code of the Sea."

"Well, lucky for us that you were so close at hand."

"Hardly lucky, since you were quite obviously following us."

Trencherman didn't answer this, but he did direct a nervous glance at Leonora, who stood there, saying nothing and staring intently at Sebastian. There was an uncomfortable silence; then Trencherman transferred his attention to the Kid.

"So the little whelp's luck has finally deserted him," he said.

"I'm still big enough to give you a kicking!" retorted the Kid, raising his fists in a pugilistic stance. "Come on, let's see you hit me, droopy drawers!"

"Impudent cub!" snarled Trencherman. "Still, small as he is, he'll hang as readily as his crew." He turned to shout over his shoulder. "Fetch ropes—we'll string these sea rats up now!"

Sebastian was appalled by this decision. He took a step forward. "You can't just hang him!" he protested. "He's only a boy."

Trencherman's steely eyes appraised Sebastian for a moment; he did not seem to like what they saw. "Sir, I do not know who you are, but let me remind you that this 'boy' has just done untold damage to my vessel . . . so much so that we are taking on water and will have to return to Ramalat for repairs."

"Yes!" hissed Cornelius, raising a fist in a gesture of triumph.

Trencherman glared at him. "This news seems to please you, little man."

"Er . . . no, not at all," Cornelius assured him. "I was, er . . . just thinking about . . . a joke I heard yesterday."

Trencherman sniffed. "Whatever," he said. "I feel I

am owed some token of revenge before I depart. And it would please me to see this so-called captain and his filthy crew hanging from the yardarms. After all, they came at me in an utterly unprovoked attack, obviously looking for plunder."

"Unprovoked, my backside!" yelled the Kid. "What about the four times you've attacked my ship? I suppose that doesn't count for anything."

"You're a dirty little pirate," retorted Trencherman. "It's my right to attack you any time I see fit."

"Oh yeah? Well, maybe I just wanted to show you how it feels. I lost three good men in your last attack. Blasted to bits by your cannons. And plunder didn't even come into it, mate. There's nothing on your poxy ship that I want. Just my revenge."

"You see how he speaks to me?" roared Trencherman. "Let's see how cocky he is with a noose around his neck!"

"You won't hang him while I still stand here," Sebastian assured him. "These men may be pirates but they deserve a proper trial before they are punished. It's not for the likes of you to dispense the law."

Now Trencherman's eyes blazed with anger. "You are impertinent, sir. I am a sea captain out of Ramalat, and on the high seas we *are* the law. What say you, Captain Swift? Is it not my right to give retribution where I see fit?"

Jenna smiled coldly. "My apologies, Captain, but I agree with my friend Mr. Darke. It's not for us to be judge, jury and executioner. We'll keep these pirates under lock and key until we return to Ramalat, and only then will they be exposed to the full measure of the law."

Trencherman scowled, but though he seemed determined to keep a rein on his temper, he could not control the malignance that glittered in his eyes. "Very well, Captain Swift, since you have the advantage of a seaworthy vessel, I must bow to your decision. But . . . please allow me to take the pirates back to Ramalat with me, so that their punishment will be all the more prompt."

Jenna shook her head. "I don't think so. Something tells me that the moment you're out of our sight, these poor devils will be dancing a merry jig at the end of a rope."

Trencherman gave her an oily smile. "And if I were to give you my word that they will remain unharmed until we reach shore?"

Jenna smiled grimly back at him. "Forgive me, Captain Trencherman, but I have had occasion to note earlier occasions when your word has appeared to stand for very little. You tried every dirty trick in the book to get control of the *Sea Witch* when my father could do nothing to help himself, and I shall never forget that. So I shall take custody of the

pirates, and if I were you, I'd hasten back to Ramalat before your ship takes on too much water."

At this there were cheers from Jenna's crew, who clearly disliked Trencherman as much as she did.

Trencherman bunched his hands into fists but somehow managed to keep his temper, even when he saw that the Kid was pulling faces at him. He seemed to remember something else and he gestured at Leonora. "I have no time to stand here arguing with you. I must be on my way. But this good lady has chartered my ship for a certain destination. I wonder if you would be willing to take her as a passenger?"

Cornelius gave a long whoop of incredulity at this. "You are joking, I hope! Take her? I'd as soon accept a large barrel of Golmiran pit vipers. No, Leonora, I'm sorry, but you're going to have to go all the way back to Ramalat. Such a shame!"

Leonora spoke for the first time, staring at Sebastian as she did so. "Sebastian," she said, "you're surely not going to let them make me do that, are you?"

"Er . . . no," he said. "I mean, yes! That is, I'm afraid I don't . . . really have much choice . . . do I?"

"Of course you have a choice! Just tell them, Sebastian; tell them you refuse to leave me out there on that dangerous ship. Tell them you insist that I come with you."

Sebastian stared at her, and it was as though her

beautiful tawny eyes were getting bigger and bigger as he stared into them. He knew what he ought to say, but somehow he couldn't make his mouth and tongue shape the necessary words. "C-C-Cornelius!" he gasped. "Surely it would be all right . . . if . . . if we took her with us?"

Cornelius stared up at him in amazement. "Don't be ridiculous!" he snapped. "Of course she can't come with us. She's the enemy."

"Yes, but . . . I'd be responsible for her. I mean, I could keep her locked up in my cabin so she couldn't get out. I mean, she's not really so bad, is she?"

Cornelius gave a long disgusted sigh. He beckoned to Sebastian with one stubby index finger. "Lean down here a moment," he said. "I want to explain something."

Sebastian lowered his head. "What is it?" he asked his friend.

"Take that hat off a minute," said Cornelius.

Sebastian obeyed him without thinking. "Why?" he asked; and felt a powerful thud against the top of his head as something hard and heavy came down on top of it. Then the deck started wheeling and soaring around him like a child's carnival ride, and he saw a sea of astonished faces staring at him. He tried to take a step toward Leonora, but his legs buckled, unable to support the weight of his body. He felt himself falling.

Then, as he hit the deck, it seemed to turn soft and

vaporous and he fell right through it, into a deep and total blackness beyond.

He was lying on his back on a soft blanket of heather in the depths of the forest of Geltane. It was late afternoon, and long fingers of sunlight were breaking through the canopy of the treetops overhead to illuminate patches of verdant undergrowth around him. Unseen birds were singing, a sweet, restful sound that seemed supernaturally loud in the half-light; and he was aware that somebody was beside him, stroking his head with a gentle hand.

He opened his eyes to find that it was Leonora who was tending to him. She was smiling down at him, studying him with those big eyes, and he saw nothing but adoration in them. He smiled back at her, basking in the warmth of her affection, and for the first time in ages he felt a sense of contentment settle over him. When he was with her, all his anxieties seemed to just melt away.

But then her smile suddenly faltered. Her mouth straightened into a tight little line of disapproval, accompanied by a frown of annoyance. He stared up at her in dismay, wondering what was the matter. Had he done something to upset her? He wanted to sit up, ask her what was wrong, but he couldn't seem to move, and when he tried to speak, his mouth simply would not obey him.

Now Leonora's lips parted, as though she was snarling; and as Sebastian gazed up in mute terror, her mouth fell open and her teeth seemed to elongate into two jagged fringes of glistening ivory, pushing the lips back, making the jaws distend wider, wider than any human jaws were ever meant to go. And a sound came from the open mouth: a deep, guttural roar that seemed to fill Sebastian's head. He struggled to command his limbs, realizing that he had to get away from there as quickly as possible. But then the open mouth was lunging down at his face, jaws wide to tear at him—

Sebastian woke with a yell of terror and jerked bolt upright from the bed, colliding with somebody who was leaning over him. Still locked in the dream, he panicked and tried to push the figure aside so he could scramble to safety. It was only after a brief struggle that he realized that this was not Leonora. It was Jenna, looking down at him indignantly, a wet cloth clutched in one hand.

"Well, that's a fine thank you, I must say!" she said.

He stared at her helplessly. "I'm sorry," he gasped. "I thought you were a . . ."

"A what?" she prompted him.

"A big . . . cat . . ." He was suddenly aware of a splitting pain in his skull and he fell back onto his pillow with a groan.

Jenna smiled and held the cold cloth against the bump on his head, making him wince. "Well, I've been accused of looking like some strange things in my time," she said, "but never a cat."

"No, not you . . . I was talking about—" A sudden jolt of memory hit him. "Leonora!" he gasped. "Where is she?"

"Gone," she assured him. She put an arm under his shoulder and raised him into a sitting position. He found himself looking through some leaded windows at the stern of the ship. Sure enough, there was the *Marauder* limping away into the distance. Somewhat closer, he could see the mauled remains of the *Black Hand*, the ship listing very low in the water and surrounded by a horde of sailors in rowing boats.

"The pirate ship's sinking," Jenna told him. "We're getting off as much of the cargo as possible before she goes down."

"But what about the *Marauder*? That could sink too before it reaches Ramalat."

"Oh, I doubt that. Trencherman will have to keep his crew at the pumps the whole time, but he should make it back all right."

Sebastian looked at Jenna. "You're sure?" he whispered.

"As sure as I can be." She smiled, as if amused by the serious expression on his face. "And what would you do if I said I *wasn't* sure? Would you swim after them? Are you that much in love with her?"

He gazed at her blankly for a moment. "Of course not," he said, as though he had never heard such a ridiculous notion in his entire life. But his voice didn't sound convincing even to his own ears. He glanced around quickly, the motion sending fresh spasms of pain through his head. "Where am I exactly?" he asked.

"In my cabin. It was quicker than carrying you down to your own." Jenna eased him back onto the pillow and pressed the cool cloth against his head. "I can't say I blame you," she said.

"What?"

"Leonora. She *is* extraordinarily beautiful."

Sebastian shrugged. "What's that got to do with anything? She's enchanted me. It wouldn't matter if she had a face like a Berundian wine merchant, I'd still feel the same way about her. I can't help myself."

"You think so?" Jenna looked doubtful. "I imagine the way she looks has plenty to do with it." She sighed. "Must be nice to have that effect on a man."

Sebastian studied Jenna for a moment. She had taken off her hat and her magnificent auburn curls were tumbled around her shoulders, glowing copper-red in the sunlight from the window. Not that he was interested, of course. "You're the . . . best-looking sea captain I've ever seen," he muttered.

She laughed aloud at that. "That's not difficult! Most of them have beards and eye-patches!"

"Er . . . yes, but I didn't mean—" Another jolt of pain lanced through his head and he gave up trying to explain himself.

"What happened to me?" he asked her. "I remember being up on deck after the fight and Cornelius said he wanted to tell me something. . . ." His eyes widened in realization and he tried to sit up yet again. "He hit me!" he cried. "That sneaky little Golmiran whacked me over the head with something!"

"The hilt of his sword," said Jenna, pushing Sebastian firmly back down. "And he *had* to do it— you were trying to get us to take the witch aboard."

"For the last time, she is not . . . a . . ."

"You try to defend her, but that is because you are in love with her."

"I'm not," he assured her. "I'm enchanted. There's a big difference."

"I wish I knew the secret of such an enchantment."

This struck Sebastian as a very odd thing to say, and he was just about to remark upon it when the door of the cabin opened and Cornelius stepped into the room, closely followed by the Kid.

CHAPTER 19

THE KID SPEAKS

Cornelius strolled over to the bed, an amused expression on his baby face. He was carrying Sebastian's tricorn hat.

"So you're awake at last!" he observed.

"Yes, no thanks to you!" snapped Sebastian. "You nearly split my skull open with that sword hilt!"

"Sorry about that, lad, but I had to move quickly. The way Leonora had you dancing to her tune, you'd have ended up fighting me to try and get your own way. So a little tap on the noggin seemed in order. At least I didn't damage your new hat." Cornelius threw the tricorn onto the end of the bed, then pulled himself up to perch beside it. The Kid found a chair and sat down moodily.

"You could have just spoken to me about it," growled Sebastian. "Like any civilized person."

"I really don't think you'd have been in the mood

to listen. Don't take it so personally. Besides, I did you a favor."

"You did?"

"Yes. Typically, you've missed all the hard work. We've been salvaging what we can from the *Black Hand*. It won't be long now before she sinks." He threw a commiserating look toward the Kid. "No treasure, I'm afraid; all they had was food and general provisions. It seems the ship stopped off at Lemora two days ago and left all the booty with contacts on the island. The *Marauder* was to be their first victim since leaving there."

"Would have been too," said the Kid, who was slumped in his seat, hands in his pockets, "if you lot hadn't come along when you did. And like I said, it wasn't about plunder with Trencherman. It was *personal*."

Sebastian studied the Kid thoughtfully. "What's *he* doing in here?" he asked. "Shouldn't he be locked up?"

Cornelius shrugged. "Well . . . after careful consideration I would like to ask, Captain Swift, for your permission to allow the boy to remain on deck rather than be kept down in the cells with what's left of his crew."

Jenna frowned. "Do you think that's a good idea?" she murmured.

"We'll see. I've warned him that at the first sign of

disobedience, he'll be thrown down there with the rest of them. Call me old-fashioned, but somehow I can't bring myself to lock up a boy of fourteen summers . . . not unless it becomes absolutely necessary."

Sebastian studied the Kid for a moment and tried to ignore the throbbing pain in his head. "Well, what do *you* say?" he asked. "Will it be necessary?"

The Kid shrugged his shoulders beneath his too-large jacket. "Course not. You think I want to spend time with that lot? They hate me. There's no telling what they'd do if they got their hands on me, specially now the *Black Hand* is lost."

This remark was puzzling to say the very least.

"But . . . you're their captain," observed Jenna. "Why would they hate you?"

"Oh . . . because they never really wanted me to be captain in the first place. See, after my dad disappeared there was two men laying claim to the *Black Hand:* the first mate, Bones, and the bosun, a man called Sully. But pirate law says the captain's eldest son has rights to the ship. Well, I was his only son, wasn't I? Twelve summers old when I started and as green as grass, but it fell to me." As he talked, the Kid's little face was a picture of misery beneath the brim of his three-cornered hat.

"Then why accept the position?" asked Cornelius. "If you didn't enjoy it, surely you could have declined the offer."

"Yeah, but I found out that Bones and Sully were planning to sell the ship to a rich buyer in Ramalat. Take a wild guess as to who that might have been."

There was a brief silence while they considered this. Then Jenna said, "Captain Trencherman."

"Got it in one! My dad would have gone mad if he'd come home and found a creep like him in charge of his ship. It's his pride and joy. And Dad always said he wanted me to take over the family business when he was gone. . . . It's just that neither of us expected it would be quite so soon."

Sebastian and Jenna exchanged glances. They both knew what that felt like and could easily sympathize.

"But you made the best of things, I suppose," said Cornelius.

"Tried to," said the Kid. "The rest of the crew tolerated me, but Bones and Sully was always looking for ways to get rid of me. They was forever trying to get the other men to mutiny. In the end I had the two of them thrown off the ship at Lemora. That made life a bit easier, but the crew kept criticizing me if I didn't get them plenty of plunder, so I had to attack anything that moved."

"But that's what pirate ships do, isn't it?" said Sebastian.

"Yeah, I know that, but it never sat easy with me. Dad always said I had too much of a conscience to be a good pirate. Maybe he was right." The Kid shrugged before continuing.

"And then Trencherman started in on us. He harried us from port to port. He didn't want to sink the ship—just get rid of me and take it as a prize. I lost a lot of good men to his guns. In the end I got tired of running; decided to try and catch him unawares." He glanced at Jenna. "I was giving him a right good stuffing before you sneaked up on me," he said proudly.

"That you were," she agreed. She looked at him warily. "But even in the heat of battle, you should always keep an eye out for the unexpected."

"Yeah, well, thanks for the tip. But you didn't play fair."

Jenna looked at him in disbelief. "You're saying I cheated?"

The Kid studied his feet for a moment, his face red. "I'm saying it was sneaky," he insisted.

She smiled at him. "Well, if it's any consolation, you managed to do quite a bit of damage to the *Sea Witch*. So much that we're going to have to put in to Lemora to make some repairs."

Cornelius and Sebastian looked at her in surprise.

"Is that a good idea?" muttered Sebastian.

"Frankly, no. But it's either that or we turn round and follow the *Marauder* back to Ramalat and undertake repairs there."

"How serious is it?" asked Cornelius.

Jenna frowned. "When we bumped hulls with the *Black Hand*, somebody got off a round of shot at close range. It breached us just below the waterline. At the moment we've got a slow leak down there. I've had a temporary patch put on, but it's only going to get worse. It needs to be fixed properly."

"So surely somebody can do that?" said Cornelius.

Jenna shook her head. "I won't send men to do it in these waters—there are too many kelfers around. There'll be even more of them once the *Black Hand* goes down with all those dead pirates aboard." She glanced apologetically at the Kid, but he waved a hand in dismissal. "No, we need to pull into a dock to do the job properly. We can be in Lemora by early tomorrow morning. I still have a few friends among the carpenters there."

Sebastian sniffed. "Pirate carpenters?" he said.

"Carpenters who *work* with pirates," Jenna corrected him. "But to be fair, they'll work with anyone who has the money to pay. They're just trying to make a living, the same as anyone else."

Cornelius shrugged. "Well then," he said, "Lemora it is. You know, I've always had a fancy to take a look at that place, but everyone says it's dangerous."

"Oh, it's not so bad," said the Kid. "People keep themselves to themselves in Lemora. It's only out on the ocean that they show their true colors. That's when you have to look out for yourself."

Sebastian studied the Kid for a minute. "Look," he said, "what's your real name? We can't go on calling you Kid all the time, can we?"

The Kid looked uncomfortable at this. "Sure you can," he said evasively. "I'm not bothered."

"No, come on, it's ridiculous. You must have answered to another name before you took over your father's ship, surely?"

"Well, yes . . . but . . . it . . . well, it's a stupid name, that's all."

"Nonsense," said Cornelius. "It's the name your parents gave you; you should be proud of it. Now come along, tell us what it is." He gave the Kid a probing look. "I could always go down and ask some of those pirates in the cells," he threatened.

The Kid sighed, looked at his feet for a moment, then shrugged. "It's . . . Beverly," he said glumly.

"Beverly?" Sebastian felt an impulse to laugh out loud and quickly glanced around at the others. "Well . . . er . . . that's a perfectly good name, isn't it?" he said, a little too loudly.

"Marvelous name," said Cornelius quickly.

"Yes, very nice," added Jenna. There was a brief pause. "Though if he prefers Kid, I see no reason why we shouldn't continue to call him that."

"Oh no, absolutely," said Cornelius. "If that's what he wants."

"Of course," added Sebastian. "Whatever."

The Kid regarded them sullenly. "See?" he said. "I told you it was a stupid name."

"So listen, what exactly happened to your father?" asked Sebastian, trying to change the subject. "Jenna told me that he was killed but you said—"

"He *disappeared*!" cried the Kid angrily. "He didn't die, he just went missing!"

"I see." Sebastian tried to pick his words as carefully as his throbbing head would allow. "So . . . how long has he been . . . er . . . missing?"

The Kid's glum expression seemed to deepen. "Over two summers now. He was out on the Deeps, south of Lemora. I wasn't with him on that trip; I'd stayed home 'cause I had a fever. Bones and Sully told me that they attacked a merchant ship they came across, and during the fight Dad was knocked overboard."

Cornelius studied the boy for a moment. "You've already said you don't trust those characters," he observed. "You're sure they told you the truth?"

The Kid glared at him. "They wouldn't know the truth if it bit them on the backside," he said.

"You said that they wanted control of the *Black Hand*," Cornelius reminded him. "It could be that they made damned sure your father didn't return from that voyage. Maybe they even ran a sword through him in the heat of battle—"

"No!" Now the Kid's eyes were blazing with anger. "You think two dogs like them could beat my father in a fight? No way! He's missing, that's all. And he'll be back one day. I know he will."

There was an uncomfortable silence. Sebastian tried to think of something to say but couldn't come up with anything appropriate; and then, at the worst possible moment, the cabin door opened and Lemuel stuck his balding head into the cabin.

"The pirate ship's going down if anybody's interested," he said.

The Kid's face registered shock, and for a moment Sebastian thought he was going to burst into tears; but somehow he managed to hold his emotions in check. "Why not?" he said quietly. He got up from his seat and made his way out of the cabin. The others followed, Jenna supporting Sebastian, who was still feeling decidedly dizzy.

Up on deck they watched the *Black Hand*, which was listing so badly to starboard that water was starting to creep in over the rails. A couple of sailors flung out a last few bits of salvage and then jumped into the water, where their comrades pulled them aboard a boat and started rowing frantically back toward the *Sea Witch*. At the last moment there was a commotion as numerous rats came scurrying out of their hidey-holes in the pirate ship and leaped into the sea, where they started swimming desperately toward the rowing boat, or climbed aboard bits of floating debris.

"Always happens at the very end," observed Jenna thoughtfully. "It's the only thing that will shift them."

The ship's timbers gave a mighty creak, and then the bows dipped dramatically beneath the surface of the water, churning the sea into violent bubbling motion. The waters closed over the decks, taking the *Black Hand* into a cold, deadly embrace, and then, in eerie silence, the hull of the ship began to slide slowly into the depths.

Sebastian glanced at the Kid and saw that despite the look of grim determination on his face, there were tears in his eyes and his hands were clenched into fists. It couldn't have been easy for him, seeing his father's ship go down like this.

"At least now Trencherman will never get his greasy hands on her," he said quietly.

The last they saw of the *Black Hand* was the very top of her foremast, where the skull and crossbones still flapped defiantly. But then she slipped beneath the surface and was gone. For a little while Sebastian could make out the dark shape of the ship's hull, going down, down into that seemingly bottomless ocean, and for the first time he felt a chill of real apprehension ripple through him, for he realized that it could so easily have been the *Sea Witch* sinking like that.

A series of huge bubbles came floating to the surface from its wake, gurgling obscenely, and then Sebastian saw the bodies of the dead pirates drifting up from the decks like life-sized rag dolls. And then he noticed a last chilling detail: a series of triangular fins cutting the surface of the water as the kelfers came cruising in, looking for a meal.

The others turned away in disgust and started toward the cabin, but glancing back, Sebastian noticed that the Kid remained standing at the rail, staring down at the swirling waters where the *Black Hand* had passed, as though hoping against hope that she might somehow rise again.

CHAPTER 20

ALL ASHORE

Early the following morning the *Sea Witch* nosed her way through a slight mist toward the harbor of Lemora. Scores of ships of every shape and size rode at anchor in the bay, but the dock seemed deserted. Standing on the prow, Cornelius and Sebastian eyed the wooden wharf and its grubby collection of waterside shanties with understandable suspicion. The memory of their visit to the lawless city of Brigandia was still fresh in Sebastian's mind and he remembered only too well how they had only just escaped with their lives.

"Seems quiet," observed Cornelius. "There's hardly anyone about."

"They're probably in hiding," replied Sebastian. "Waiting to jump out at us with knives and swords."

"Oh, you're too pessimistic."

"Even so, there's no real reason to go ashore, is there? Unless . . ."

"Unless what?" asked Cornelius.

"I've been thinking about the Kid."

"Oh yes?"

"I was reminding myself that if we do take him back to Ramalat, they'll hang him. I don't know about you, but the thought of letting a young lad go to the gallows is not one I can easily accept. Especially when it turns out he never really wanted to be a pirate in the first place."

Cornelius smiled and nodded. "I'm with you on that," he said.

"So maybe we *should* have a quick look around Lemora."

"Yes. And while we're there, it might just be that young Beverly manages to escape from us. All those narrow streets and everything . . . Well, it would be pointless looking for him in a labyrinth like that, wouldn't it?"

Sebastian grinned. "Sounds like a great idea. What about his crew?"

Cornelius's expression hardened. "Oh no, they're adults. They're also robbing, murdering scum. I've no problem with seeing the likes of *them* hang."

"You're all heart," said Sebastian.

Jenna came walking toward them from the stern. "What are you two conspiring about?" she asked as she approached.

"Nothing!" said Sebastian, a little too quickly.

"We were just saying," said Cornelius, "that Lemora seems like an interesting place to explore."

Jenna looked doubtful about that. "I wouldn't recommend any stranger to go into that hellhole," she said flatly. "Not without a small army to back them up."

"Oh, but we'll have an expert guide," said Cornelius. "Where is the Kid this morning?"

"Still eating his breakfast, I believe. You know, that boy could charm the birds out of the trees. He's got Thaddeus to whip him up a batch of pancakes. I've never known that cantankerous old coot to do that for anyone." She looked suddenly thoughtful. "You know, I've been doing some thinking. . . ."

Sebastian and Cornelius exchanged knowing glances.

"If you insist on taking the Kid into Lemora, you might want to consider coming back *without* him."

Cornelius raised his eyebrows. "What? But he's a pirate, Jenna. He and his crew would have plundered the *Sea Witch* without a thought if they'd had the opportunity!"

"I know, but . . . well, he's just a kid."

Sebastian shook his head. "Pay no attention to him. We've already planned to let him get away."

Jenna smiled, which seemed to light up her entire face. "I'm glad," she said. "I was dreading the thought of taking him back and letting Trencherman have his revenge. Well, I'll leave the details up to you. I'll be here, supervising repairs." She studied Cornelius for a moment. "You'll be stepping into a den of thieves. Perhaps you'd like to leave the treasure map with me for safekeeping?"

Cornelius shook his head, smiling. "Oh no," he said. "I think I'd rather keep that with me."

"Really, Captain Drummel!" she cried, in mock horror. "Anyone would think you didn't trust me." She chuckled. "Anyway, I'd better go and see about bringing this old tub into harbor." She started to turn away but Sebastian put out a hand to grasp her arm.

"Captain Swift?" he said. "Er . . . Jenna? Could I ask a small favor?"

She turned back to look at him, her dark eyes flashing, and smiled in a way that was designed to make his heart flutter but was wasted on a man so enchanted. "Of course. What is it?"

"Do you think . . . well, do you think that Max might be allowed to accompany us into Lemora?"

"Max?" She looked puzzled, as though struggling to remember the name.

"My buffalope. He's going crazy cooped up in that hold. I had a long conversation with him last night—"

"I can imagine," murmured Cornelius, rolling his eyes.

"—and he told me that if he didn't get his feet on dry land soon, he would go crazy. And, well, when a buffalope goes crazy, he's liable to smash into anything that gets in his way. Could cause a lot of damage down there."

Jenna frowned. "We don't want any more damage than we already have," she said. "Well, yes, I'm sure somebody in the harbor will have a hoist. I could use the opportunity to send somebody down there to do some mucking out."

"Oh yes, he's very embarrassed about that," Sebastian assured her. "But there really was nowhere else for him to go. And besides, he was frightened. The noise of the sea battle and everything . . ."

Jenna nodded. "Oh dear," she said. "I'm sorry if I . . . embarrassed your buffalope." She gave him a strange look: either she found him interesting or she thought he was some kind of dangerous lunatic—it was difficult to tell which. Then she strode away, shouting orders to her crew, as the *Sea Witch* swept into the shallow waters of the harbor.

Sebastian turned back to Cornelius to find that his friend was giving him a cool look of appraisal.

"She's really after you," he said.

Sebastian gave him a look of total innocence. "Oh, I seriously doubt it."

"Come on, man! I haven't much experience of

affairs of the heart but . . . I think she's very interested in you, Sebastian. What a pity you're already committed to another."

"Huh? What are you talking about?" Sebastian glared at him. "If you're referring to Leonora, you know perfectly well that whatever hold she has on me is against my will."

"I wasn't, actually."

"Then who?"

"That ruddy buffalope!" Cornelius shook his head in disbelief. "Taking him out for a stroll? You'll be tucking him in and reading him a bedtime story next!"

"That's not fair! Max has been in the Darke family for a very long time. . . . And in case you've forgotten, he's saved your neck on one or two occasions."

"I appreciate that," admitted Cornelius. "But you seem to forget, Sebastian, that he's just a simple beast of burden, not some relative of yours. Little wonder that Jenna gave you such a strange look!"

"I thought you said she was interested in me?"

"That was before you came up with the bit about Max being embarrassed."

"But he is!" insisted Sebastian. "Max is not your average, run-of-the-mill buffalope. He's . . . special."

"Perhaps. But he won't be around forever, my friend. And you need to remember that."

A shout went up from behind them as the *Sea Witch* swung round out of the wind. The crew hauled on the ropes, furling the sails, and the ship slowed as she crossed the shallows. Sailors ran to grab the mooring ropes as she came smoothly alongside the wooden jetty to make berth in Lemora, City of Pirates.

CHAPTER 21

IN LEMORA

Max complained bitterly about being hauled out of the hold in such an undignified fashion, but he was nonetheless grateful to get his hooves back onto dry land. He stood there on the jetty, blinking uncertainly at Sebastian and Cornelius, his eyes clearly unused to the full glare of sunlight. A couple of crewmen removed the leather harness from around his shaggy body, and he shook himself, flared his nostrils and took a deep breath of sea air.

"Dry land!" he cried, almost in exultation. "I was beginning to think I'd never see it again." He stamped one hoof repeatedly on the wooden boards beneath him. "Look at that," he said, as if in amazement. "It doesn't move under your feet. It's solid!" He stamped again and a wooden board snapped beneath him. "Well, fairly solid," he muttered, and moved along a few steps. He glanced around at the tumbledown dwellings that clustered along the jetty, then noticed Jenna and Lem entering what looked like a carpenter's shop. Max stared suspiciously at his friends. "Where are we exactly?" he asked. "This isn't the treasure island, surely?"

"No. It's the island of Lemora," said Cornelius matter-of-factly.

"The island of—" Max's mouth dropped open in dismay. "Lemora? Isn't that the place where all the pirates live?"

Sebastian frowned. "Umm . . . yes, but—"

"Oh well, that's typical, isn't it! The first chance I've had to get ashore in ages and where do you bring me? A place that's infested with pirates."

"We didn't have much choice," Sebastian assured him. "The ship was damaged in the battle; we had to come here."

"Don't talk to me about that battle. The noise of it! It's a wonder I wasn't deafened. Permanently!"

"You're safe now," Cornelius told him.

Max looked doubtfully at his surroundings. "Think so?" he muttered.

Sebastian saw that doors were opening all along the waterfront and various people were stepping out of their homes to inspect the new ship in the harbor. Some of them looked disreputable, to say the least. Sebastian could see a profusion of long coats and cloaks, tricorn hats, eye-patches, earrings and other piratical paraphernalia. It seemed to him that many eyes were studying the *Sea Witch* with what looked like an unhealthy interest.

The Kid came strolling down the gangplank and approached the three friends. He was sauntering along as though he hadn't a care in the world, waving to a few of the people on the jetty as he went by. He grinned at Sebastian.

"Welcome to my hometown!" he said. He looked at Max with interest. "Who owns this old fleabag?" he asked.

Sebastian winced. "Kid, allow me to introduce my friend, Max. He's been down in the hold for most of this voyage, so you won't have seen him. Max, this is the former pirate Captain Kid."

"Delighted to meet you, I'm sure," said Max icily. "And for your information, sonny, nobody officially *owns* me. My original master is dead and I choose to serve his son, Sebastian, out of the goodness of my heart."

The Kid stared at him in amazement. "It spoke!" he cried. He looked around at the others and pointed at Max, just in case they hadn't noticed. "It said *words*."

Sebastian chuckled. "Haven't you ever seen a talking animal before?" he asked.

"Well . . . yeah. I saw an equine once that could say 'Howdy do,' . . . but this one talks like a person."

"Yes, that's it," said Cornelius. "A person. A very rude person."

Max tossed his head dismissively. "Huh! Look who's talking! Mr. Mouth Almighty from the kingdom of Golmira!" He studied the Kid for a moment. "Did Sebastian say 'former pirate'?"

The Kid nodded. "That's right. I was pretty good at it too, till Captain Swift came along and sank my ship."

It dawned on Max what must have happened. "Oh my goodness!" he exclaimed. "The battle I heard. That was you?"

The Kid nodded proudly. "Like my father before me," he said. "A pirate bold and true."

"I see. . . ." Max looked at Sebastian. "Could we have a word?" he said quietly. "In private," he added meaningfully.

"Er . . . yes, I suppose so." The pair of them walked a short distance along the jetty until they were out of hearing. "What's the matter?" asked Sebastian.

"*What's the matter?*" Max looked at him in sheer disbelief. "Are you stupid or something?"

"I don't believe so. . . ."

"Well, for goodness' sake, think about it! The Kid is a *pirate*. You've just brought him ashore to his hometown, a city full of *pirates*. By rights, he should be down in the hold, shackled hand and foot. All he has to do here is snap his fingers and he'll have a crowd of thugs coming to his rescue."

Sebastian shrugged. "That's OK," he said. "It's kind of what we're hoping for."

Max glared at him. "What are you talking about?"

"None of us want to take him back to Ramalat, because the authorities will hang him and he's basically a nice lad."

"A nice lad? How do you arrive at that conclusion? He attacked our ship, for goodness' sake."

"No, he didn't! He attacked the ship that was following us, and in a way he did us a service, because he threw Leonora off our trail. We attacked *his* ship and he just fought back."

"You have lost me," said Max. "Completely."

"Just trust us," said Sebastian. "We know what we're doing."

"Really? That would be a novelty."

Sebastian moved back to join Cornelius and the Kid, and Max trailed reluctantly after him. Just then, Jenna and Lem came out of the carpenter's shop and made their way across the jetty.

"We're in luck," announced Jenna. "These carpenters have agreed to undertake repairs immediately."

"At an inflated price," growled Lemuel. "There are many ways to rob somebody, and maybe being a pirate is the most honest method. At least you're not pretending to be anything other than a crook."

Jenna spread her arms in a gesture of helplessness. "What can we do but accept their terms?" she said. "We are in a difficult situation. And we don't have the luxury of shopping around for a better deal." She thought for a moment. "Have the men mount guard around the ship while the work's being done. We don't want any of the inhabitants to get any closer than they need to." She lowered her voice. "Remember, we've half the crew of the *Black Hand* chained up in the brig. If news of that gets out, we'll be scuppered." She looked at Sebastian. "You still intent on going into Lemora?" she asked.

"We thought we would," said Sebastian. He glanced down at the Kid. "If this young man will agree to accompany us and keep us out of trouble."

The Kid grinned. "No problem," he said as he started off along the waterfront. "I know all the best places. Just follow me."

Sebastian was about to do so but Jenna put a hand on his arm.

"Be careful out there," she said quietly. "And don't be too long. I want to be out of this harbor the moment repairs are finished."

"Relax," he told her. "We've got the Kid with us. What could go wrong?"

"How I wish you hadn't said that," muttered Max. Sebastian turned and strolled after the Kid.

Cornelius and Max fell into step on either side of him.

"Leave him plenty of room," whispered Cornelius. "With any luck he'll make a run for it soon. . . ."

The problem was, the Kid *didn't* make a run for it, though the three friends gave him every opportunity. The idea of escape didn't even seem to have occurred to him. He showed Sebastian, Cornelius and Max the sights of Lemora, and though they hung back and turned away, and at one point even suggested that he go to the other side of the main square to buy some fruit, he nonetheless came straight back to them, as though he had decided that he was now a member of their gang.

Lemora turned out to be a big, sprawling place, replete with busy markets, coffeehouses, taverns and dwellings of every shape and size. As they wandered around, people recognized the Kid and stopped to pass the time of day with him. Suspicious glances were thrown at his companions, but it seemed that most people were happy to accept anyone who was in the Kid's company, even if they were total strangers. The hours passed as they trooped around the crowded streets until Cornelius announced that he was hungry and the Kid offered to take him to "the best tavern in Lemora."

As they headed toward it, Cornelius took the

opportunity to give the Kid a gentle push in the right direction.

"It's certainly very crowded here," he observed brightly. "You know, it's a good job you're staying close to us, because it would be very easy for you to lose yourself amongst all these people."

"I suppose," agreed the Kid, without much enthusiasm.

"Or when we're in the tavern," suggested Sebastian, "it would be a breeze for you to excuse yourself for a moment, to go and use the latrine or something. And if for some reason you didn't come back, well, we wouldn't have the first idea where to look, would we, Cornelius?"

The Kid nodded. "Well, don't worry, that's not going to happen," he said.

Sebastian and Cornelius exchanged exasperated looks.

"I think what my friends are clumsily trying to suggest," said Max, "is that you should push off. That way, they don't have to take you back to a public hanging in Ramalat."

"You're . . . trying to get rid of me?" The Kid's bottom lip began to tremble. "But I thought you *liked* me!"

"We *do* like you!" Sebastian assured him. "That's why we don't want to see you hang. I mean, look, I can't say it any plainer than this. Why don't you just slip away and go back to your mother?"

"My mother's dead," said the Kid. "She passed away when I was a baby."

"Oh . . ." Sebastian felt decidedly awkward. "Well then, some other relative. Brother, sister? Uncle, aunt? Grandmother, grandfather?"

The Kid just kept shaking his head.

"There must be *somebody*," insisted Cornelius.

"No," said the Kid. "I'm all alone in the world. The crew of the *Black Hand* was the closest I had to family, and you sent most of them to the bottom of the sea. Now I've only got you lot."

"Us?" Max looked horrified. "You think of us as family?"

"Well, maybe not *you*," said the Kid bluntly. "But Sebastian and Cornelius . . . and Captain Jenna, of course. You could have clapped me in chains and sent me back with Captain Trencherman, but instead you gave me a chance, you trusted me, and I don't think anybody ever did that before. So why would I want to run away from you? You're my mates." He paused for a moment and studied them. "Look, I know what you're trying to do. But we won't be heading back to Ramalat for quite some time, will we?"

"Well, no . . . ," admitted Cornelius.

"So *that* will be the time to jump ship, not now when we're heading off on an adventure! Don't worry, I've no wish to end my days dangling from a rope. And when I decide to slip the leash, nobody in the world will be quick enough to catch me. Now come on, I'm starving!"

He indicated the doorway of a tavern just ahead of them, a low, ramshackle, thatched building with a sign over the ancient wooden door that announced it as the Salty Dog.

"This place makes the best fish pie you've ever tasted," said the Kid enthusiastically.

"Sounds good," said Sebastian. He glanced at Max. "Max . . ."

"I know, I know, wait here! Don't worry, I'm used to it by now. Just make sure you bring me out a bit of this pie—I don't see why I should miss out on everything."

"You can't eat fish pie," said Sebastian. "You're a buffalope."

"He's eaten worse before now," said Cornelius. "Remember on the great plains that time? He tucked into—"

"Shush!" said Max. "Do we have to go into that every time the subject of food comes up? Can I help it if I have the kind of inquiring nature that longs for new experiences? I've never tasted fish pie; I don't think a mouthful would hurt."

"Rest assured, shaggy, we'll bring you some out," said Cornelius. "We'll just have to make sure we stay upwind of you."

"I can't imagine what you mean," said Max primly.

Everyone laughed at his disapproving expression; and then the Kid pushed open the tavern door and led the way inside.

CHAPTER 22

THE SALTY DOG

They found themselves standing in a dark, crowded interior, packed with seafaring types all drinking ale, smoking pipes and talking in a raucous babble consisting mostly of "oohs" and "arrs." A rich aroma of cooking hung in the air, making Sebastian realize how hungry he was.

The three of them pushed through the crowds and found a vacant table at the far end of the room, screened from the bar by a high wooden stall which gave them a little privacy. They sat down and a serving girl came in to take their orders. She was elvish, petite and curvaceous, with big black eyes and a tangle of dark curly hair spilling over her shoulders. She noticed Sebastian's pointed ears and favored him with a warm smile.

"Welcome to the Salty Dog, gentlemen," she said. "What's your pleasure?"

They each ordered the fish pie and a tankard of ale.

"You'll like the pie," she told Sebastian. "Made it with my own fair hands, I did. The recipe's an old family secret."

Sebastian smiled back at her. "I'm sure it's delicious," he said.

"You could do with putting a little fat on your bones," added the wench. "I like a man to be slim, but you'd blow away in a strong wind. Maybe I'll get you an extra-large portion."

Cornelius coughed impatiently. "If you wouldn't mind getting a move on," he said. "We're in a bit of a hurry."

"At once, sir," she said, and turned away, but not before directing another admiring look in Sebastian's direction.

"I think Megs is sweet on you," observed the Kid as the girl made her way to the bar. "You want to watch out for her—she's a man-eater."

"What, you mean she's a cannibal?" Sebastian gasped.

"No, you twit! I mean she's already had three husbands."

"Well, she won't be making me the fourth," Sebastian assured him.

"We'd best not tarry too long," Cornelius reminded them. "Jenna thought those repairs would only take a short while and she'll be anxious to get away from here."

"There's always enough time to eat," Sebastian assured him. "Besides, it will make a welcome change from Thaddeus's lumpy porridge."

The Kid pulled a face. "I don't know how you eat that stuff," he said. "I got him to make me some pancakes instead."

"Yes, how did you manage that exactly?" asked Sebastian.

"I've got big appealing eyes," said the Kid. "Like a puppy dog. Works every time."

Megs returned with three frothing tankards and set them down on the tabletop. As she leaned forward, she directed a wink in Sebastian's direction and he immediately felt his face coloring.

"I found an extra-large bowl, just for you," she told Sebastian. "And I'm going to pick out the nicest, juiciest pieces of fish I can find."

"That's, er . . . very kind of you," said Sebastian, squirming in his seat. "But really, there's no need."

"You going to be in Lemora long?" she asked. "Only it's my evening off and I'm not doing anything special. Maybe you'd like to—"

"We're only here for a short while," Cornelius told her bluntly. "Until our ship is repaired. And as I mentioned earlier, we are in something of a hurry, so . . ."

"Hmm? Oh . . . yes, sir! Of course, sir!" Megs turned

away with visible reluctance and trudged off toward the kitchen.

The Kid grinned, enjoying Sebastian's discomfort. "She's after you," he taunted. "You two are gonna get married!"

"Are not!" said Sebastian.

"Are too!" said the Kid. "Gonna get married and have babies!"

"Are not!"

"Are too!"

"Oh, shut up!" protested Cornelius. He shook his head. "What do women see in him?" he asked the room in general. "We can't seem to go anywhere without some dratted female fluttering her eyelashes at him."

"You're just jealous," said Sebastian, and now it was Cornelius's turn to go red in the face.

"Nonsense!" he protested. "You know I have no interest in women! They're nothing but a blasted nuisance!"

"Ah, but I bet if a *Golmiran* wench had brought the ale, you'd take a very different view."

"Pah! There's no such thing as a Golmiran wench! And a Golmiran *lady* wouldn't lower herself to wait on tables in a dump like this!"

"Hey, this is the best tavern in Lemora!" protested the Kid.

"Number one, a boy your age shouldn't be

frequenting taverns and drinking ale," said Cornelius. "And number two, if this is the best, I should hate to visit the worst. I mean, just look at the customers!"

The three of them studied the other drinkers. Sebastian had to agree that the ones they could see were a pretty motley crew—and that didn't include the hardened drinkers who were standing at the bar behind them, hidden behind the stall. In fact he realized it was an ideal spot to eavesdrop on their conversations, and the three friends started listening with interest when they detected a bit of a stir back there. Somebody had just entered the tavern and pushed his way straight over to the bar.

"Hey, lads!" said the newcomer, shouting above the hubbub of voices. "You'll never guess what I've just heard!"

"What's that?" asked another voice, sounding barely interested.

"The *Black Hand*'s been sunk and most of her crew killed!"

"What?" There were sounds of disbelief all round.

"You're making it up," said a third voice.

"It's true, I tell you! There's a galleon in the harbor, out of Ramalat—the *Sea Witch* she's called, put in for repairs. I got talking to the son of Ben Thomas, the ship's carpenter. He says as how his father's patching her up. One of the crew let slip that they got the damage during a fight with a ship called the *Black Hand*. Ben reckons that those of her crew who weren't killed are caged belowdecks like animals."

There were gasps of astonishment and anger at this news. Somebody suggested that if that was the case, they should raise a party of armed men and go and free the prisoners at once. There were several cries of agreement. Sebastian gave Cornelius a worried look and wondered if maybe it would be a good idea to forego the fish pie and make for the exit as quietly as possible. But then another voice spoke, a deep croaky voice filled with spite and arrogance; and Sebastian was aware of the Kid freezing beside him, his tankard halfway to his lips.

"What about that young brat of a captain? What happened to him?"

"Sorry, Bones," said the newcomer. "The man didn't say."

Now they heard yet another voice, soft, breathy, but in its own way every bit as unpleasant as the one that had spoken before.

"With any luck he'll be inside the belly of a kelfer."

"I'll drink to that, Sully!"

"Shame on you!" said a third voice. "He's only a youngun."

"Young 'un or not," growled Bones, "the cheeky little rip had me and Sully put ashore only a few days ago. Said we was disputing his authority."

"You should be glad about that. It could be you two floating around in the ocean like sprats at feeding time."

"It would never have come to that," whispered Sully. "Not if we'd got control of the ship. We'd be rich men now, living in the lap of luxury. And the *Sea Witch* would have a new owner."

"Whatever do you mean," asked the newcomer, " 'a new owner?' "

Sebastian leaned cautiously out to peer round the end of the alcove seat. The two pirates stood at the bar amidst a crowd of their cronies, grasping pints of foaming ale, both of them red-faced, their tongues doubtless loosened by the drink. They were a nasty-looking pair. The one called Bones was a tall, thin, almost cadaverous fellow, with greasy black shoulder-length hair. He wore a filthy striped tunic under a leather waistcoat and a plumed hat that had once been rather grand but now looked like it needed to be taken outside and buried. Sully was shorter and plumper. He was almost completely bald and had lost the end of his nose at some point in his career. When he grinned, he displayed the fact that he barely had a tooth left in his head.

"A contact of ours in Ramalat was ready to pay us a thousand gold crowns apiece for the ship," said Sully, in that soft, honeyed voice. "All we needed to do was get control of it. We had it all worked out.

First of all we made sure that the Kid's father didn't come back from his last trip."

"What are you saying?" asked the newcomer, who clearly wasn't all that bright. "I heard he fell overboard."

"You heard right," said Bones gloatingly. "What you didn't hear is that we gave him a helping hand over the side."

" 'Twas in the heat of battle," whispered Sully.

"That's when things get overlooked," said Bones.

"Nobody's paying attention," added Sully.

"Good time for accidents," said Bones. "And of course, that's exactly what it was. An *accident*."

"Yes. We 'accidentally' smacked him across the head, and he 'accidentally' fell into the water. Then, when the fight was over, we 'accidentally' forgot that we saw him fall in."

There was a brief silence; and then the drinkers at the bar burst into peals of raucous laughter.

"So who is this mysterious contact in Ramalat?" asked the slow-witted man.

"Can't you guess?" said Bones. "Trencherman, of course! He's been helping us sell our stolen goods to respectable folk for years. He's also a collector of ships and he's had his eye on the *Black Hand* for a long time. We figured the way was clear to sell her to him, but then Jack Donovan's brat turned up and claimed her for his own. I thought the rest of the crew would mutiny, but no, they agreed to abide by the Code of the Sea. Imbeciles! So instead of earning a fortune, we got thrown off the ship, and now she's at the bottom of the ocean where she can profit nobody. So I hope the Kid *did* go into the water. And I hope he was torn to pieces by hungry kelfers before he gave up the ghost. Good enough for him, I say!"

Sebastian turned to look at the Kid, his mouth open to tell him to stay quiet; but the seat beside him was empty. Looking up, he saw that the Kid was already leaving the stall.

"Wait!" he whispered, and hurried after him, closely followed by Cornelius.

CHAPTER 23

A HASTY DEPARTURE

As they stepped out from the cover of the stall, Megs appeared in the doorway carrying a tray of food. The Kid snatched up two steaming platters of fish pie and kept right on going. By the time Sebastian and Cornelius caught up with him he was standing in front of the men at the bar.

For a moment they carried on laughing and drinking. Then somebody noticed who had arrived and an abrupt silence fell over the crowd. It took a little while for Bones and Sully to take heed and then they too turned their gaze toward the Kid. Bones's surprise was so complete, he sprayed a fountain of ale out of his mouth. Sully just stood there, staring at the Kid in utter dismay.

It was Bones who found his voice first.

"K-Kid . . . ," he said. "Thank . . . thank goodness you're safe. . . ."

"Oh, worried about me, were you?" said the Kid, grinning wildly.

"What . . . what are you doing here?" whispered Sully. "We . . . we was afeared you was drownded or something."

The Kid smiled at them. "Oh no, I'm fine, thanks. But the *Black Hand*'s gone, sunk in battle."

"Sunk, you say?" Bones affected a look of complete amazement. "Oh, that's terrible news, ain't it, Sully?"

"Yes," whispered Sully. "That's terrible."

"It gets worse," said the Kid. "I've had to take on other work. I'm working here at the Salty Dog . . . as a waiter."

"A waiter?" murmured Sully.

"Yes." He indicated the two steaming bowls in his hands. "I brought the fish pies you ordered."

"But," said Bones, "we didn't ord—"

That was as far as he got. A scalding bowl of slop hit him full in the face; a moment later the other one crashed into Sully's ugly features. The men screamed and reeled back, clawing at their faces, and in that same instant the Kid nimbly grabbed the hilt of a sword from the scabbard of a bystander and slid it out. Sebastian just had time to register a sense of disappointment— he'd been looking forward to tasting that pie—and then he too was drawing his sword and he sensed, rather than heard, that Cornelius had done likewise.

There was a terrible silence at the bar. Bones and

Sully stared at the Kid, their eyes malevolent in their half-scalded faces.

"You cheeky little pup," snarled Bones, reaching for his sword. "I'll run you through for that!"

"You can try," the Kid told him. "But unlike my dad, I've had a bit of warning about your cowardly ways. Now, this is just between the three of us. What say we go outside and settle this man to man?"

There was another short silence while Bones and Sully considered this. They looked at each other for a moment. Then they burst out laughing.

"You are joking, of course!" said Bones, sneering. He gestured to his cronies and they all began to unsheathe their swords, until the dark interior seemed to glitter with a whole forest of razor-sharp blades. Then: "Get them!" roared Bones.

Sebastian didn't have time to think after that. A big bearded man came lunging straight at him, swinging a blade that seemed to be the size and weight of a small tree trunk, and when Sebastian raised his own blade to intercept the blow, the impact nearly drove him to his knees. He lashed back and managed to slice the plume off the top of the bearded man's hat. But sword blades were lashing at him from every direction and there was simply no room to move. It quickly became evident that they couldn't hope to hold out very long against such an onslaught in these cramped conditions.

"Cornelius!" Sebastian hissed over the clanking of blades. "There's too many of them!"

"Oh, you noticed that too, did you?" Cornelius lunged forward and drove the point of his blade through somebody's thigh; but then had to leap back as a storm of blades came hacking down at him in retaliation. "We can still take them!"

"But we must get back to the ship and warn Jenna!"

Cornelius scowled. "You go! I'll hold them here."

"No! This isn't the time for heroics. We have to return to the ship!"

"OK, then *I'll* hold them!" yelled the Kid.

"Nobody is going to hold anybody!" yelled Sebastian, hacking desperately at the circle of blades that were jabbing relentlessly at him. "We're simply going to tell Jenna what's happened!"

"I suppose you're right," admitted Cornelius reluctantly. "But I want it on record: running away was not *my* idea!"

Sebastian, Cornelius and the Kid began to retreat toward the door, fighting as they went. Sebastian's shoulders thudded against wood, and he pushed backward and stepped out into the street, with Cornelius and the Kid right behind him. They immediately slammed the door on the advancing horde and put their backs against it.

"Where's my pie?" asked an indignant voice. Max was standing there, regarding them suspiciously.

"Never mind the pie!" cried Sebastian. "We're in a spot of bother."

Even as he spoke, the door began to move as the angry crowd within exerted their combined weight on it.

"What have you been up to in there?" said Max, rolling his eyes. "Honestly, you've only been out of my sight for a short while."

"Forget that," snapped Sebastian, gritting his teeth as he struggled to hold the door shut. "Max, old friend, we need a bit of time to make an escape. I don't suppose . . ."

Max sighed. "Oh, right, so it's 'old friend' now, is it? Funny how you only ever say that when you're in trouble."

"Max, *please!* We don't have time for this."

"I suppose I'll help," he said. "But I still say you could have grabbed a bit of pie for me."

"I'll make it up to you," Sebastian assured him. "If it's any consolation, we didn't get any either."

"Very well." Max shrugged his massive shoulders and stepped closer to the door, where the three friends were rapidly losing their struggle. "Right," he said. "I'm going to count to three . . . and when I do, I want you to step quickly aside, all right?"

"Whatever," agreed Cornelius through gritted teeth.

"All right then." Max lowered his huge horned

head and pawed the ground with one hoof. "Ready? One . . . two . . . *three!*" he roared; and Sebastian and the others jumped smartly to either side of him. Max threw himself at the door with all the speed and power of a gigantic battering ram. At first it looked as though he had left it too late. The door was swinging open and the crowd within were spilling through like shaken-up ale spurting from a bottle. But then Max's head connected with the door, making a sound like a thunderclap and driving it shut again. The door was wrenched straight off its hinges, slamming backward into the crowd of pirates pressed up against it. Propelled by Max's lumbering body, the door and the people behind it were thrust back into the tavern and there was a great crash from within.

The others didn't wait to see what had happened. They turned on their heels and began to run back in the direction of the harbor. After a few moments Sebastian glanced over his shoulder and saw a rather dazed-looking Max trotting away from the inn, pursued by a few battered pirates. But they were urging other people in the street to come and help them, and several seemed to be responding.

"This way!" yelled the Kid, and he turned left into a narrow opening. "Shortcut!" Sebastian plunged after him and found himself racing along a narrow cobbled alley crisscrossed by countless washing lines heavy with pegged-out clothes. While Cornelius and

the Kid simply ran underneath them, Sebastian was obliged to keep ducking down under the washing.

"Master, wait for me," bellowed a voice behind, and glancing back again, Sebastian saw what, in different circumstances, might have been a comical sight. Max was galloping after them, his horns snagging every line of washing that he encountered, snapping the twine and heaping the damp clothing onto his head. After a few such collisions he was virtually running blind, his head encased in what looked like a great multicolored turban.

Some way behind Max came a yelling mob of sword-waving pirates, and as they gave chase, they seemed to be gathering more and more members to their cause. Sebastian shouted to Max to keep going, and at that same instant he burst out of the alleyway and was shocked to find that the ground dropped away in a steep flight of stone steps. He missed the first of them, tripped and fell headlong, narrowly missing Cornelius and the Kid. Sebastian went sprawling past them, the sharp-edged stones grazing his knees and elbows. He lost his sword, which clattered away from him, but somehow managed to halt his fall. He lay for a while, dazed and breathless.

"For goodness' sake, get up and stop messing about," said Cornelius as he went running past. "This is serious."

"I know that," snapped Sebastian. "I just didn't realize that—"

He broke off as he saw Max's huge body come lumbering out of the mouth of the alley, his head now so thoroughly encased in washing that he had no hope of finding his footing. He leaped out into empty space, and for a long time it seemed as though his impetus had given him wings. He soared for quite some distance, his legs pedaling madly as they sought to gain purchase on something substantial. Then his hooves came down onto the slippery edge of a step, his knees buckled, and he was flipped head over heels onto his back.

For a moment he seemed to stop right where he was. But then he began to slide. He came whizzing down the steps like a huge, shaggy toboggan, and Sebastian, transfixed by the sight of him, was unable to scramble out of the way. Max's haunches struck him in the legs, knocking him clean off his feet. He came crashing down, face-first, onto Max's chest, and clung in desperation to the buffalope's front legs. Once again he overtook Cornelius and the Kid, who stared in amazement as he and Max went rocketing past them. Looking back, Sebastian saw that the crowd was now spilling out from the alley and descending the steps in hot pursuit.

"Where am I?" grunted Max's muffled voice, speaking through layers of washing.

Sebastian was about to say, "On some steps," when, quite suddenly, Max's progress came to an abrupt halt and Sebastian was flung backward through the air to some unknown landing place. He steeled himself for a terrible impact but felt only the shock of cold water against his back. His first thought was that he must be in the harbor, but thrashing around, he found that the water only came up to his knees and that he was in the middle of some kind of circular fountain. Standing all around the rim were some surprised-looking women, who had been doing their washing and were now soaked to the skin.

Max's back end had connected with the stone rim of the fountain, but luckily his ample layers of fat had prevented him from doing himself any real injury. He scrambled to his feet, thrashing his head madly, and Sebastian helped him to divest himself of the last of the washing. The buffalope stared around in astonishment, trying to work out how he had got here. Sebastian looked back toward the steps and saw Cornelius and the Kid descending the last of them. Behind them, the angry mob had swelled to a great crowd, all yelling and gesticulating and looking very nasty indeed.

"Where did all that lot come from?" asked Max.

"Never mind," gasped Sebastian, scrambling over the low parapet of the fountain, hampered by the fact that the women, having recovered from their surprise, were now pelting him with handfuls of washing.

"Stop that!" he protested, but that only made it worse. He and Max joined the other two as they reached the foot of the steps.

"This is no time to go swimming," observed Cornelius.

"Which way?" grunted Sebastian.

"Follow me!" yelled the Kid, racing past him across the square. "It's not far now."

"I hate running like this," complained Cornelius, who was sounding a little breathless. His short and rather bandy little legs were not designed for the purpose.

"How would you prefer to run?" asked Max. "On your hands?"

"You know what I mean! Now we're on open ground, perhaps we should stand and fight."

"Are you kidding?" gasped Sebastian. "Have you seen how many of them there are now? Besides, we have to warn Jenna!"

Right on cue, they burst through an opening between two cottages and found the harbor straight ahead of them. They spilled down the slope onto the wooden jetty. Up ahead of them they could see Jenna, standing on the jetty, talking to the ship's carpenter.

"Jenna!" yelled Sebastian. She turned to look at him, a smile on her face; a smile that faded when she registered that he and the others were running at full tilt; a smile that disappeared completely as she looked behind them and saw what now looked like half the town racing in pursuit. She hesitated for only a moment, said something that looked very unlady-like and threw the carpenter a bag of coins. Then she turned and began to run back toward the *Sea Witch*, shouting orders as she went. The ship's crew, already on the lookout for any sign of trouble, reacted promptly and raced up the gangplank onto the ship. On deck there was feverish activity as crewmen heaved on ropes to let out the sails.

The four friends were only a short distance from the gangplank now, and Sebastian was just thinking that they might make it to the ship when something struck him hard between the shoulder blades, pitch-ing him forward and making him lose his footing. He hit the wooden boards, rolled awkwardly and came to a halt, lying on his back, stunned. Beside him lay the heavy cudgel that somebody had thrown with deadly accuracy.

A great cry of triumph went up from the approach-ing crowd, and Sebastian saw with a jolt of dismay that his friends had not noticed he had fallen. They were following Jenna up the gangplank to the safety of the *Sea Witch*. He sat up and turned back to face his adversaries. He had lost his sword during the pursuit and could only get wearily to his feet and stand there with his fists raised as the mob closed in on him, weapons at the ready. He saw a rather battered-looking Bones and Sully in the lead, grinning malevolently at the thought of catching at least one of their tormentors.

The mob came to a halt a short distance from him and a terrible silence descended.

"All right," said Sebastian, trying to sound defiant. "Who's going to be first?"

And then there was a weird bellowing sound, and something came spinning through the air above his head, a whirling blur of motion that carried a sword in either hand. There were several short, sharp screams as pirates flew in all directions, clutching at their arms, their sides, their faces. The blur stopped spinning and fell to the ground, where it revealed itself to be a little warrior called Cornelius.

He gave a mocking bow. "That, gentlemen," he announced, "was called the Golmiran death leap. It's a speciality of mine." He stooped, snatched up a fallen sword and threw it to Sebastian. "And now we've evened up the odds a bit, who's next?" He nodded to Bones. "You, sir?" he suggested; and then to Sully, "What about you?"

Bones and Sully began to advance slowly, their faces grim.

"It ain't you we have the argument with," muttered Bones.

"It's the Kid," whispered Sully.

"What if you was to hand him over to us?" snarled Bones.

"Then there needn't be any more trouble," added Sully.

"You can forget all that," Sebastian told them. "He's with us now."

A shout came from behind them: Jenna's voice.

"Hurry aboard! We're ready to leave."

Cornelius looked up at Sebastian. "Off you go," he said.

"But what about you?"

Cornelius smiled. "I'll be along presently," he said. "Now *go*—that's an order."

Sebastian frowned, but started to back toward the gangplank. He began to ascend it slowly, keeping his eyes on his friend.

"So," he heard Bones say, "it's just you and us now . . . shorty!"

Sebastian winced. Big mistake, he thought.

There was a minute of deep, deep silence. Then Cornelius went into action, his sword arm moving so fast that it became a blur of chain mail and leather. Sebastian didn't exactly see how it happened, but when the arm slowed again, both Bones and Sully were standing there looking quite ridiculous, their clothes hacked to shreds, their breeches around their ankles, Bones's hat crownless and hanging around his neck like a collar.

Sebastian stepped from the gangplank onto the deck and realized that the ship was already moving away from the quayside: that the gangplank was going to collapse at any moment. "Cornelius!" he bellowed. "Come on!"

Cornelius gave a mocking little bow to the crowd. "Gentlemen," he said. "Until we meet again."

Then he turned and made a dash for it, climbing the gangplank as fast as his little legs would carry him. At the last moment it fell away from the hull and Cornelius was obliged to jump, pumping his arms and legs to gain extra momentum. Sebastian caught his outflung hand and hauled him across the divide as the *Sea Witch* pulled away into deeper water, out of reach of the bellowing crowd on the quayside.

"Wow!" said the Kid. "You were incredible, Cornelius. You gave them a right good kicking!"

"Oh, I'm full of surprises," said Cornelius with a grin. "Pity I didn't have a bit more time to finish off those two rascals."

Jenna came stalking over, looking far from pleased. "I thought I told you to keep a low profile in Lemora," she said. "Not to come back with half the flipping population baying for your blood. It's a good job we'd just finished the repairs when you arrived."

"They'd heard about the *Black Hand*," said Sebastian. "They were coming down here to try to rescue the crew. We held them up a bit, otherwise they might have got here before you were ready to leave."

"Well, if that's supposed to make me feel better, I—" Jenna broke off in alarm. The ship had quite suddenly stopped making progress and there was a terrible creaking sound, a shuddering sensation that seemed to travel the length of the hull. "What on earth . . . ?" Her eyes widened in sudden realization. "The mooring ropes!" she cried. "Somebody forgot to cast off!" She grabbed a discarded axe and started to run back toward the stern; but in that same instant there was a thunderous roar from behind them as the straining rope refused to stretch any further and simply pulled the side of the wooden jetty clean out from under the feet of the angry crowd. There were cries of panic, a splintering of wood, and then the whole lot of them were tipped into the cold gray water of the harbor.

Sebastian and the Kid laughed delightedly but Jenna lifted a hand to cover her forehead in a gesture of despair.

"Oh, perfect," she observed. "Good work, boys. Now every pirate in Lemora will be after us."

"Load up the cannon," suggested Cornelius glee-fully. "We'll sink all the other boats in the harbor while we've got the chance."

"I don't think so," Jenna told him. "I vote we sim-ply put as much distance between us and them as possible." She turned away, shouting to Lemuel, "Full speed ahead! Put on extra sail if we need to. I want to be far away from here!" She handed him the axe. "And for goodness' sake cut the mooring rope before we find ourselves towing half of the jetty behind us."

"Aye, aye, Captain," said Lemuel, and hurried away.

Sebastian took the opportunity to lean against the rail and get his breath back while he studied the floundering people who were trying to pull them-selves back up the tumbled wreckage of the jetty.

"So that was Lemora," he said. "Nice place to visit, but I wouldn't want to stay." He glanced at the Kid. "I thought you told me you had plenty of friends back there."

"I did, until a short while ago. Must have fallen in with the wrong crowd, I guess." He shrugged. "I sup-pose they all think I've gone over to the other side."

"I rather think they may be right," said Cornelius with a knowing smile.

"One thing's for sure," said the Kid. "Trencher-man's an even bigger villain than I thought. It was *his* idea to get rid of my dad. If I ever see his ugly face again, he'd better be ready to fight. And he'll get no mercy from me."

"Good lad," murmured Cornelius. "You were right to harbor suspicions about that slimy toad."

Max was gazing glumly over the side of the boat. "Well, at least they haven't put me back down in that stinking hold," he said. "I'm up here breathing the fresh air and everything."

"Right," said Sebastian. "So why the long face?"

Max shrugged his huge shoulders. "I'm starving," he said. "What time's din-dins?"

The *Sea Witch* sped onward across the shimmering depths of the ocean, heading due south from Lemora and rapidly shortening the distance between herself and the mysterious island where, according to the ancient chart, the pirate treasure was hidden.

CHAPTER 24

SHIPS IN THE NIGHT

They sailed south for five days and five nights and saw little else but the unending stretch of restless ocean. Occasionally some massive sea beast would rise from the deep, blasting out great plumes of water, then sink back again without a trace. But other than that, life was tedious and Sebastian found himself looking forward to being back on dry land. Every night Jenna would come up on deck to take readings from the stars with the quarterstaff; then she and Lemuel would return to her cabin and huddle over their charts, making intricate measurements and conferring in whispers.

On the morning of the sixth day Jenna called Sebastian and Cornelius down to her cabin and told them that if she and Lem had made their calculations correctly, they should come upon the island by late that afternoon. Sebastian was very excited by the news, though Cornelius played it down, as though he found treasure islands every day of his life.

However, Sebastian noticed that, from midday onward, the little warrior stationed himself in the ship's prow and didn't budge from there. Down on the main deck, Max, who could usually be relied upon to make irritating conversation at such times, was unusually silent, as though he too was waiting for a glimpse of land. But the afternoon came and went, twilight descended upon the *Sea Witch*, and still they found nothing. To add to their problems, a thick sea mist rose up around them and they were more or less sailing blind.

Cornelius finally gave up his vigil and announced he was going down to the cabin to study the chart. Sebastian told him he'd be along in a little while, but in fact, the stuffy confines of the cabin were not an option at the moment. A terrible restlessness had come over him, mounting steadily through the day, and he was now in a state of high excitement. So he continued to pace the deck, wrapped in a long cloak against the evening chill. There was a strange calm— hardly a breath of wind—and the *Sea Witch* was moving at a much slower pace than usual. Everywhere was silent save for the creak of ropes and the faint splash of waves breaking against the prow. He walked along the main deck and climbed the steps to the bow, where he strained his eyes staring into the thick, undulating banks of fog up ahead, but he could see nothing. Looking up at the crow's nest, he could just make out the figure of a crouching sailor who was no doubt in a much better position to see something if it was out there. Any moment he might give a cry of "Land ho!" but the time passed and he remained silent.

Not for the first time, Sebastian wondered if the treasure map that Cornelius had paid five gold crowns for was genuine. Maybe the island was a figment of somebody's imagination. Maybe it was some elaborate practical joke. How long would they go on sailing south before Jenna concluded that the island they were seeking simply wasn't there?

Sebastian was walking back toward the stern when he noticed the big shaggy shape of Max looming out of the fog. The buffalope was backing carefully up against the rails, trying to maneuver his huge rear end over the top of them. Sebastian approached, smiling.

"What are you doing?" he asked.

Max looked startled and then vaguely sheepish. "What do you think I'm doing?" he snapped. "I'm trying to have a quiet poo. I thought I was alone," he added primly.

"But why bother?" persisted Sebastian. "Just do it on the deck—somebody will come along and shovel it over the side."

Max shook his head. "I'm not running the risk of upsetting Captain Swift. She's had it in for me ever since I came on board."

"Oh, Jenna's not that bad. You must admit it is a bit strange having a buffalope wandering around the deck of a ship."

"What's so strange about it?" persisted Max. "As a member of this expedition, I feel I have every right to be here."

"I'm not saying you don't. But you can see her point of view, surely? A great clumsy beast, wandering the decks, getting in everyone's way. It's not ideal, is it?"

"No, but I suppose they just have to put up with you!" quipped Max.

"Oh, very funny!" Sebastian gave Max's huge shoulder an affectionate punch. "She's just saying that buffalopes and ships don't go together."

"Hmph! I might have known you'd take her side."

"What's that supposed to mean?"

"It's quite apparent from the way she stares at you that you've made a big impression. And I suppose you've gone all gooey over her."

"No I haven't. I can't think about anyone these days, except . . ."

Max gave him a disparaging look. "Leonora," he said.

"Yes. Is that so wrong?"

"About as wrong as it could be."

"Yes, but I can't seem to help myself. I mean, I close my eyes and I see her face, staring at me."

Max shivered. "It's enough to give you the creeps," he said. "I wouldn't fancy having her leering at me like that. It'd give me nightmares."

As if cued by his remark, a dark figure with a pale, grizzled face came looming out of the mist. Max gasped in terror but it was only Lemuel, wrapped in a warm blanket. He grinned, displaying his many gold teeth.

"Ah, Mr. Darke, there you are! Captain Swift asked me to tell you she'd like to see you in her cabin." He nodded and went on his way.

"Just friends, eh?" said Max, looking at Sebastian accusingly.

"Yes, of course!"

"Then why do you suppose she wants to see you?"

"I don't know. Perhaps she wants to show me some map references."

"Oh, is that what you call it? You'd better hurry along, she's waiting."

"Look, it's not what you think."

"Oh, just go, will you, and give me a bit of privacy!"

Sebastian stared at him, not understanding. "Why do you want privacy?" he asked.

"Because . . . you *know*!" Max turned his head to

nod back toward his rear end. "What I was doing when you happened along? I'm *bursting!*"

"Oh, I see!" Sebastian grinned. "You're getting very prim and proper in your old age, aren't you?" He turned toward the stern of the ship, wondering why Jenna had asked to see him. Cornelius was always saying that the captain was sweet on him, and she did seem to stare at him rather a lot. The problem was, he felt absolutely nothing for her other than a sense of friendship. He hoped she wasn't looking for anything more than that. He'd only taken a few steps when he heard an explosive sound of rushing wind from behind him, followed by a groan of relief from Max.

"Charming!" he called over his shoulder. "There's nothing quite so inspiring as the sound of a buffalope voiding his bowels!"

"Sorry," murmured Max. "I'm not getting enough greens in my diet." He thought for a moment. "In fact, I'm not getting *any* greens. You know, while you're down there with Captain Swift, you might mention the fact!"

"I might," muttered Sebastian, under his breath. "But I seriously doubt it."

CHAPTER 25

TRUE CONFESSIONS

Sebastian descended the wooden steps, strolled the short distance to the captain's cabin and rapped on the door.

"Who is it?"

"Jenna, it's Sebastian. Lem said you wanted to see me."

"Sebastian!" There was an unmistakable smile in her voice now. "Oh, er . . . yes, wait a moment!"

"If it's a bad time, I can always come back later."

"It's a perfect time. I'm just . . . not quite ready, that's all."

There were rustling noises from within, as though somebody was hurriedly getting dressed. "Just give me . . . a moment longer."

Sebastian heard the sound of heavy boots clumping on the floor. "Are you all right in there?" he asked.

"I'm fine. I'm changing out of my work clothes."

"Well, don't change on my account."

"I wasn't!"

There was a long pause and then the sound of Jenna humming a half-remembered tune. "Won't be a second," she said at last. "Just brushing my hair!"

"Oh really, there's no need for any of that. Look, maybe I should come back another time."

"No! I'm nearly ready. . . ."

"The thing is, Jenna, if it's about the expedition to the island, we can always—"

He broke off in mid-sentence as the door swung open, revealing Jenna, dressed in a long embroidered robe of rich red velvet tightly belted around her slender waist. Her freshly brushed chestnut curls spilled over her shoulders, and she had outlined her eyes with a dark brush and rubbed a little rouge into her cheeks. Out of her usual captain's uniform, she looked quite stunning, and she was wearing a powerful fragrance that smelled of wildflowers.

Sebastian just stood there and stared at her in surprise. "Wow," he said. He couldn't think of anything else to say for a moment.

"Sebastian," said Jenna. "Please come in."

He stepped into the cabin and closed the door behind him. Jenna gestured to an upholstered couch in a corner of the cabin.

"Please," she said, "have a seat. I'll get you a goblet of wine."

She went across to her desk, the movement making the full velvet gown flare out behind her, and Sebastian noticed her bare feet moving across the wooden boards. They were dainty little feet, hardly what you might have expected to find inside a sea captain's heavy boots.

Jenna poured out two goblets of red wine, carried them across to the couch and sat down beside Sebastian.

"Now," she said softly. "What can I do for you?"

"Er . . . sorry? I thought you wanted to talk to me."

"Yes. Yes, I do. Sorry." She took a large swallow of her wine. "I've been thinking," she said.

"Thinking?" he echoed.

"Yes, I've been thinking . . . about you. And about me. Well, about both of us, really."

"What about us?"

"Well . . ." Jenna paused to take another gulp of wine, as though she was trying to summon some courage. "I asked Lem to call you down here. I hope you weren't doing anything important?"

"Oh, I was just talking to Max. . . ."

"Ah. Max." Jenna's face fell, as though the very mention of the buffalope had cast a cloud over the proceedings. "Your beloved buffalope. And how was . . . Max?"

"If you must know, he was having a poo over the side of the ship." Jenna's eyes widened and Sebastian immediately wished he hadn't mentioned it. "But that's not important! What *is* important is that we talked about Leonora. . . ."

"Oh!" Jenna sat back in her seat as though he had punched her and took another large gulp of wine. "Leonora," she said. "The witch."

"No, you mustn't call her that. She's not a witch, she's just . . . misunderstood. And she is devilishly good-looking—you said so yourself. And her eyes . . ." He shook his head. It was all getting horribly mixed up. "Anyway, that's enough about her," he said. "I wonder, Jenna, do you think I could . . . ?"

"What?" asked Jenna softly.

"Do you think I could have some more wine?"

Jenna snatched his goblet from his hand and stalked across to the desk, where she replenished it for him. There was an uncomfortable silence.

"So did you and Max talk about me at all?" she asked him.

"Yes, yes we did. He was having a poo over the side and we started talking and he had this ridiculous notion about you."

"Did he now?"

"Yes. He thought that you . . . Well, don't laugh or anything, but he thought that you liked me."

Jenna came and sat beside him again and thrust the goblet of wine none too gently into his hand.

"Well, for once I have to agree with Max. It's true, I do like you."

"Yes, obviously you like me. But, you know, he was trying to say that you *really* liked me."

She glared at him. "I *do* really like you."

"Yes, of course, but he said that you really *really* liked me."

"Oh, for goodness' sake!" Jenna drained her goblet of wine, wiped her mouth on her sleeve and set it aside. Then she took his goblet and put it down beside hers. "Come here, Sebastian Darke," she said. She grabbed him by the lapels and, pulling him toward her, leaned forward to kiss him—

Right on cue, the door burst open and Cornelius came running into the room like a madman. "Land ho!" he roared. "Land ahead—we've found the—"

He stopped in his tracks and stared at Sebastian and Jenna in amazement. "What's going on?" he gasped.

Sebastian stared back at him. "I haven't the faintest idea," he said. "I think . . . I think Jenna was trying to explain something."

There was a pause. Then Jenna sighed, a long regretful sigh. Her shoulders slumped. "Go up on deck," she told Sebastian. "I'll be there in a moment."

"But—"

She reached out her fingers to his lips to still them.

"Later," she told him. "We'll have time to talk about this. For now, we need to see if this is the island we've been looking for."

Sebastian shot a baffled look at Cornelius. But he got up from the sofa and followed the little warrior out of the cabin.

"I thought you said you weren't that interested in Jenna," hissed Cornelius as soon as they were outside.

Sebastian looked at him blankly. "I'm not," he said. "But between you and me, I think she might have a bit of a soft spot for me."

Cornelius groaned and slapped his forehead. "Oh, the croat's finally dropped, has it?" he said.

"Yes, well, I think that's what was on her mind. But, you know, when it comes to stuff like that, I can't stop thinking about Leonora. I keep seeing her eyes looking at me. I pretty much told Jenna that."

"I bet that went down well. Sebastian, you have got to get some help," Cornelius told him.

"Help? What, you mean to find Leonora?"

"No, you idiot! To cast her out of your mind forever and start seeing what's really important. It's quite obvious that Jenna is mad about you. I've been telling you that for ages."

"Have you? It's funny, because Max said pretty much the same thing." Sebastian made a gesture of dismissal. "But I mean, who'd listen to Max anyway?"

"You usually don't have any problem doing that," Cornelius told him.

"Yes, but on affairs of the heart I think I know a bit more than he does. And you see, I just have this powerful feeling that Leonora and I are meant to be together. It's just our fate."

Cornelius groaned again. "Sebastian," he said, "it's tragic. You can't even think straight anymore."

"Oh, forget all that for now!" said Sebastian. "This is *far* more exciting. Let's go and have a look at this island of yours. And I hope for your sake it turns out to be the right one. There are going to be a lot of disappointed faces around here if it's not."

CHAPTER 26

MYSTERIOUS ISLAND

They made for the bow of the ship, where they found the Kid sitting on a crate, staring through the twilight mist at the approaching outline of a large island. Cornelius took a seat beside him and Sebastian went to lean on the ship's rail.

There was a long silence and then the Kid spoke.

"What's going on?" he asked.

"Well, let me see now, where should I start?" murmured Cornelius. He thought for a moment. "Sebastian's under an enchantment, which makes him hopelessly in love with the most evil woman I've ever met."

"You're a born exaggerator," Sebastian told him. "There must be much worse women in the world than Leonora."

Cornelius ignored him and continued. "And to make matters worse, he's having a romance."

"A romance?" The Kid looked astounded. "Who with?"

"Well, there's only one female on the ship, so take a wild guess."

"Not Captain Swift?"

Cornelius nodded. "Got it in one," he said. "I don't like these entanglements, Sebastian, they make everything so much more complicated."

Sebastian rested his elbows on the rail. "But we're not having a romance," he argued. "I think Jenna is interested in me, yes, but it's not as if I've done anything to encourage her."

"You're in love with the captain!" sang the Kid, in a mocking falsetto voice.

"Am not!" said Sebastian.

"Are too!"

"Am not!"

"Are—"

"Oh shut up!" said Cornelius.

They heard a creaking noise on the steps behind them and a big shaggy shape loomed out of the mist. They saw Max's mournful face staring at them. His nostrils were flared and he was snuffling the air, as though he could smell the approaching island.

"Did I hear someone shout 'Land ho?' " he muttered.

"Yes. But how on earth did you get up here?" Sebastian asked him. "The steps . . ."

"Very slippery," Max assured him. "It's a wonder I wasn't killed. I've a good mind to complain to Captain Swift." He studied Sebastian for a moment. "What did she want, by the way?"

"Never mind," said Sebastian.

"I was right, wasn't I?" said Max triumphantly. "She's after you."

"She's not after anyone!" protested Sebastian. "Look, could we please change the subject?"

"You *were* right, Max," said Cornelius. "I caught the two of them down in her cabin. Canoodling."

Max wrinkled his nostrils in a show of distaste. "I knew it," he said. "I could tell. It's a gift I have."

"Will you all please just mind your own business?" yelled Sebastian. He turned at the sound of boots climbing the steps behind him, and there was Jenna, back in her more familiar garb of waistcoat and boots, strolling toward him, her face deadly serious. The Kid started to snigger and Cornelius jabbed an elbow into his ribs, silencing him.

"So, gentlemen," said Jenna. "The moment of truth."

They all turned their attention back to the approaching island. In the gathering darkness they could see very little save for the outline of some rolling hills, heavily clad with jungle. A few dark shapes flapped silently above the treetops and were gone.

"Birds?" murmured Sebastian.

"Bats," Cornelius corrected him. "Filthy things. They come out at night and suck your blood."

Max glared at him. "Ever since the grundersnat, I can't tell if you're making stuff up or not," he complained.

"Oh, I'm deadly serious," Cornelius assured him. "I've seen those things descend on a troop of men and suck them dry as husks in the blink of an eye."

"You see," cried Max. "He does it on purpose! There I was, looking forward to being back on dry land, and you have to go and tell me something like that."

"You'll be all right, old shaggy," said Sebastian, reaching up and rubbing the buffalope's nose affectionately. "No bat is going to get its fangs through your thick hide."

Jenna moved in to rest on the rail beside Sebastian, but kept a discreet distance from him. "It's getting too dark to do anything right now," she said. "We'll go ashore at first light."

"So where exactly is the treasure hidden?" asked the Kid. Everyone turned to look at him.

"Who said anything about treasure?" said Cornelius. He glanced accusingly at Sebastian. "Did you tell him?" he growled.

"I didn't say a word," protested Sebastian.

The Kid laughed. "There's no need for anybody to say anything," he said. "You've come to some mysterious island in the middle of nowhere. Of course there's a treasure. And I suppose you have a map?"

Cornelius patted his breastplate, making a dull clanking sound. "Oh yes," he said. "There's a map. You wait and see. In a few hours' time we'll all be rich beyond our wildest dreams."

There was a long silence and then Max sighed. "I do wish people wouldn't say things like that," he said. "I mean to say . . . it's asking for trouble, it really is!"

PART THREE

CHAPTER 2 7

TREASURE HUNTERS

The following morning saw scenes of feverish activity aboard the *Sea Witch* as the crew made preparations to send the treasure-hunting party ashore. They had begun by making slow passes along the shore, looking for the right place to land. Cornelius had sat up in the prow, watching intently, and suddenly indicated a stretch of beach.

"There!" he announced. "That's where we go ashore!"

"How do you know this is the right place?" Jenna asked him, but he simply patted his breastplate and told her he'd explain later; so she ordered the anchor dropped and the longboat lowered.

It had already been decided that Jenna and the Kid would accompany Sebastian and Cornelius on the expedition, but naturally Max wanted to go along as well, and that was going to prove difficult. For one thing, the shallow waters that surrounded the island teemed with schools of kelfers; and for another, there was no longboat in the world that would carry Max without tipping over.

"You'll just have to wait here for us," Sebastian told him.

"I'm not staying here a moment longer," protested Max. "I've been skulking around this old hulk for days. I want to feel the good earth beneath my hooves—something that doesn't sway up and down when you stand on it."

"Well, what do you intend to do, *swim*?"

In the end Max insisted that he would do just that, staying alongside the boat as it was rowed to shore. There was no dissuading him, so the crew dutifully rigged up some pulleys and a system of ropes, which they passed under Max's belly. Once the boat was sitting in the water and the expedition party was safely aboard, Max was lifted from the deck and lowered gently alongside it. Then the ropes were released and Max was left bobbing like a hairy island in the crystal clear water. Sebastian looked anxiously down at his old friend, painfully aware that a series of triangular fins were already cutting through the water only a short distance away. He and Cornelius had armed themselves with long paddles, with which they intended to dissuade any kelfers that came too close, while Jenna had brought her bow and arrows.

"Whatever you do, don't stop for anything," Sebastian told the buffalope.

"Don't worry, young master," said Max through gritted teeth. "I'm not quite ready to be fish food just yet." And with that, he kicked off and started heading toward the island. Lemuel and Cassius, who had come to ferry the party ashore, dipped their oars into the water and began to row, while the others sat in their seats, ready for action if it should be required.

It wasn't long before the first inquisitive kelfer came nosing through the surf. Sebastian could see its shiny striped flanks and the great jagged opening of its jaws. As it swerved toward Max, Sebastian thrust his oar into the creature's snout and it veered away, startled. Sebastian glanced at Jenna and saw that she was staring into the water with an expression of intense loathing on her face. She slid an arrow from her quiver and nocked it, ready to fire.

When a second kelfer came speeding toward the swimming buffalope, she let go a feathered shaft right into its snout, and a few moments later the stricken beast was writhing in the midst of a whole school of its former comrades who, lured by the fresh blood, were intent on tearing it to pieces. As they watched the frenzy in the water, a much bigger fin cruised by, and they saw what must have been the biggest kelfer ever, a huge white creature that was twice the length of the rowing boat. It rose momentarily to the surface, its soulless black eyes staring ahead, and Sebastian noticed a long-healed, straight scar running across its side.

"That fellow looks like he's been in the wars," he said grimly.

"I hope he stays well away from us," muttered Lemuel. "He'd turn us over with one flip of his tail." Happily the giant creature didn't come any closer, but sped on by at an astonishing rate.

The fighting kelfers caused just the diversion they needed. A few minutes later Max's pumping legs touched the sea bed and then the boat was nosing into the shallows beside him. The treasure-seekers hopped out into the water and hurried up onto the beach, where they found Max dancing about on the sand like a skittish calf, relishing the feel of real sand beneath his hooves.

"Land!" he cried. "Real land. What joy!" He shook himself vigorously, spattering his companions with salt water as they approached.

"You made it, Max!" observed the Kid brightly.

"Yes," agreed Cornelius. "Let's hope he does as well on the way back." He handed the Kid a knapsack.

"What's this for?" asked the Kid.

"For the treasure of course," said Cornelius. "If we find it, we'll need some way of carrying it back." He handed two more packs to Sebastian and Jenna and strapped one on himself.

Sebastian turned to Max. "Are you all right?" he asked.

Max tossed his horned head contemptuously. "It'll take more than a few oversized sprats to stop me!" he boasted. "I was just hoping one of them would come within range of my horns."

"Did you see the big fellow, though?" said Sebastian. "I wouldn't like to get too close to him."

"He didn't scare me," said Max.

Jenna instructed Lemuel and Cassius to take the longboat back to the *Sea Witch*. "I don't want to risk leaving it on the beach," she told them. "We don't even know if this island is inhabited. But keep an eye open for our return, just in case we need to come back in a hurry."

"Aye, aye, Captain," said Lem. "Good hunting!" He and Cassius started rowing back to the ship.

Sebastian, meanwhile, was studying the thick ranks of jungle foliage ahead of them. There was one spot where a narrow track led into the greenery, and this was flanked by two tall pillars of gray stone. Cornelius must have spotted them from the ship.

"Enter through the narrow way, past two tall sisters dressed in gray," said Cornelius quietly. He reached

beneath his breastplate and pulled out the ancient chart. "It's written right here in somebody's blood."

"Sisters, eh?" Jenna studied the stone columns doubtfully. "They look more like brothers to me."

"I think you'll find I'm right," Cornelius told her. "Come on."

He led the way forward and the others trailed after him more cautiously. Only a few yards past the columns, the track narrowed and the jungle pressed in closer around them. There was only room for them to walk in single file. Jenna followed Cornelius, with Sebastian and Max bringing up the rear. In the gathering heat they all began to sweat profusely. Sebastian wondered how hard the going would get if and when their packs were full of treasure.

"Are you sure this is right?" grumbled Max, who had already acquired a tangle of leaves and thorns draped around his horns. "I'd hate to think we were wasting time wandering down the wrong path."

"Wrong or not, somebody else has used it recently," said Cornelius. He pointed to a piece of muddy ground at his feet and everybody crowded around to look. They could see, quite clearly, the imprint of a man's bare foot.

"Who could it be?" asked Sebastian. "Some primitive tribe perhaps?"

Cornelius shrugged. "Who can say? We'd better

keep our wits about us. We don't want anybody leaping out at us on this secluded track. They could cut us to pieces before we have time to move a muscle."

"You really are a ray of sunshine," grumbled Max.

Cornelius glanced back over his shoulder and gave him a tight little smile. "I try to make an effort," he said.

They continued on their way, and after trudging along for quite some time they came to a place where the undergrowth thinned dramatically and found themselves in a small clearing. Ahead of them they could see what could only be a manmade structure, a little hut built out of branches overlaid with what looked like palm leaves and grasses. A short distance from the hut was a campfire, still burning; and scattered around it were a few odd bits and pieces, all made from natural materials. There were a couple of hollowed-out fruits that were obviously used as bowls, some crudely carved wooden implements that might have been for eating, and a log had been covered with the hide of a wild animal for use as a seat.

The party approached the hut cautiously, pulling out their swords and holding them ready for action. But there was nobody at home.

"Can't be much of a tribe," muttered Max. "They've only got one hut; and that looks like it's about to fall down."

"I don't think we're dealing with savages," said Cornelius. He stooped and picked up the crudely carved implements from beside the fire. "Whoever heard of a savage making himself a knife and fork to eat his dinner?"

"Perhaps he has ideas above his station," suggested Max.

"You'd know all about that," said Cornelius.

"It's not a savage," said Jenna. She had found something else beside the fire, and she opened her hand to show it to them. It was dented and battered but there was no disguising the fact that it was an old silver pocket watch. "If he managed to make this out of coconuts, then he's not your usual run-of-the-mill wild man."

"Here, let me look at that!" said the Kid, and took the watch from her.

"Wherever he is, he can't be far away," said Sebastian. "The fire's still burning and—"

He broke off as a figure emerged from the trees on the far side of the clearing, a tall, skinny man dressed in ill-fitting clothes made from animal hides. He had a thick growth of red beard and was wearing a strange wide-brimmed hat that appeared to have been made from the leaves of a palm tree. Sebastian noticed that he had a long spear slung across his shoulders and a bundle of firewood under one arm. He was strolling back toward the hut, seemingly without a care in the world, but then he suddenly noticed the group of people standing around the fire and reacted as though he had seen a bunch of ghosts.

He shrieked, dropped the firewood and went into a defensive apelike crouch. He pulled the spear from across his shoulders and, holding it protectively in front of him, started backing off, moving toward the trees from where he had emerged.

"Wait!" shouted Sebastian. "We mean you no harm!"

The man stopped in his tracks and tilted his head to one side, a curious mannerism that put Sebastian in mind of some wild animal. The man grunted in apparent amazement. He stood there for what seemed ages, staring at them as though he simply couldn't believe his eyes.

"Are you all right?" asked Cornelius. The stranger flinched as though he'd been struck. Then, quite suddenly, he whooped at the top of his lungs and came running toward them, tossing the spear aside as he did so.

"You . . . you is civilized men!" he cried. "You is sailors! Hoop dee hoy! I don' believe it! I must be 'sleep and dreamin'!" He stopped a short distance away and began to circle them, his eyes wide and staring, as though he was trying to burn every little bit of them into his memory. Then he began to pinch himself, and when that didn't settle the matter, he

gave himself a series of hard slaps in the face, almost knocking himself off his own feet. "No, reckon I'm 'wake all right," he giggled.

Up close, Sebastian could see his mad blue eyes and his dark skin, baked and lined by exposure to the sun. He was grinning like a maniac and was so painfully thin that his teeth seemed rather too big for his mouth.

"It's no dream, sir," Jenna assured him. "We have come here in the *Sea Witch*, a merchant ship. I am the captain and—"

The man stopped still for a moment and pointed a finger at her. "Captain?" he said. "Captain? I knows that word! And I knows that accent. You . . . you is from Ramalat!"

Jenna smiled, puzzled. "Well, yes, but how—?"

"Hoop dee doo! I don' believe it! My dreams have been answered, you've come at last!" He fell onto his back and started kicking his skinny legs in the air like a lunatic. Sebastian and Cornelius exchanged worried glances.

"You . . . are from Ramalat too?" ventured Jenna.

"No, from Lemora! But I know Ramalat well enough—sure, haven't I sunk many a merchant ship out of that port?" The man sat up, cross-legged, still grinning. "Aye, a Lemoran born and bred. But I been here on this stinking island for . . . for . . . I dunno how long. See, I was a captain too. My ship was—"

For the first time his gaze fell on the Kid, who was still staring at the watch he was holding. The thin man seemed to freeze again. His jaw fell open and he stared at the boy for a very long time. Then a big fat teardrop slipped from the corner of his eye and rolled down his thin face.

"Beverly?" he whispered. "Is it really you? Or have I gone mad?"

There was a long, deep silence. Sebastian looked at the Kid and saw that the answer was only just beginning to dawn on him.

"M-my dad had a watch like this," the boy whispered. "It had the same picture on the front of it. I used to play with it when I was little."

"Beverly?" The man spoke again, his voice firmer now. "Don'tcha know me?" he said. "Don'tcha recognize me?"

The Kid stared at him for a long time. Then: "D-Dad?" he said.

And the man was nodding, grinning, holding out his arms to the boy. "Aye, 'tis me, Beverly, though I don't doubt you stare at me so. Reckon I'm a changed man since you last saw me! And you! How you've grown! I wouldn't hardly have recognized you!"

"*Dad!*" yelled the Kid, and he ran forward and threw himself into his father's arms, while the others looked on in delight.

CHAPTER 28

BACK FROM THE DEAD

"Will somebody please tell me what's going on here!" cried Max. "Why is the boy calling that weird-looking fellow *Dad*?"

Jenna gave him a weary look. "Take a wild guess," she said.

Max continued to look at her blankly. "Is it some kind of father figure the boy's looking for?" he asked.

"That *is* his father, you idiot! Captain Jack Donovan. He went missing during a sea battle . . . must be over two summers ago."

"Is that how long it is?" gasped the wild man. "Two summers? You can't tell in this accursed place—the weather's always the same. Seems a lifetime. I tried scratching a record on a tree, one notch fer every day in this miserable hole. But one night a big storm came and blew that tree clear into the ocean, and after that

I . . ." His eyes were full of tears and he was hugging the Kid as though his life depended on it.

"Everyone thought you were dead," said Jenna.

"That ain't no surprise," said Donovan. "I very nearly was. It was those two bilge rats, Bones and Sully, who did for me. Flung me over the side in the middle of a fight, they did, and left me to drown. But I spotted this island on the horizon. Just a dot it was, but I swam for it. Nearly didn't make it." He gave that strange, deranged giggle and pulled aside his crudely made jacket to display a fearsome long-healed scar across his ribs. "A kelfer did that to me. It would have finished me too if I hadn't stuck my knife into it." He jabbed wildly at an imaginary beast with an equally imaginary knife. "Great big beast, it was, the biggest kelfer you ever saw!"

Sebastian and Cornelius exchanged looks.

"He's still out there, you know!" continued Donovan. "You'll recognize him by the scar I put across his side. Cruises by the beach every day, hoping that I'll venture out. That's how come I ain't as well fed as I might be. Any time I try and wade out into deeper water, it comes a-lookin' fer me. Holds a grudge, see. Twice now it's nearly had me in its jaws. Twice!"

"I think we saw your kelfer," said Cornelius. "When we were coming in to shore, a huge white fellow—"

"Aye, that's the lad! Kelfers are not just pure evil,

they're cunning with it—they've got it all goin' on up here." Donovan tapped his sun-blasted head with a shriveled forefinger and Sebastian felt a shiver go through him. Clearly the long years of loneliness had taken their toll on Jack Donovan.

"So you made it to shore and . . ."

"I very near died from loss of blood, but 'twas hunger for revenge kept me alive. And the thought of seeing my boy again." He pulled away from his son, placed his hands on the Kid's shoulders and gave him a fierce look. "Bones and Sully," he said. "Tell me those two aren't still aboard my ship."

The Kid looked very uncomfortable. "It's a pity they're not," he said, "for the *Black Hand* is at the bottom of the ocean, Father, sunk in a battle only a few days ago." He hung his head in shame. "I'm sorry," he said.

But Donovan shook his head and stroked the boy's hair. "Tell me, son, did she go down fightin'?"

The Kid nodded and wiped his eyes on his sleeve.

"Then that's all that matters. And who sank the ship?"

There was a brief uncomfortable silence. Then Jenna took a step forward.

"That would be me, Captain Donovan," she said. "I took your ship on in a fair fight and sent her to the bottom of the sea." She reached out a hand and put it on the Kid's shoulder. "Your son put on a brave show, but in the end he was overcome. We took him aboard rather than leave him to his fate. If we could have saved your ship, we would have, but she was too badly damaged in the battle."

Donovan stared at her for a moment with those mad blue eyes, as though deliberating what his response should be. Then he nodded. "There's no shame in losing a fair fight," he said. "And no blame to be apportioned. You have rescued me, and for that I will be forever grateful." He looked at his son. "Bones and Sully?" he asked.

"They're still around. We had a run-in with them in Lemora. Gave them a right good kicking, we did."

Donovan's eyes widened. "But . . . you didn't kill either of 'em?"

The Kid shook his head.

"Good! That's for me to do. It's all I've lived for these last two years."

"There's more, Father," said the Kid. "There was somebody who paid Bones and Sully to do their dirty work. A captain out of Ramalat called Trencherman. He wanted the *Black Hand* for himself and he didn't care how he went about getting her."

Donovan looked grim. "Then he too is my mortal enemy," he said. "And I'll settle with him when I meet him face to face." He released the boy and sat back. His mood changed abruptly: now he was grin-ning happily and rocking backward and forward where he sat. "Hoop dee doo!" he cackled. "This is a good day. One I thought I'd never live to see!" He looked around at the others. "So what brings you good people to this island?" he asked.

"They've come seeking treasure, Father!" said the Kid excitedly. "They have a map and everything."

Captain Donovan gazed at them and then gave a lopsided grin. "Treasure?" he said. "You mean to tell me that I've been sitting on a fortune all these years and never even knew it?"

"If my chart is correct, yes," said Cornelius. "It is our belief that the fabled treasure of Captain Callinestra is hidden somewhere on this island."

Donovan stared at Cornelius for a moment and then burst into a laugh that was only just on the right side of sanity. The sound of it made Sebastian shiver.

"Captain Callinestra? Hoop dee doo! Not one of those fake treasure maps they've been selling for years in every port in the land, is it? You wouldn't fall for a story like that, would you, sir? Why, if I had a croat for every time I'd been offered one of those things, I'd be a wealthy man today!"

Cornelius looked uncomfortable. "I have no reason to doubt the map's authenticity," he said.

Donovan managed to calm himself a little. "Well, how did you come by it?" he asked.

"It was given to me—" began Cornelius.

"*Sold* to you," Sebastian corrected him.

"Er . . . quite so. Sold to me by an old dying sailor in a military hospital."

"Sold to you?" cried Jenna. "You never mentioned that before!"

"I always said it sounded funny," muttered Sebastian. "A dying man selling a map—what's that all about?"

Cornelius made a small gesture of irritation. "It's been right so far, hasn't it?" he snapped. *"The two sisters dressed in gray . . ."* He frowned and shook his head. "Anyway, we've come this far; we may as well follow it to the end and see. If the map turns out to be wrong, then you may ridicule me as much as you like." He smiled at Captain Donovan. "Of course, Captain, since you are already here, you are most welcome to join us in our quest; and should we be successful, and provided my partners agree, I am prepared to offer you a share of whatever we find."

Captain Donovan looked at him for a moment and then slipped an arm around his son's shoulder. "I've just found my treasure," he said. "And to be honest, I wouldn't be much use to you. I'm weak from not eatin' proper. So if it's all the same to you, Beverly and I will sit this one out."

The Kid looked at his father in dismay. "Oh, but Dad—" he began.

"No arguments, son. We've got some catchin' up to do." He looked at Jenna hopefully. "I hope you do not think me rude," he said, "and I 'preciate I'm a former pirate who was a sworn enemy of ships like yours, but I would relish the opportunity to rest aboard your ship. And if your cook would have a bit of grub to spare . . . I've kept myself alive on whatever bits of fish and meat I could hunt for myself, but I've never had what you might call an abundance of food."

Jenna looked doubtful at first; she was obviously wondering about the members of Donovan's old crew, still caged belowdecks; but then she studied the skinny, almost cadaverous figure in front of her and realized that he was barely capable of lifting a sword, let alone using one. She seemed to relax a little.

"Kid, help your father down to the beach and hail the longboat. Tell Lemuel that Captain Donovan is my guest and that they are to give him whatever he wants to eat and drink. And tell Lem to break open the best rum."

"Aye, aye, Captain," said the Kid. He reached out a hand and helped his father to his feet.

Suddenly Donovan seemed to remember something. "If your route takes you inland, I should warn you . . . ," he said. "There are creatures in there. Yarkles . . ."

Cornelius raised his eyebrows. "Yarkles?" he said. "What manner of beast are they?"

"Something from the lowest reaches of hell. I

named them that for the noise they make when they call to each other. Some kind of upright lizard, I'd say, but bigger than three men standing on each other's shoulders. It's one reason why I haven't explored inland much. Any time I've tried it, they've come a-calling and I've had to run for my life." He giggled as though the notion struck him as funny. "Teeth like razors, they have," he said. "And they seem to hunt in pairs. Luckily they don't venture into the deep jungle. They prefer to stay in the long grass around that peak." He pointed through the treetops to the crest of a hill in the middle distance.

Cornelius consulted his chart and frowned. Then he glanced at Sebastian. "It would seem Nathaniel's story wasn't so far-fetched after all," he said. "He mentioned walking toward a high peak when he was attacked. And that's exactly where we're headed."

"Oh, goody," muttered Max. "It had to be."

"Don't you complain," Sebastian warned him. "You could have stayed safe aboard the *Sea Witch*, but no, you insisted on coming with us."

"A good thing by the sound of it," retorted Max. "What would your mother think if I let you face these sparkles without my help?"

"Yarkles," Donovan corrected him.

"We'd better get moving," Jenna told them. "Time's passing, and if we're going to encounter these beasts, I'd rather we did it in daylight."

"Good point," said Cornelius. He nodded at the two who had elected to stay behind. "Captain Donovan, Bever—Kid, hopefully we'll see you later."

"Good luck," said the Kid. "Watch your backs."

"Yes," said Donovan, grinning like a maniac. "Look to the long grass and keep listenin' out for steps behind you. I'll say a prayer for your safe return."

The Kid looked at his father in surprise. "A prayer?" he cried.

"Oh yes. Many things have changed since I last saw you, boy. I pray a lot these days. How do you think you found your way back to me?"

He draped an arm around his son's shoulders and the two of them turned away and started along the track that led back to the beach.

"Amazing," said Sebastian. "To come all this way and find a lost soul. Even if we don't discover the treasure, the trip's already been worthwhile."

Cornelius looked somewhat unconvinced by this. "But rather *more* worthwhile if we end up getting our hands on a fortune in gold and precious jewels," he said.

"I wouldn't get your hopes up too high," Max warned him. "You heard what Donovan said about that so-called treasure map. Not to mention those vicious beasts that hide in the long—"

He broke off at the sound of a distant shriek that made everybody lift their heads to listen. Two bloodcurdling notes echoed on the air, and Sebastian understood exactly why Captain Donovan had named the creatures yarkles: that was exactly the sound they made.

Max swallowed noisily. "I don't suppose there's any point in suggesting that we turn round and head back to the ship?" he ventured.

"None whatsoever," said Cornelius, starting forward toward the edge of the clearing.

"No chance," added Jenna, striding after him.

Sebastian didn't say anything. He smiled ruefully at the buffalope, shrugged his shoulders and followed the others.

"Yes, well, I just thought I'd ask," said Max dolefully. "I might have known I was wasting my breath." He lowered his head and began to plod dutifully after his friends.

CHAPTER 29

YARKLES

Beyond the clearing, the jungle reared up again and the narrow track twisted and turned through dense ranks of vegetation. The heat intensified, making them sweat profusely, and the air buzzed with a multitude of insects, intent on feasting on the blood of these unexpected visitors. Off in the mysterious green depths, unidentified creatures yelped, howled and croaked, the constant sound fraying their nerves.

But they did not hear the yarkles again for quite some time.

They walked for what seemed like hours with no real change of scenery, the undergrowth crowding in oppressively on either side. Then, just as they were beginning to think that the trail would lead on forever, they came to a place where a steep rocky slope rose up and left the jungle behind. They struggled up the incline to the top of a ridge and found themselves looking down into a valley that was completely cloaked in a covering of long yellow grass, which swayed rhythmically in the wind. On the far side of the wide meadow, the foothills of the mountains rose steeply.

Cornelius consulted his map and read aloud:

"Now you leave the narrow pass
And move across a sea of grass,
And if the treasure you would seek,
Walk toward the highest peak."

"Hmmph!" said Max. "Not what you'd call great poetry, is it?"

"Never mind the poetry," said Cornelius. "We're not here for an education." He glanced at the others. "Remember what Donovan said. Those lizard things may be out there. If anything comes at us in that grass, our best chance is to stick together." He gazed toward the mountain and pointed with his sword toward what was quite clearly the highest peak. "Let's go," he said. And they moved down the slope into the long grass.

It was incredibly disorientating. The grass grew higher than Sebastian's head, and it was only because the crest of the mountain remained in sight that they knew they were heading in the right direction. They fanned out to walk abreast rather than going in single file and kept their ears alert for any sounds approaching them. It soon became apparent that big creatures had recently passed through these grasslands, because there were ragged trails where the grasses had been crushed flat by the passage of something heavy. Nobody spoke, not even Max, because they knew instinctively that any noise might attract the creatures that guarded this place.

Then they came to a terrifying sight: a great pile of dung was heaped in the middle of one of the trails. They all looked at it in dismay. It was as big as a boulder and covered by a great mantle of buzzing flies.

Of course, it was Max who voiced what everybody was thinking.

"If that's the size of its poo, how big is the beast?" he muttered apprehensively.

Nobody answered him. They edged round the dung pile and continued on their way in silence.

They must have been halfway across the valley when Sebastian heard it: a dry rustling sound away to his left, as though something was pushing through the grass toward them—something big, judging by the noise it was making. Sebastian reached down and tapped Cornelius's shoulder, then pointed in the direction the noise was coming from. The little warrior paused to listen and nodded grimly. He could hear it too.

They quickened their pace, but doing so meant that

they made more noise and, sure enough, the rustling sound seemed to be homing in on them. And then, to make matters worse, Sebastian heard more sounds coming from the right, and he remembered what Donovan had said earlier:

Yarkles hunt in pairs.

The noises to either side intensified, and now Sebastian could make out thudding sounds, as though heavy feet were propelling massive bodies forward through the grass. He didn't really want to look back over his shoulder but somehow he just had to. And he was doing exactly that when, quite suddenly, the nearest of the beasts came into view, and he felt a thrill of terror go through him, because he was looking at something from his wildest nightmares.

It was a huge gray-green lizard, three times the height of a man, that ran upright on two incredibly powerful back legs. Its forelegs were tiny, sticklike things that looked barely capable of holding anything, but it had a massive loaf-shaped head that seemed to hinge through the middle into a set of jaws that were fringed with what looked like hundreds of razor-sharp teeth.

The beast was looking down at the creatures running before it, its tiny eyes glittering with predatory malevolence. As it moved closer, it opened its mouth and let out an ear-shattering roar, bathing the runners with the stench of raw meat. It towered over them, its head moving from side to side, as though uncertain who to attack first.

Then its companion closed in from the other side, equally big, equally fearsome. The beasts were trying to trap their prey in a pincer movement.

The first yarkle seemed to reach a decision. It shifted position slightly and lunged downward with its great jaws. Sebastian felt the heat of the beast's breath enveloping him and instinctively threw himself to one side, just as a scaly snout slammed against him, the great teeth locking with a click inches from his ribs. As he fell, he lashed out with the sword and felt the blade glance off the scaly flesh of the beast's nose; heard a corresponding bellow of mingled pain and surprise.

Then Sebastian hit the ground, rolled forward and came up onto his feet again. As he did so, Cornelius and Jenna turned back and took up defensive positions on either side of him. Max wheeled round too, his horns ready to charge.

The yarkles came at them, shrieking in indignation. Clearly they were not used to having their prey fight back. The first of them lunged down with its snout and was met by three swords, which slashed at its nose and jaw. It reeled back with a frustrated bellow and swung round. Something came cutting through the long grass like a great fat scythe, and Sebastian just had time to register that it was the beast's tail before he was knocked backward off his feet. He lay stunned, realizing that Jenna was lying beside him, and he saw the creature's great clawed feet come crashing down on either side of him. He started to struggle upright—

And then he saw Cornelius go racing in beneath the creature's splayed legs, and as Sebastian watched in amazement, the little warrior took a flying leap toward the back of one of those legs and his sword hissed round in a deadly arc, cutting through the yarkle's hamstring. The roar that issued from the beast was almost deafening and it tipped backward, its tiny front legs clawing at the air as it fell.

But there was no time to watch what happened next because the second yarkle was closing on Sebastian and Jenna, roaring vengefully. Calmly Jenna selected an arrow from her quiver and took careful aim. She fired, and the arrow bounced off the yarkle's skull. She gave a tut of irritation, then reached for another arrow.

"You can do it," Sebastian told her.

She didn't answer but drew back the bow and aimed a second time. The arrow flew low and pierced the bottom part of the creature's jaw, causing it evident pain but not doing much to slow it down.

"Rats!" said Jenna.

"It's getting close," Sebastian warned her. He cringed as a huge roar came from behind him and, turning his head, he saw that Cornelius had just plunged his sword into the first yarkle's throat, finishing it off. He turned back to look at Jenna, who was calmly nocking another arrow to her string. "It's getting *very* close," he added nervously.

Again she didn't reply but drew back the bow a third time and stood there, waiting calmly as the yarkle approached, closer, closer, its huge jaws opening to claim her.

Cornelius appeared from behind them, his baby face splattered with blood. "Let it go now," he whispered. "That's close enough."

But still Jenna waited, and now that awful hot rawmeat stench was engulfing them and they all had a grandstand view of the creature's open jaws and into the fleshy caverns beyond.

"Let it go!" yelled Sebastian.

And then, with a loud crack, the bow snapped in two, leaving Jenna standing there, looking in dismay at the useless length of broken wood she held in her left hand.

There was a moment when it seemed that they were as good as dead. Sebastian recovered first. He threw his arms around Jenna and pulled her back out of harm's way just as the yarkle's teeth came lunging down at her, snapping shut a hair's breadth in front of her face; but in that same instant the creature shook as though from an impact. It leaned back and looked down, and there was Max, slamming his horns repeatedly against the beast's haunches, the sharp tips sinking into the scaly thighs and drawing blood. The yarkle swung round to strike at its tormentor, but before its open jaws could close around the buffalope's shaggy neck, three swords had moved in to defend him, and the beast met with a flurry of blows that struck against its head, neck and nose.

It snorted in anger and launched a kick at its tormentors, the great claws of its hind feet as sharp as daggers. Jenna and Cornelius were swept aside like a pair of rag dolls, but the claws just missed Sebastian and he saw his way free to slip inside the outstretched leg. He raced in and, using both hands, plunged his sword up into the softer, vulnerable belly of the beast.

The scream that issued from the yarkle was terrifying. Sebastian left the sword where it was, buried to the hilt, and started to run. The crippled yarkle was staring stupidly down at its punctured belly. It made a few pathetic attempts to reach down with its tiny forelegs and then, acknowledging the futility of that, set off in pursuit of Sebastian, intent on revenge. But it had only taken a few halting steps before its huge back legs stumbled and lost their footing, and the creature pitched abruptly forward. Sebastian felt the creature's shadow looming over him and he instinctively veered to one side.

The yarkle fell in a curious kind of slow motion and slammed into the ground, the impact so great that its head and chest half buried themselves in the soft earth. Sebastian turned back to look at the fallen creature, holding himself ready to run again if he needed to. But though the yarkle's chest rose and fell a few more times, it was clear that it was finished. The fall had driven the sword deep into its bowels. The back legs gave a single convulsive shudder, scraping two deep furrows in the soil, and then it lay still.

As Sebastian stood there, gasping for breath, the others came running up.

"Are you all right?" Jenna asked him, and he nodded.

He gestured to the yarkle's body, lying embedded in the churned-up earth. "Not much chance of getting my sword back from under there," he said bleakly.

"Let's hope we have no need of it," said Cornelius. "Donovan mentioned two of the beasts, but we can't be sure there aren't more." He surveyed the dead yarkle for a moment, then thumped Sebastian's hip with a clenched fist. "That was a brave move," he said. "Slipping inside his guard like that."

"I saw my chance and took it," said Sebastian quietly.

"Yes, but you only got the chance because I distracted the beast," said Max tetchily. "I hope you all noticed that I gave him the old one, two!" He tossed his head, proudly displaying his horns, the points of which were caked in gore.

Cornelius smiled. "We all did well," he said, "because we worked as a team."

"Yes, but I think I did especially well," persisted Max.

"I suggest we move on," said Jenna coolly. "While we're all standing here congratulating ourselves, time is passing. And we don't know what other dangers may lie ahead of us." She began to walk, heading toward the mountain.

Max pulled a disapproving face at her back and glanced at Sebastian. "Excuse me, I'm sure," he said.

Sebastian and Cornelius followed Jenna through the long grass, but Max hesitated a few moments before stepping up to the yarkle and giving it a swift poke with one of his horns. "Take that, you big scaly bully," he snorted.

A last convulsive hiss of air emerged from the beast's open mouth, sounding almost like a growl. Max retreated quickly.

"Wait for me!" he yelled, and hurried after the others.

CHAPTER 30

ONWARD AND UPWARD

On the far side of the sea of grass, the land rose in green moss-covered slopes. At first the incline was gradual, but it quickly grew steeper and rockier, and soon it became quite a struggle to climb. It was hard enough for the two-legged members of the expedition, who could at least use their arms to haul themselves up; but it was even worse for Max. His hooves kept failing to find a purchase on the slippery rocks, and time and again he slipped back down the incline, dislodging little avalanches of shale, his heavy body threatening to keep going until he was back at the foot of the slope. Eventually there was nothing else for it but to leave him behind. Of course, he wasn't very happy about it.

"I've come this far," he protested. "I don't want to miss out on the final stretch."

"We all appreciate that," said Sebastian. "But what

are we to do? We can hardly get up these slopes ourselves and we can't carry you." He pointed up to the
rocky heights. "If you slipped from up there, there'd
be no hope for you."

"Yes, but if I stay here, I'll be unprotected." Max
looked scornfully at Cornelius. "So much for all that
twaddle about working as a team."

Cornelius frowned. "Max, we couldn't have got
this far without your help," he said. "But you surely
can't expect us to give up the quest simply because
you can't go any further?"

"Well . . . no . . . ," began Max.

Cornelius looked around for a few moments and
then pointed to a narrow gully in the rocks. "I suggest you back yourself in there," he said. "Then if
anything should come at you, you'll be facing it. You
know," he added slyly, "there's no creature living
that could match you in combat."

"I *am* a force to be reckoned with," admitted Max.

"It's settled then," said Cornelius, turning away.
"We'll be back for you as soon as we can. And don't
worry, you've earned your share of the treasure.
You'll still get your cut."

"Provided there *is* a treasure," muttered Max. "And
there'd better be after all that blooming exertion."

Cornelius ignored the remark. He began to climb
and Jenna followed him. Sebastian hesitated for a
minute. He realized that there was nothing he could

do, but nevertheless he felt guilty about leaving his old friend behind.

"I'm sorry, Max," he said. "You know that if there was any other way—"

"Yes, yes," said Max brusquely. "You go on. Don't mind me. Though of course, if anything should happen to me while you're up there—"

"I'm sure nothing will," said Sebastian, a little too quickly.

"—don't make any special efforts on my behalf. Just leave me where I'm lying and carry on with your life. I don't expect anybody to waste any effort mourning me. I mean, one would like to be remembered, of course . . . talked about when tales of heroism and adventure are being recounted . . . perhaps a special mention could be made of my valiant struggle with the yarkles . . . but as you know, I've never been one for blowing my own trumpet. In the end, it's just . . ."

Sebastian turned away and began to climb, aware as he did so that Max was still talking, his voice droning on and on as it gradually receded into the distance. Sebastian made a considerable effort and managed to catch up with his two companions.

Jenna gave him a knowing look. "Well, well," she said. "Out in the world, without your constant companion. How *will* you manage?"

"Frankly, I'm sorry to see the back of him," said

Cornelius. "Max can be irritating, but he's got plenty of muscle." He peered up toward the misty mountain peak. "We may need some of that before we're through."

Nobody had an answer to that, so they continued to climb in silence.

They climbed for what seemed like hours, the way ahead growing ever steeper. Sebastian, who had no great head for heights, found that he had to concentrate all his attention on finding hand- and footholds in the smooth gray rock. Several times his boots slipped and he found himself hanging on by his fingers, horribly aware of the great void behind him; and when on one occasion he had the misfortune to glance back over his shoulder, it was to see the great stretch of grassland far below him and the two crumpled bodies of the yarkles looking like a child's discarded toys.

All in all, it was quite a relief when they finally reached a plateau, a great stone ledge in the side of the mountain, sparsely dotted with tall coniferous trees. The three friends slumped down on the ground, glad of the opportunity to get their breath back as they examined what lay ahead of them. A narrow sheer-sided ravine cut through solid rock, as though it had been hammered out of the stone by a giant chisel.

Cornelius reached beneath his breastplate and pulled out the map. He unfolded it carefully and read the next instruction aloud.

"If our secrets you would know,
Into the chasm you must go
Until you find the special place
Where footsteps venture into space."

"Into space?" repeated Sebastian. "What do you suppose that means?"

"Only one way to find out," said Jenna, getting back to her feet. She held out a hand to help Sebastian up. He took it gladly, because the long climb had exhausted him.

"Think we're getting close?" he asked the others hopefully.

Cornelius looked at the map and nodded. "Shouldn't be much further," he said, standing up. "Come on."

The three of them headed into the ravine and it was as if the sun had suddenly been extinguished. The ground was littered with a deep covering of loose shale, which made progress difficult, and the sound of it clattering underfoot seemed to echo eerily in the enclosed space. The three adventurers found themselves looking up at the overhanging crags above, nervous of anything that might appear at the tops of the slopes, ready to attack them. But they saw no signs of life, save for a few ragged black shapes flapping overhead. Not birds, but the huge leathery-winged bats they had seen from the ship.

As they walked, they noticed that the ravine was growing narrower and narrower, as though the walls were gradually crushing them. Sebastian's keen ears caught a sound up ahead, a prolonged crashing, which after a while he recognized as the noise of falling water. As the cleft closed in, so the sound rose to a thunderous roar, and finally the ravine ended in a narrow opening in the high walls of rock, only just wide enough to admit one person at a time. Cornelius went first and Sebastian heard him say, "Shadlog's beard!" Jenna was next and her reaction was a sharp intake of breath. Then it was Sebastian's turn.

He stepped through the gap, not knowing what to expect, and found himself suddenly bathed in brilliant sunlight. He stood there blinking, his mouth open, staring in wonder at the unexpected landscape that surrounded him.

They had emerged into a great natural basin in the heart of the mountain and were standing on a narrow stone ledge, which ran for a short distance ahead of them and then ended abruptly in a wide crevasse. This ran left and right across the expanse of smooth gray rock like a jagged scar, each end dropping away into a deep void. At one time the rock must have been all one piece, but somewhere back in ancient history a mighty movement in the earth had caused the rock to split across the middle, creating the gap.

It was far too wide to jump across but Sebastian saw that it had been bridged by the trunk of a tall but slender tree, which had been carefully positioned with its ends resting on either side of the crevasse. On the far side there was another narrow ledge, and then the mountain rose up sheer again to a dizzying height. Cascading down its face, a short distance to the left of the tree trunk, was a mighty torrent of water, which came crashing onto the far ledge in a seething fury of foam and spray and then went gushing into the crevasse to lose itself in the seemingly bottomless drop below. In the tumult of spray that filled the air, the sunlight had created a magnificent rainbow, which arced high above the mountain peaks, making the scene even more incredible.

Sebastian turned to the others and saw that they were every bit as amazed as he was. "This place is—" He broke off, unable to find the words to do it justice. For the first time since they had set off on their journey, he was convinced that the map was genuine; and he tried to imagine how Captain Callinestra and his crew must have felt all those years ago when they'd first stumbled upon this remote spot. He could easily understand why the famous pirate had chosen it as the hiding place for his treasure. Only the most intrepid adventurer would find his way to this place;

and only the boldest would dare to risk crossing on that slender, slippery tree trunk.

"They must have cut down a tree at the top of the ravine," said Cornelius. "Then carried it along to place it across the gap to make a bridge. It would have taken a whole crew to do it."

Now Sebastian walked warily to the edge of the crevasse and dared to look into its depths; but what he saw down there made his stomach lurch and he stepped back quickly, bumping into Jenna, who had come up behind him. She moved round him and peered over the edge. She gave a low whistle.

"That's a long way down," she shouted, above the roar of the waterfall.

"Maybe there's another route," said Sebastian, licking his suddenly dry lips. They looked to left and right but it quickly became apparent that there was only one way across the chasm, and that was to walk along the tree trunk.

"It looks all right," yelled a voice behind them, and they turned to see that Cornelius was already clambering up onto the end of the trunk, clearly with the intention of crossing over the gap.

"Hold on a moment," said Sebastian nervously. "Let's not rush into this. Who says we need to go across there in the first place?"

"The map," said Cornelius calmly. *"Where footsteps venture into space."*

"Yes, but that doesn't necessarily mean that we're supposed to walk across that thing."

Cornelius gazed around slowly and then looked back at Sebastian. "How else are we supposed to get across?" he asked. "Fly?"

Sebastian frowned, all too aware that it was his own reluctance to step out above such a terrible drop that was prompting him to delay the matter. But he just couldn't help himself. He was afraid of heights, and his desperate fight with King Septimus at the top of Keladon's highest tower hadn't done anything to help him conquer his fear.

"The tree could be completely rotten," he argued. "Who knows how long it's been lying here soaked by the spray from that waterfall? It could snap like a rotten twig and send us tumbling to our doom. And besides, you can see there's nothing on the other side but a sheer rock face! How are we supposed to climb up that?"

Cornelius studied the map again. "I don't think we'll need to," he said. "There's just the one verse left, so we must be very close now." And he read out:

"If the treasure you would hold,
Then let courage make you bold.
Ignore the blows that sting and hurt
And look behind the gray maid's skirt."

Cornelius raised his eyes from the page and looked at Sebastian. "That's all there is," he said. "It's the final clue."

Sebastian stared back at him in exasperation. "Well, what's it supposed to mean?" he cried. "*The gray maid's skirt!* Do you see any women standing around over there, waiting to be searched?"

"No . . . ," admitted Cornelius.

"Then . . . what?"

"I haven't any idea," Cornelius assured him. "But it's obvious we're meant to go across this crevasse— it's as simple as that. Maybe we'll find more clues on the far side." He tested the end of the tree with one foot. It swayed a little, but seemed strong enough. "I think it'll take the weight," he said. "Provided we go one at a time. Now, if you two are not up to this, you can always wait here."

"No way!" cried Jenna. And she too clambered up onto the trunk. Sebastian stared after her for a while and then realized that he would have to follow or be forever tortured by the thought that he'd lost his nerve in front of his two friends.

A moment later he was standing on the tree beside Jenna, staring apprehensively over her shoulder as Cornelius set off across the void.

CHAPTER 31

ACROSS THE ABYSS

"The trick is not to look down," announced Cornelius calmly, as though he was about to take a gentle stroll across a meadow. "Just keep your gaze fixed firmly on the way ahead and then you won't—Oops!"

He tripped on the broken-off nub of a branch and fell facedown on the huge log, which sagged visibly beneath him. Sebastian winced and watched, hardly daring to breathe, as Cornelius wrapped his arms around the slender trunk and waited a moment for it to stop quivering. "On second thoughts," he said, "maybe it's not a bad idea to look down *occasionally*."

He got himself back onto his knees and then, very carefully, his feet. He straightened up, spreading out his arms to keep his balance, and began to move slowly forward again. As he reached the very middle of the trunk, the spray from the waterfall began to soak him and he suddenly stopped walking.

"Shadlog's beard!" he cried.

"What's wrong?" gasped Sebastian nervously.

"*The gray maid's skirt!* It's the waterfall, isn't it? We're to look behind the waterfall!" He began to move again, placing his feet carefully on the wet, slippery wood, edging slowly forward step by step until, after what seemed like an age, he reached the far side and the safety of the stone ledge. Sebastian let out a long relieved breath, but then, almost instantly, Jenna started forward.

"Wait!" Sebastian grabbed her arm. "Maybe there's no need for you to go over there," he said. "Why don't you leave the rest to Cornelius?"

She flashed him a disbelieving look. "Are you kidding? I didn't come this far to give up at the last hurdle. I'll be fine. You've got to remember, I've been shinning up masts since I was a little girl." She studied him sympathetically for a moment and lowered her voice. "But look, if *you* can't handle heights, nobody will think any the worse of you if you wait here."

"Me?" Sebastian gave what he hoped was a devil-may-care laugh. "Oh, *I'm* all right. I was just worried about you. . . ."

"So maybe you do care about me a little?" she said.

"Oh, er . . . I didn't mean . . ."

Jenna laughed at his embarrassment. "Relax, Sebastian," she said. "I'm only pulling your leg." She glanced briefly down into the abyss. "Maybe not a good idea, right now."

She turned back toward the trunk, extended her arms and started moving forward as though she did this kind of thing every day. She was heavier than Cornelius and the supple trunk bowed alarmingly when she got to the midway point, but she didn't slow her pace, even when the spray began to hit her, and in a matter of moments she had made it to the far side. She turned, smiling, to look back at Sebastian; and he realized with a cold sense of dread that he was going to have to try and make it across.

A thick sweat of terror broke out all over him but he made himself move forward, placing one foot carefully in front of the other. He tried to keep his attention fixed on Jenna's face, but remembering how Cornelius had tripped, he kept glancing down. As he moved out over the edge of the crevasse, he couldn't help but catch a glimpse of the dizzying depths that waited below. He gritted his teeth and kept going, hoping that his terror didn't show on his face—though Jenna's serious expression suggested that it did.

"Are you all right?" he heard her shout.

He tried to give her a reassuring grin but it must

have come out wrong, because now she looked really concerned.

"Sebastian, maybe you'd better go back."

"I'm fine!" he assured her.

But he wasn't fine. He was terrified. In his mind's eye he kept seeing himself falling from the trunk into the dark depths below; in vain he tried to shake off the image.

He took another step forward and the trunk sagged beneath him with a crack. His blood seemed to turn to ice in his veins, but perspiration was running into his eyes and he could hardly see where he was going. He stood there in an agony of indecision for a long time and then decided to take another halting step forward. The midpoint of the log was slippery with the constant soaking from the spray that billowed out across the cavern, and finding a secure footing was difficult.

"Just keep moving forward!" Jenna shouted to him. He nodded and took another step. Then his foot slipped sideways off the wood, and for a terrible moment he thought he was going to fall. But instead, he came down heavily astride the trunk and grunted with the pain of it. He was in danger of tilting sideways, but he managed to wrap his arms around the tree and hang on for dear life. He crouched there, trying not to think about what lay directly beneath him. He was shaking from head to foot, soaked by the icy spray from the waterfall, and he doubted that he had the strength to move from where he was. In the ensuing silence, the roar of the falling water seemed to rise to an earsplitting crescendo.

Then the trunk sagged even more and, glancing up in alarm, he saw that Jenna was coming back, one hand held out to him.

"Jenna," he warned, "it's too dangerous—go back."

"Not without you," she said firmly. She was beside him now, right in the middle of the trunk, and the wood was bending beneath their combined weight.

"Be careful, Jenna," called Cornelius from the far side. "I don't think it will take both of you!"

"It's all right," said Jenna, without looking back at him. She held out her hand to Sebastian, gazing at him all the while. "Now," she said. "Forget about trying to stand up again. Just move yourself forward any way you can."

Sebastian shook his head. "No," he whispered. "I'll have to stay here."

"You can't," she told him. "We'll all need to come back this way once we've found the treasure."

Sebastian nodded. "The treasure," he murmured. "Yes. Of course." The thought of it gave him a little courage. He took a firm grip on the tree trunk and scooched himself forward.

Jenna moved back a little to give him more room. "Good," she said. "And again . . ."

He repeated the move. Another cracking noise came from the wood and he cringed, convinced that it would splinter and break beneath them, tipping them into the void.

"It's all right," said Jenna soothingly, pulling him upward. He got one foot up onto the trunk and raised himself to a crouch. Then he was standing, looking directly into Jenna's brown eyes. "Now come on, follow me," she whispered. "It isn't far."

Jenna continued to move slowly backward, never taking her eyes from his; and Sebastian had no option but to go with her, inching his way forward. And gradually, in this way, the two of them made it to the far side.

Sebastian nearly wept with relief when he got his feet back on solid rock. He hugged Jenna so tightly she had trouble drawing breath.

"I'm so sorry," he yelled into her ear, because on this side of the crevasse the thunder of the waterfall drowned out every other noise. "Thanks for coming back for me! I was useless out there!"

She dismissed the matter with a wave of her hand. "Everybody is afraid of something," she shouted back. "I'll just have to remember not to send you up to the crow's nest when we're back aboard the *Sea Witch*."

"*If* we ever make it back," yelled Sebastian.

"Of course we'll make it back," she assured him.

They turned to look for Cornelius, but he was already moving on. He was standing as close as he could to the waterfall and they noticed that he had one arm up to protect his face. They moved to join him and then they understood why. Sebastian felt something glance off his cheek and lifted his own arm to shield his eyes.

"Ignore the blows that sting and hurt," yelled Cornelius. "There must be stones coming down in that water the whole time." As if to illustrate the point, something clunked off the top of his helmet and careened off into the falling water. "But I think"—he pointed into the seething, pounding cascade—"I think I can see an opening back there, behind the waterfall."

Sebastian stared hard and realized that Cornelius was right. He could discern a kind of shadow back there. But how to get to it? The rushing water was too powerful to just step through: it would most likely sweep him off his feet and fling him headlong into the crevasse. No, there had to be another way.

"Maybe there's a gap between the water and the rock," suggested Jenna. "If we put our backs to the wall and move sideways . . ."

Cornelius nodded. "That makes sense," he agreed. "Here, I'll go first."

"No," said Sebastian, who was still feeling bad

about his poor showing over the crevasse. "*I* will."
He pushed past Cornelius and pressed his shoulders
up against the sheer rock face. Then he started edging
closer to the water. After a few steps he could see that
Jenna was right. There *was* a narrow gap between
water and rock, but unfortunately heavy pebbles
were raining down and he had only gone a little way
when the first one bounced off his tricorn hat,
making him wince. He lifted his arms over his head
and shouted a warning to the others over the roar of
the water. He kept moving, and now it was his hands
and arms that took the brunt of the stinging blows.
Soon he was behind the thundering veil of water and
then, in the strange bluish half-light back there, he
saw what Cornelius had glimpsed—a small opening
in the rock wall. He ducked gratefully inside, and the
sound of the waterfall diminished in volume.

He found himself in what seemed to be a large cavern, but it was pitch dark in there and he couldn't see
very far. In the dim light around the doorway he
spotted a couple of old lanterns, still with tallow candles in them. He felt in his pockets for his tinderbox
and, kneeling down, set about trying to light one of
them. Then Jenna, backing in through the opening,
nearly fell over him.

"What are you doing?" she asked him.

"Trying to get some light in here," he told her. He

321

struck sparks from the tinderbox, and in the sudden flashes of light he could see that the cave was much bigger than he had first imagined. He managed to get a candle alight just as Cornelius backed into the cave.

"I'm nearly knocked out!" he muttered. "Even with my helmet on, some of those stones are big enough to—"

He broke off in surprise as Sebastian lowered the glass of the lantern and stood up, illuminating the interior. They were looking at a hideous grinning face, peering at them from the shadows to one side of the entrance. Sebastian had to bite back a gasp of astonishment, and he felt Jenna's hand tighten on his arm in silent terror. But then they realized that they were looking at a skeleton, slumped against the wall of the cave and still dressed in the ragged finery of a pirate. A plumed hat was pulled down just above the empty eye sockets and a tattered silk shirt covered the rib cage. Sebastian let out a sigh of relief and Jenna released her grip.

"Looks like they left somebody behind to guard their treasure," observed Cornelius. "An old pirate custom, I believe."

They turned to survey the interior of the hideaway. They were in a huge high-roofed cavern, extending deep within the rock. Great multicolored stalactites hung from the ceiling, looking like the remains of giant wax candles that had been allowed to melt; and further back, in the shadowy hollows of the roof, they could see hundreds of tiny glittering eyes staring balefully down at them.

"The bats we saw!" exclaimed Cornelius with an expression of disgust. "Filthy things—this must be their home."

"Never mind *them*," said Sebastian impatiently. "Where's the treasure? Are you sure the map doesn't give any more clues?"

"Of course I'm sure. But it has to be here somewhere."

"Look," said Jenna. She was pointing across the uneven floor to the very center of the cave, where a flat-topped stalagmite jutted up to waist height. Lying on top of it was a small wooden chest.

They moved closer and Sebastian held out his lantern to get a better look.

"That can't be the treasure," he muttered. "It's too small."

"Perhaps there's another clue inside the chest," suggested Jenna.

"Maybe." Sebastian reached out a hand for the box but Cornelius grabbed his arm.

"Not so fast!" he said. "Don't you think it's a bit obvious, just sitting there like that? It's as though somebody *wants* you to pick it up."

"Well, of course," said Sebastian. "What else?"

"Let me find a stick or something. It could be booby-trapped."

"Oh, come on," said Sebastian. "How likely is that?" He pushed Cornelius's hand away and picked up the box.

They all heard the loud click from the top of the stalagmite.

CHAPTER 3 2

X MARKS THE SPOT

Sebastian opened his mouth to say something, but in that same instant Cornelius dived at his legs and threw him to the ground. A second later, something big and heavy came hurtling out of the darkness and scythed the air above their heads. Sebastian felt the wind of its passing and the shadow seemed to take an age to pass over him. He saw with a feeling of relief that Jenna was standing far enough back to be safe from the booby trap. He started to sit up but Cornelius put a hand on his head and pressed him to the ground.

"Stay still, you idiot!" he snapped.

Immediately the big shape came swinging back again and only now did Sebastian realize what it was. A heavy tree trunk, suspended from the ceiling on ropes and somehow set to hit whoever picked up the wooden chest. As it swung backward and forward overhead in a series of gradually diminishing arcs, he saw that some charmer had fixed a series of metal spikes to the leading end of the trunk, and he shuddered to think what would have happened to him if they had met their target. He glanced at Cornelius, who was glowering at him in the light of the lantern, which by some miracle hadn't been broken.

"How likely indeed!" hissed Cornelius.

"Sorry." Sebastian picked up the lantern and they crept out from beneath the tree trunk. Sebastian set the wooden chest on the ground and they all crouched down to examine it. They could see that it was secured with a stout padlock. There was no evidence of a key anywhere, so Cornelius found a large stone and pounded the clasp until it broke open. The others watched in silent expectation as he opened the chest, stared at its contents in silence for a moment, then placed it carefully on the floor at their feet.

The chest held nothing more surprising than a dagger. Not a fabulous golden dagger with a jewel-encrusted hilt; just a rusty old thing with an odd metal handle fashioned in the shape of an X. Sebastian stared at it in disbelief. He couldn't believe they had risked so much and come so far for this.

"Is that it?" he cried incredulously. "The famous treasure of Captain Callinestra?" He reached into the chest and lifted out the dagger. "This old thing?"

Cornelius spread his hands in a gesture of helplessness. "I don't understand," he said. "How *could* that be it? Who'd go to so much trouble to hide something like that?"

"Look at it!" cried Sebastian. "It hasn't even got a proper blade! You couldn't cut butter with it!"

"Let me see that," said Jenna calmly. She took the dagger from him and studied it for a moment.

Sebastian didn't even notice. He was intent on giving Cornelius a piece of his mind. "I knew there was something wrong with that map!" he cried. "The instant you told me that man in the hospital sold it to you, I knew it had to be some kind of confidence trick. Five gold crowns you paid for it!"

"But . . . the map was genuine enough. It led us to this place, didn't it? And whoever put the dagger here had to brave so much. The yarkles . . . the sheer climb . . . that walk across the void. Somebody went to a lot of trouble to place that dagger here. But why?"

"Why? How do I know why? Perhaps somebody was stark staring bonkers!"

"Or perhaps it's not just a dagger," said Jenna. She picked up the lantern and walked across the cave to a section of wall opposite them, where somebody had scratched a short sentence deep into the gray stone.

X marks the spot, it said.

"It has a very distinctive shape, the handle," observed Jenna.

"So?" snarled Sebastian. "What's that supposed to mean?"

Jenna didn't reply. She was examining the wall closely now, outlining the deeply etched words with her fingertip. She traced the whole sentence before returning to the X at the start of it, which seemed to be incised much more deeply than the rest of the words. She looked at the handle of the knife for a moment, then back at the hole in the wall again.

"Jenna, what do *you* think the dagger is?" asked Cornelius, intrigued.

"I think it's a key," she said; and with that, she slotted the handle into the X on the wall and pushed it hard. It went in with a satisfying click.

There was a long, deep silence. Then the cave filled with the sound of an ominous rumbling, as unseen machinery began to work for the first time in many long years. As they watched in stupefied silence, in a great swirl of dust a whole section of the cave wall to the left of where Jenna was standing began to rise, revealing another opening.

Sebastian opened his mouth to shout something but the noise of the machinery had disturbed the legions of bats above them and, quite suddenly, they came flapping down from the ceiling in a great repulsive leathery-winged cloud—so many that, for the moment at least, he could see nothing. He gave a grunt of revulsion as dark shapes flapped past him, inches from his face, and instinctively threw up his hands to cover his head. The shrieking bats whirled round the astonished intruders and then, as one, zoomed out of the cave through the opening in the rock. For a while it was impossible to see anything other than the dark flapping shapes. But finally the creatures were gone.

And as the dust settled and the light from the lantern began to penetrate that inner darkness, they saw an amazing sight. A great glittering mound of booty was piled haphazardly on the ground in front of them. Sebastian's jaw dropped and he could barely suppress a cry of astonishment.

He was looking at more wealth than he could ever have imagined.

CHAPTER 33

CALLINESTRA'S SECRET

There was a long moment of total silence before they came to their senses. Sebastian's eyes took it all in, and he could barely believe what they told him. In front of him, in a careless heap, lay a fabulous hoard of treasure that must have been looted from every corner of the known world.

There were gold coins in their thousands, great dazzling mounds of them, pressed with the imperious faces of long-dead kings and queens; there were heaps of precious stones, shimmering with every color of the rainbow. There were beautifully crafted weapons of many kinds: silvery swords in velvet and gold scabbards, their hilts decorated with emeralds and rubies; fancy daggers with inscribed blades; massive embellished battle-axes; fearsome spears; and ornate shields made of hammered bronze that glowed dull red in the light of the lantern. There were pieces of armor that must once have been worn by mighty warriors; there were metal figurines and beautifully crafted ornaments, golden goblets inlaid with sapphires and diamonds, and dark wooden chests holding who knew what other wonders.

The three adventurers were rooted to the spot for a long while, hardly daring to believe that their expedition had paid off so handsomely. It was Sebastian who recovered first. He started to move toward the opening.

"Wait!" Cornelius's barked command stopped him in his tracks. "Let's not let excitement overrule our caution," he said.

"But, Cornelius"—Sebastian pointed a shaking finger toward the vast pile of wealth—"it's right there," he finished lamely. "The . . . the treasure." Whatever he called it could not hope to do justice to the sight that lay before them.

"I appreciate that," said Cornelius. "But we've almost walked into one trap; who's to say there isn't another?" He thought for a moment, glanced quickly around the cavern and then went over to the entrance to pick up the skeleton that was slumped against the wall. Beside it he found an old spear and, hooking this into the dead pirate's rib cage, he lifted the skeleton in front of him and raised it to the height of a man. Turning back, he walked toward the opening with the frightful thing held out before him.

"Sorry about this," he told the pirate. "But whatever happens, it isn't going to make much difference to *you*." He stepped up to the opening and thrust the skeleton over the threshold, into the inner chamber. Nothing happened and Cornelius shrugged, then smiled self-consciously. "Maybe I was being overcautious," he said, and took another step forward.

There was an abrupt twang from somewhere to his right and a great wooden spear came flying out of a hole in the cave wall. It pierced the skeleton's rib cage with such force that pieces of bone flew off under the impact, and the pirate's remains were ripped from Cornelius's spear and propelled across the chamber to smash to pieces against the far wall.

There was a short but very deep silence and Cornelius let out a slow breath. "And then again, maybe I did the right thing," he observed. He gave Sebastian a disparaging look. "*Now* I think it's safe to go inside," he said.

Sebastian swallowed and nodded.

Cornelius edged through the opening, looking left and right, holding himself ready to dive to the floor if anything else should come at him. But after several long moments of indecision he allowed himself to relax; then he was down on his knees beside the treasure, his hands experiencing the unfamiliar feel of immeasurable wealth.

"Bring the lantern," he said.

Sebastian and Jenna hurried to join him. Sebastian set down the lantern and they crouched there in silence, searching feverishly through the loot in the warm glow of light, picking up pieces that caught their eye and examining them in more detail. Then the three of them seemed to realize all at once what was happening. They looked at each other and exchanged grins of sheer delight.

They had done it! They had set out to find the treasure of Captain Callinestra, and against all the odds they had succeeded. They began to laugh delightedly, the sound of their voices echoing around the cavern. Sebastian grabbed a gold tiara and, removing Jenna's three-cornered hat, set it in place on her head. He found an ornate bronze helmet and threw off his tricorn to jam it down on his own head.

"We're rich," he announced delightedly. "Richer than we could ever have believed possible. Cornelius, I'm sorry. I was a fool to ever doubt you!"

Cornelius chuckled. "No need to apologize," he assured his friend. "To tell you the truth, I had more than my fair share of worries along the way. When we found that dagger . . . well!" He glanced at Jenna. "It took someone smarter than both of us to work out what that was for."

Jenna smiled. She set the tiara at a rakish angle. "What do you think?" she asked Sebastian. "Perhaps

I'll give up the ways of the sea and become a lazy noblewoman, with servants to do my every bidding."

"Why not?" said Sebastian. "You can be whatever you want to be now. We all can."

"We'd better not get ahead of ourselves," said Cornelius soberly. "We still have to get what we can carry back to the ship." He gestured to the mountain of wealth in front of them. "We'll hardly be able to shift a fraction of this," he said. "We'd better load as much as we can into the packs."

Sebastian frowned. "It's hard to know what to take," he said. "There's so much of it."

Cornelius nodded. "I'd advise you to concentrate on the precious jewels. They're lighter than gold and worth much more than the coins and statues. But don't forget, now we know where this place is, we can come here any time we like."

They set to the task of cramming as much as they could carry into their packs. Sebastian followed Cornelius's advice about the jewels, but he did choose for himself a splendid sword with a gold-embellished hilt to replace the weapon he had left buried in the belly of the yarkle. Cornelius insisted that his two companions each take a metal helmet to guard their heads against the stinging stones of the waterfall when they made their way back. The packing accomplished, they stood up, backed away and gave the interior of the treasure chamber one more awed look before stepping out into the main cavern.

"I don't much like the idea of leaving it all on display like this," said Sebastian, lifting the lantern to take one last look.

"Maybe we don't have to," said Jenna. She reached up to grip the blunt blade of the dagger where it stuck out from the opening in the wall and, with a grunt of effort, pulled it free. At first nothing happened. Then there was a rumbling sound, and the wall began to descend again until it hit the ground with a loud thud. There was no longer anything to tell a chance traveler what lay behind that ingenious screen.

Jenna slipped the dagger into her belt. "Now nobody can get at the treasure but us," she announced gleefully. "It's perfect."

Cornelius studied her for a while and Sebastian thought he was going to order her to hand over the dagger. But the moment passed and he seemed to dismiss the notion.

"Come on," he said. "We'd better get moving. Sebastian, you lead the way."

Sebastian hefted his heavy pack onto his shoulders, jammed the metal helmet down securely onto his head, then moved obediently to the entrance. He set down the lantern. "Last one out, put out the light," he said. Stooping, he climbed out into the already unfamiliar glare of daylight and began to edge his way past the rushing torrent, painfully aware that his loaded knapsack obliged him to lean forward. But though his clothes were soon soaked, the bronze helmet protected him from the falling stones. He could hear the dull clunks as they bounced off it, and he wondered how much time Captain Callinestra and his crew had spent ferrying their precious booty to its hiding place.

He glanced back and saw that Jenna was following him, looking decidedly odd in the oversized warrior's helmet she was wearing. She grinned, gave him a thumbs-up, then winced as an extralarge pebble bounced off her armor-plated head. Cornelius followed close behind her, and soon the three of them had edged their way out from behind the waterfall and were heading back toward the huge crevasse, where the narrow tree trunk stretched ahead, daring them to risk crossing it a second time.

"I'll go first," announced Sebastian, still haunted by his poor showing on the way across and determined not to put this off a moment longer than necessary. Jenna and Cornelius exchanged doubtful looks, but then Cornelius nodded, and they said nothing as Sebastian climbed up onto the trunk and prepared himself to cross.

"You'll be all right," Jenna assured him. "Just keep moving forward." She gave him a brief, nervous smile.

"I'll be fine," he told her.

He moved quickly out across the terrible space, his arms extended on either side to maintain his balance. The spray from the waterfall was soaking him with its icy chill and he was horribly aware that the heavy pack had increased his weight considerably. It seemed to him that the slender trunk was bowing more alarmingly than before as he moved toward the center, but he seemed to be handling the crossing well.

He lifted his gaze to stare at the far end of the trunk, and that was when he saw a figure emerge from the narrow opening in the rocks up ahead. It was a woman dressed in a long hooded cloak. She came to a halt a short distance from the edge of the crevasse and lifted her hands to pull the hood back from her face. She stood there, smiling, her eerie tawny eyes burning into his.

"Hello, Sebastian," she said. And he froze in his tracks, staring back at her, unable for the moment to move a muscle.

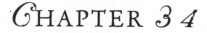

CHAPTER 34

ICE-COOL REUNION

Sebastian was frozen to the spot, staring at Leonora in dull surprise. He couldn't believe she had managed to find them again, but he also knew that he wasn't imagining things. She was studying him intently, her full lips curved into a wicked smile.

"Well, well," she said quietly. "I was beginning to think I'd never catch up with you. But here you are at last."

He looked beyond her, fully expecting to see Captain Trencherman and his crew massing for an attack, but for the moment at least, Leonora seemed to be alone. Sebastian just stood there, not knowing what to do.

"Did you find what you were looking for?" she purred.

"I don't know what you're talking about," said

Sebastian, aware as he did so that big beads of sweat had broken out on his forehead.

She laughed at that, throwing back her head and cackling, sounding more like an old hag than a beautiful young woman.

"Oh come now," she said. "You know you can't lie to me." Her expression changed suddenly and her voice became hard and commanding. "Bring me that pack you're carrying."

Sebastian shook his head, but already he was aware of his feet moving to obey her. He took a step forward, but then Jenna's voice made him stop again.

"No, Sebastian! Turn round and come back!"

He paused and looked over his shoulder, but the action nearly made him lose his balance. His legs wobbled and he threw out his arms, flailing wildly before he recovered himself. He was horribly aware of the terrible distance below him, and once again his heart was pounding in his chest.

"Sebastian!" Leonora's voice again. He looked back at her and her eyes seemed to be shining with an eerie malevolence. "You cannot disobey me. I order you to cross over to me."

Sebastian's head seemed to fill with a dull red glow and there was a whining noise in his ears. He licked his dry lips and told himself that he *could* deny her, but again he felt his feet shuffling forward as though they no longer belonged to him. Then the tree trunk dipped alarmingly beneath his feet, and he thought it was going to break and drop him into the empty air that waited below.

A few seconds later he was shocked to feel a hand grasping his arm from behind. He realized that Jenna had walked out onto the trunk and was now standing right behind him. Her mouth brushed against his ear.

"Sebastian," she whispered. "Listen to me. We're going to cross back to the other side. Just move with me—"

"No!" Leonora's face contorted into an expression of dark rage and she pointed an accusing finger at Sebastian. "He's mine; he does as I say!"

"Not this time," Jenna told her. And she began to ease Sebastian backward along the trunk, keeping one hand on his arm.

Leonora gave another shriek—or rather, it began as a shriek but suddenly turned into a long, thunderous growl. Sebastian looked back at her in terror and saw that she was changing, shifting her shape within the loose-fitting cloak, her body melting like hot wax. In an instant, it was no longer Leonora he saw, but the long, lithe body of a cat, shrugging itself free of the cloak and advancing toward the tree trunk, eyes glittering, teeth bared.

"Jenna," whispered Sebastian. He didn't need to say anything else because he heard her gasp, felt her body stiffen beside him. "Run," he advised her with a calmness that amazed him. "I'll be right behind you. . . ."

She took him at his word, turning on the narrow trunk and moving back the way she had come, the movement making the tree trunk judder. Sebastian would have followed, but he had underestimated the speed at which the new Leonora could move. She had leaped up onto the end of the trunk and was racing toward him. Caught between trying to turn away and facing up to her attack, Sebastian chose the latter, and took the full force of the leap against his chest. He fell backward and his backpack slammed against the tree trunk. Leonora carried on, clearly focusing on Jenna, but Sebastian desperately twisted round on the trunk: hanging on with one arm and reaching out with the other, he grabbed the big cat's tail.

Leonora gave a screech of anger, turned round and lunged at Sebastian, her claws raking at his head. He let go of her tail and lifted the arm to cover his face as the needlelike claws shredded the fabric of his tunic and bit deep into the flesh beneath. The pain almost made him relinquish his grip on the tree trunk; but then he felt it dip alarmingly again and he realized that Jenna was coming back to help him. At the far end of the log he could see Cornelius, watching grimly but unable for the moment to do anything to help.

"Jenna, stay back!" he yelled. "This tree's nearly gone!" But she ignored his warning. As she came forward, she pulled something from her belt. Sebastian just had time to register that it was the dagger they'd used to reach the treasure; but then all hell broke loose, and he had to concentrate on hanging on grimly as Leonora launched herself at him again, her mouth open.

At the same instant Jenna closed on the big cat, and her arm lifted and fell, sinking the blunt blade deep into Leonora's tawny flank. The cat-woman bellowed in agony, a great howl of pain and anger. She tried to twist round to face her attacker, but was now losing her grip on the tree trunk. She slipped backward, her claws gouging great furrows in the wood. Her back legs swung out over the abyss and she hung there for a moment while Jenna aimed a kick at her face. Leonora's front paws tore into tree bark in a vain attempt to hold on, but then she began to fall backward, past Sebastian.

For a fraction of a second he experienced a great sense of elation. He would be free of her at last! But then there was a terrible impact as something yanked on the strap of his backpack, nearly pulling him from his perch. He locked his arms desperately around the tree trunk, but a terrible weight was dragging him down. Twisting his head to peer back over his shoulder, he saw that a woman's hand was clamped around one of the straps. The hand and arm were human, but below them the body was still that of a big cat. Even as he looked, it was changing back to the shape of a naked woman. The eyes still glared up at him with a terrible malignance, and from a mouth that was not quite cat and not quite human came a voice that had elements of both creatures.

"You're coming with me," it growled. "Be sure of that."

Sebastian held on grimly, his arm muscles screaming in pain as he struggled to hold Leonora's weight. He knew that he could not hope to hang on for more than a few minutes. But then Jenna was reaching down past him with the dagger, using the blunt bloodstained blade to saw at the strap of the backpack.

"No use," he gasped. "Can't . . . hold on. . . ."

"You've got to!" gasped Jenna. "I'm nearly there. . . ."

Sebastian's muscles were stretched to the breaking point. He opened his mouth to yell against the pain of it—

And suddenly the weight was gone and Sebastian cried out in relief as the half-cat, half-woman fell into the void, still clutching the backpack. He risked another glance down and saw her changing body turning over and over in the air as she fell into those terrible depths. And he saw something else falling beside her, something that glittered in the sunlight— an ancient weapon with an oddly-shaped handle.

"The dagger!" he whispered.

Jenna nodded but said nothing. She was starting to help Sebastian up onto the tree trunk when something seemed to shake him to the very core and he almost lost his grip a second time. A vivid brightness flared within his head, and suddenly it was as though he was seeing everything for the first time. He noticed the incredible detail of the tree bark around which his arms were clasped. He noted the gold brocade of the sleeve of Jenna's jacket as she reached down to help him up, and he saw the beauty of her brown eyes as they stared into his.

He realized at once what had happened. Leonora's body had just crashed onto the jagged rocks far below and, in dying, she had finally freed him from the enchantment that had claimed him for so long. He clambered up onto the tree trunk and flung an arm around Jenna's waist.

"I'm free, Jenna!" he cried. "That witch has gone from my head at last!"

She was about to answer but an ominous crack from below alerted them to the fact that the tree trunk was finally losing its battle against their combined weight.

"Quickly!" she gasped, and they scrambled on their

hands and knees to the far side. Sebastian was so relieved to be on solid ground again, he felt like hugging it. They both turned back to stare across the crevasse at Cornelius. He was standing there, looking doubtfully at the tree trunk.

"You can't risk it!" Jenna shouted across to him. "It's barely holding together."

"I *have* to risk it!" he bellowed back. "There's no other way across that I can see. I'll just have to be fast. Make room for me!"

"Cornelius, wait!" shouted Sebastian. "Perhaps we could—"

But it was too late. The little warrior was already running across the tree trunk, his eyes fixed on the far side. As he emerged from the spray of the waterfall and moved toward the middle, the trunk bowed again and they all heard that terrible cracking sound.

"He's not going to make it," whispered Jenna.

But Cornelius kept going, shortening the distance with each stride. Sebastian moved to the edge of the abyss and held out a hand to his friend.

"For a moment there," he said, "I thought you were going to—"

And then the tree trunk gave a final crack and snapped across the middle like a rotten twig. Cornelius's expression momentarily registered surprise; then his powerful little legs launched themselves from the tree trunk, he gave a deep bellow and his body went into the familiar spinning blur that was the Golmiran death leap. He arced across the void and crashed headlong into Sebastian, knocking him backward in an ungainly sprawl.

They lay there for a moment, catching their breath.

"Shadlog's teeth," said Cornelius at last.

Sebastian had to agree that it summed up the situation pretty well.

CHAPTER 35

OUT OF THE FRYING PAN . . .

Once he had got his breath back, Cornelius disentangled himself from Sebastian and turned to stare down into the crevasse, watching in fascination as a dust cloud slowly settled over the place where the tree had landed. "That was too ruddy close for comfort," he said. "It's a wonder that tree trunk hung on for as long as it did." He looked up at Sebastian. "I'm sorry, lad, I couldn't do anything when that shape-shifter attacked you and Jenna. I didn't dare add any more weight to the trunk."

Sebastian waved a hand in dismissal. "It doesn't matter," he said. "The main thing is Leonora's gone. She's out of my head completely and my thoughts are my own again."

Jenna came to stand beside him. "I'm glad of that," she said. "But your freedom was bought at quite a price. We've lost the dagger—and your pack and everything that was in it. Even our bridge is gone."

Cornelius moved away from the edge with a matter-of-fact shrug. "It's not the end of the world," he said. "It makes things more complicated, that's all. We can mount another expedition any time we need to. Of course, we'd have to bring some equipment and a lot more people. We'd need to cut down a new tree and carry it up the ravine for a start!"

"That would get us across the chasm," admitted Jenna. "But the treasure will be locked away behind solid rock."

"There are ways to blast through rock. Maybe we could get hold of some more of those thunder-sticks we had in Keladon. They'd smash their way through any obstacle." Cornelius threw himself down on the ground and the other two joined him. "Besides," he said, "I don't know what we're worrying about. The booty in the two packs we still have will provide enough wealth to last us a lifetime. I take it we'll still split it three ways?"

"Of course," said Jenna, without hesitation.

"*Four* ways," Sebastian reminded him. "Don't forget, Max is still expecting his cut." They all laughed at that.

"He'll be the richest buffalope in history," said Jenna.

"He'll buy lots of pommers," said Sebastian, "and get very, very fat."

"The important thing," said Cornelius, "is *we're* alive and the witch is dead." He glanced warily at Sebastian and smiled when he didn't react. "Did you hear what I said, Sebastian? I called Leonora a witch . . . a rotten, stinking witch!"

Sebastian shrugged. "Why not? That's exactly what she was."

Cornelius grinned. "It looks as though you really are cured, my friend!"

"It's as though I've been wearing blurred glasses all this time," Sebastian told him. "Now I can see everything in perfect detail." He glanced sheepishly at Jenna. "And I can finally recognize true beauty when I see it." He reached out a hand and put it on hers.

There was a brief, thoughtful silence. Then Cornelius spoke.

"The problem is, what are we going to do now?"

"We go back to the ship, of course," said Sebastian brightly. He looked at the other two and noted their frowning faces. "Don't we?"

Cornelius shook his head. "I don't think it's quite as simple as that," he said. "For one thing, Leonora couldn't have got here by herself. Which means that Trencherman and his crew must be skulking around somewhere—"

"We're closer than you might think!" announced a strident voice, and they all looked up to see Trencherman and his villainous-looking first mate emerging from the opening in the rock that was the only way in or out of the place. The two men advanced slowly. They were smiling, the kind of thin smiles that were not to be trusted.

"I feel I should thank you," Trencherman told Sebastian.

"Thank me? For what?"

"For ridding the world of that scheming witch. She worked her enchantment on me too—otherwise I would never have allowed her within a sea mile of me. And I certainly wouldn't have let her persuade me to turn round a ship that was slowly sinking to follow the *Sea Witch* to her destination. But here I am." He pointed to the crevasse. "I must say it was interesting watching that little drama unfold." He flicked his gaze across to Cornelius. "For a moment there, midgeling, I thought you were going to follow her down into those hellish depths."

Cornelius got to his feet, drawing his sword as he did so. His companions followed his example.

"I'm no midgeling, Captain Trencherman. I'm a Golmiran. And you'd best stay where you are, or you shall have my sword to answer to."

Trencherman looked somewhat amused by this comment. "You speak as though you are in charge . . . when in fact it's not like that at all. Allow me to demonstrate."

He clapped his hands, and at his signal a dozen

men appeared on the high rocks that ringed the plateau. Sebastian looked slowly around at them. Each man held a bow and every bow had an arrow nocked and pulled back ready to fire. There was a long silence while the three friends assessed the situation. There was nothing they could do. If they tried to resist, they would be dead in moments. If they turned to run, there was only the deep and terrible chasm behind them and no way of crossing it.

"I trust your treasure-hunting expedition was successful," purred Trencherman, who couldn't seem to stop smiling now that he was back in control. "I must say, I'm looking forward to inspecting the booty. It will be doubly sweet when I know that somebody else has done all the hard work for me. Captain Swift, I'll trouble you to throw your sword and your pack over to me."

"Go to hell!" snapped Jenna. "You'll take them only from my dead body."

Trencherman shrugged. "If that's what you'd prefer," he said. "It's really all the same to me." He lifted a hand to signal to his archers, but Cornelius stepped over to Jenna.

"Do as he says," he told her. "No treasure is worth losing your life over."

"But—"

"Do it!" insisted Cornelius. And he threw over his own pack and sword.

Jenna glared at him for a moment, then nodded as she acknowledged the impossibility of their situation. She followed suit with great reluctance, and Trencherman signaled to his mate to collect the packs.

"We'll take those nice bronze helmets you're wearing too," prompted Trencherman. "And, elfling— what about the jeweled sword you have at your waist? I'd say it's far too fancy for a breed like you to wear."

"Why, you—" Cornelius took a step forward but Sebastian put out a hand to hold him back.

"It's all right," he said. "Of course he can have it." It had suddenly come into Sebastian's mind to try and play the hero. Perhaps it was an attempt to make up for his poor performance crossing that tree trunk. Perhaps he had momentarily taken leave of his senses. Whatever the reason, it had occurred to him that if he could just cover the short distance between himself and Trencherman, he might be able to take the captain hostage and use him to barter a way out of there. So he pretended to be having trouble with the ancient brass catch on his sword belt while he began to edge forward.

"I found this in the treasure cave," he said as he walked. "The precious stones in it must be worth a small fortune—"

"Stay where you are!" Trencherman warned him.

"No, really, you must look at this one big stone at the end of it. I'm not sure if it's a diamond or an emerald. What do you think?"

"I told you to stand still!" snapped Trencherman.

"Sebastian, do as he says," said Jenna anxiously.

Sebastian was very close now. A few more steps and he'd be able to make his move. Meanwhile he carried on talking.

"You know, Captain, we should sit down, the two of us, and discuss a deal. You see, there's a lot more treasure. We weren't able to carry it all and—"

Trencherman made the slightest of gestures to his first mate and the big man stepped forward to intercept Sebastian, pulling something from his belt as he did so. Sebastian lifted an arm to throw a punch into the man's ugly face, but in the same instant the mate lashed out at Sebastian's head. A bright light seemed to explode in the middle of his skull and his limbs lost all their strength. He was only dimly aware that the ground was rushing up toward him, but before it could thud into him, everything turned black.

CHAPTER 36

THAT SINKING FEELING

He woke for an instant and thought that he was back on the *Sea Witch*, because whatever he was lying on was swaying and lurching rhythmically beneath him. But then he became aware of thick, springy hair under the palms of his hands and, opening his eyes, he realized that he was slumped facedown across Max's back. He vainly tried to sit up. His wrists were tied with thick ropes that passed under the buffalope's belly.

He groaned, managed to turn his head to one side and saw Jenna's concerned face looking at him. She was walking alongside Max and he saw that her hands were tied behind her back.

"He's awake," he heard her say, but he couldn't see who she was talking to and he presumed it must be Cornelius.

"Young master!" Max's voice seemed to boom

because Sebastian's ear was flat against the buffa-lope's back. "Speak to me! Are you all right? Or have those villains dashed out your brains?"

"What ... what happened?" groaned Sebastian. His mouth was horribly dry and there was a buzzing sound in his ears, as though clouds of angry insects were swarming inside his skull.

"You were hit with a belaying pin," Jenna told him. "It's a wonder your skull wasn't smashed in." She glanced around quickly. "They're taking us back to the *Marauder*. Trencherman said that he's prepared a special welcome for us."

"We ... we have to bargain with him," muttered Sebastian. He was barely holding on to conscious-ness. "He doesn't know . . . where the rest of the treasure is. . . . Maybe we can use that. . . ."

But Jenna was shaking her head.

"He searched me and found the map," said Cornelius's voice from somewhere out of sight. "He knows everything."

"But ... but ..." A great roaring redness was filling Sebastian's head, and Jenna's lovely face was fading away as unconsciousness tugged at his senses once again. He struggled to throw off the dark enveloping arms that reached up to claim him, but his strength was all gone. He slipped back into the darkness like a peb-ble falling into a bottomless lake.

* * *

He woke again, and this time he knew he really *was* aboard a ship. There was no other way to account for that familiar pitching and rolling sensation. He opened his eyes and blinked, quickly realizing that he was in a dark and dingy location, somewhere belowdecks. Two anxious faces were gazing forlornly down at him in the semidarkness. He recognized Jenna and Cornelius.

Sebastian tried to sit up and a terrible pain lanced through his temples. He groaned and fell back onto what he realized was a rough wooden board with a thin blanket thrown over it.

"Take it easy," Jenna advised him. "That was quite a whack you took. And besides, we aren't going anywhere for the moment."

Sebastian turned his head and understood what she meant when he saw a row of thick steel bars in front of him. He realized where he was: in a lockup down in the dank, dark bowels of the *Marauder*. He made an effort to put aside the pounding in his head and sat up, swinging his legs off the board and putting them down onto what he expected to be wooden planks. But he received a shock when they plunged into several inches of icy water.

"What the—?"

"Yes," said Cornelius. "I'm afraid it's every bit as bad as it could be. The *Marauder* is sinking. Clearly, enchanted as he was, Captain Trencherman didn't bother to make any repairs. That's how he was able to catch up with us so quickly. But at a terrible cost. His ship is doomed—it's only a matter of time before she goes down."

Sebastian lowered his hands to the water and scooped some up to splash in his face, which helped to bring him back to full consciousness. "Where's Max?" he asked.

Cornelius shrugged. "He was taken aboard the ship when we were," he said. "I suppose he must still be up on deck."

"But . . . if we're sinking"—Sebastian struggled to make his fuddled senses work—"then why are we out at sea?"

Cornelius frowned. "The *Marauder* was moored a short distance down the coast from the *Sea Witch*," he observed. "My guess is that Trencherman will try and make it to Jenna's ship. But knowing him, I can't see him politely asking if he and his crew can come aboard, can you?"

"He'll have his hands full if he tries anything!" said Sebastian fiercely. "Jenna's boys will give him a fight to remember!"

But Cornelius was shaking his head. "I don't think so," he said. "Not when they realize that Jenna is Trencherman's captive."

Realization dawned in Sebastian's aching head. "Of course," he said mournfully. "That's why he didn't kill us all back at the crevasse. He means to use us as a bargaining tool!" He reached up a hand and touched his fingers against a hard lump on his head. He winced. "We've got to do something," he decided. "We can't just sit here and let it happen."

"I'm afraid we don't have much choice," Cornelius told him. "I had a good look at those bars while you were sleeping. It would take a couple of thunder-sticks to make any impression on them. I tried picking the lock, but I didn't get anywhere with that approach. That's more your territory, Sebastian." He looked thoughtfully down at the water around his ankles. "The way this water is rising, we may not be sitting here for very long, anyway."

"He can't just let us drown like rats in a trap," said Sebastian.

"I wish I had your faith in human nature," sighed Jenna. "Trencherman is capable of just about anything. It's a shame I didn't ignore the Code of the Sea and leave him to perish when the *Black Hand* was attacking his ship."

Sebastian splashed more water onto his face. The pain in his head was still pretty bad, but at least the fuzziness had gone and he could now see everything with crystal-sharp clarity. He glanced at Cornelius. "Let me have a look at that lock," he said.

Cornelius splashed aside and Sebastian searched in the pockets of his belt until he found a suitable pick.

He reached through the bars and spent some time fiddling with the heavy padlock that secured the door, but without success. As he struggled, everyone was painfully aware that the level of the icy cold water was creeping gradually higher.

"It's no use," confessed Sebastian at last. He moved back to slump down on the seat. "Perhaps if my head was clearer . . ."

"We don't have the luxury of waiting for that," Cornelius told him. "Look, if I'm right about Trencherman needing Jenna as a hostage, he isn't going to let her drown. That would be stupid. And though that man may be sly and treacherous, the one thing he *isn't* is stupid. So . . . let's try something. When they come down to take Jenna out, you pretend that you're still unconscious, let them get past you and—"

"You needn't bother," said a voice from the top of the stairs on the other side of the room. Glancing up, they saw Trencherman coming down the staircase, followed by his first mate and a couple of other burly crewmen armed with swords. He was smiling again, that spiteful, all-knowing smile that Sebastian had already learned to hate. "I was about to release you anyway. But please don't try anything funny. You're all unarmed and my men have instructions to cut you down at the slightest show of resistance."

One of the crewmen stepped down into the shallow

water. He paddled across to the bars and unlocked the gate. Opening it, he stepped aside to allow the prisoners out. Trencherman beckoned to them impatiently. "Well, come along, we haven't got all day. Or would you rather remain down here until you drown? Captain Swift, you first, if you please."

Jenna scowled and strode out of the cell, the water swirling around her knees now. "Your ship's going down fast," she observed. "You should have taken our advice and gone back to Ramalat."

"Madam, I assure you I would have done so had I been in my right mind. But that witch commanded and I had to obey. Which means that I am in a fix and must resort to desperate measures." Trencherman took hold of Jenna's arm and pulled her roughly toward the stairs. Sebastian and Cornelius started after her but were immediately seized by the sailors. Then Trencherman unsheathed a vicious-looking dagger and pressed the blade against Jenna's throat. "Now, now, gentlemen, I have already told you," he growled. "No funny business. We're all going to go up on deck, nice and peaceable, and nobody is going to do or say anything that makes me angry, otherwise my hand is just liable to slip and make a mess of this pretty little neck." He turned and pushed Jenna up the staircase before him. Sebastian and Cornelius had no option but to allow themselves to be frog-marched after her.

They emerged into the brilliant sunlight of afternoon and stood blinking around for a moment. Trencherman's crew were gathered on the main deck, armed to the teeth and watching the captives impassively. Beyond them Sebastian caught sight of Max. He was lying on his side, chained around the neck to the wooden rail, and his front and back legs were roped securely together. He didn't look very happy, and when he caught sight of Sebastian, he struggled against the thick ropes but could do nothing to free himself. Sebastian tried to make a move in his direction, but the sailors held him and pushed him forward again. He saw that over by the mizzenmast a small table had been set up with paper and ink. Trencherman propelled Jenna toward it and forced her to sit down in the vacant chair.

"What's this?" she demanded, looking down at the sheets of paper.

"Those are deeds of sale," Trencherman told her. "I've just had them drawn up by the ship's clerk. They explain that you're selling the *Sea Witch* to me for a modest sum. I just need you to ink your signature here." He pointed to a blank space at the bottom of the page.

"Sell the *Sea Witch*?" Jenna glared at him. "Are you mad?"

"Not at all. I tried everything I could to persuade you to sell her to me when your father suffered his little accident, but you would not do it. Now my own ship is sinking and this time you *will* sell her, like it or not. And when I sail her back to Ramalat, I'll be able to prove that I didn't take her by force. These papers will see to it that nobody can contest my ownership."

"And what makes you think I'd agree to something like that?" snarled Jenna contemptuously.

Trencherman smiled. "I thought, perhaps, with the right persuasion—"

"You can do what you like to me, I won't sign anything," she told him.

"Hmm. Well, I expected as much. You always were far too brave for your own good."

Trencherman gestured to the men who were holding Sebastian and Cornelius. "Take them," he said. The men started pushing them across the deck to the port side. Sebastian saw, to his horror, that a plank of wood had been securely fixed to the rail, jutting out over the open water. A bearded sailor was occupying himself throwing fish scraps over the side and he gave Sebastian a ghoulish gap-toothed grin.

"Come along, lads," he said. "Don't be shy!"

Sebastian started to struggle but he could not withstand the muscular crewmen holding him. They picked him up bodily from the deck and set his feet onto the plank of wood. A moment later Cornelius was lifted, kicking and struggling, to join him. Then various swords and spears were prodding them out toward the far end of the plank. Sebastian looked down into the clear blue water and saw, with a feeling of dread, that several big kelfers, attracted by the fish scraps, were moving around in the water, their triangular fins cleaving the surface.

"It's quite simple," Trencherman told Jenna. "Sign the document . . . or your two friends become fish food."

Jenna shrugged and adopted a "couldn't care less" expression. "They're nothing to me," she said. "Do as you please."

Sebastian felt a brief jolt of shock at her attitude, but then realized that she was merely trying to bluff her way out of the situation.

Trencherman studied her in silence. Then he grinned. "Very well," he said. "Men, start with the breed."

The swords and spears began to jab with renewed intensity, and Sebastian had to flinch back from them, retreating to the very end of the plank.

"Wait!" cried Jenna. She bowed her head in defeat. "I'll sign," she said quietly.

A wave of bravado swept over Sebastian. "Don't do it, Jenna," he cried. "Don't give him the satisfaction. It was your father's ship; it means everything to you."

Jenna looked at him and he saw that her eyes were glistening. "It's not worth the lives of two men," she told him. She picked up the quill and quickly wrote her name on the paper.

"Splendid!" Trencherman grabbed the deed of sale, examined it for a moment, then folded it and slipped it into the inside pocket of his frock coat. "In a short while," he said, "we will come upon the *Sea Witch* and you will prevail upon your crew to throw down their weapons and hand the ship over to me. Do you understand?"

Jenna nodded sullenly, then looked expectantly toward the plank. "What about them?" she asked.

"Oh yes, I nearly forgot." Trencherman looked up at Sebastian and Cornelius with that cold, merciless smile. "Goodbye, gentlemen," he said. "I trust you'll enjoy your last swim." And he signaled to his men.

The swords and spears began prodding once again. Sebastian heard Jenna's shrill cry of protest.

"But . . . you told me they would go free!"

Trencherman shook his head. "I don't believe I said anything of the sort," he replied. "You simply assumed I would let them go. But they are of no value to me now."

Sebastian was dimly aware of Jenna leaping up from her seat and of Trencherman grabbing her again; but he had little time to think about helping her, because a spear's cruel point had driven him to the very end of the plank and his heels were teetering on the edge of the drop. He caught a glimpse of Cornelius's grim expression, looking up at him; and then he lost his balance and he was falling, his arms waving frantically as he tumbled feet first toward the clear blue water where the hungry kelfers waited.

CHAPTER 37

A WATERY GRAVE

The impact of the cold water hit him like a fist, driving all the breath out of his lungs, and he was sinking. At first he felt almost serene, as though he was descending into a silent, magical world where nothing could harm him; but then a lithe gray shape flashed through the water ahead of him, reminding him of the deadly danger he was in.

He panicked, attempted to snatch in a breath and got a mouthful of salty water for his trouble. He clawed his way upward and broke the surface, gasping for air. He bobbed around in the water for a moment, coughing the last of the seawater out of his lungs, and saw the *Marauder* moving away at considerable speed and the vast expanse of water all around. To his left he could just make out the distant line of the shore, but it was a greater distance than he could ever swim, even if he wasn't surrounded by kelfers.

And where was Cornelius?

As if in answer to his thought, the little warrior surfaced a few feet away, coughing just as desperately as Sebastian had. Cornelius was rarely at a loss, but he was in an unfamiliar element here and, quite literally, out of his depth. He saw Sebastian and swam closer, spitting out water as he did so. He got up close and said one word, his eyes glittering with malice.

"Trencherman," he growled.

Sebastian nodded. "If we ever get out of this . . . ," he said.

Cornelius looked apprehensively at a great triangular fin cutting the surface a short distance to his left. "It seems unlikely," he said matter-of-factly. "The best we can hope to do is sell our lives dearly."

Sebastian nodded and threw another hopeless glance after the *Marauder*, but it was already dwindling in size. "If only I had a weapon of some kind . . . ," he muttered.

Cornelius sighed. "I had a knife hidden in my boot," he told Sebastian. "I was hoping Trencherman's thugs wouldn't find it—but they did."

Sebastian looked at him for a moment and then pointed toward the distant shore. "What do you think?" he gasped. "Maybe . . . ?"

"We'd never make it," said Cornelius flatly. "It would take a champion swimmer to cross that distance. And we—"

He broke off as a huge kelfer cruised through the water to his right.

"They're getting bolder," he said. "Here . . ." He turned round in the water and pushed his back up against Sebastian's. "Better get ready," he said.

"I don't want to die like this," said Sebastian mournfully.

"I have news for you. Neither do I. But sadly, you don't always get a choice in these matters."

A kelfer came speeding up from the deep, straight at Cornelius. He threw back his arm and punched it in the nose, and it veered away, crashing the water into a frenzy of foam.

"Aim for their eyes if you can," said Cornelius. "It looks like the most vulnerable part of them."

Sebastian nodded. "It's been a honor and privilege knowing you," he told his friend.

"I'm sure it has," agreed Cornelius. "You've had your moments too."

"Remember when we—?"

Sebastian stopped talking as a great brutish snout plowed through the water toward him. He remembered Cornelius's advice and aimed a punch at one of the kelfer's eyes. The creature gave an eerie shriek and lunged aside, its great tail churning the water. And then it was gone. Sebastian remembered to breathe and continued with what he had been saying.

"—when we first met on the great plain? When you

turned up carrying that javralat? Max tried to convince me that you weren't to be trusted, but luckily I didn't listen to him."

"I would advise anyone not to listen to Max," said Cornelius. "That creature has a habit of opening his mouth before his brain has—"

Suddenly the little warrior was pulled beneath the surface by a prodigious force.

"Cornelius!"

Sebastian didn't hesitate but snatched a breath and dived down into the clear water. He saw to his horror that his friend was being dragged down by a young kelfer, which had grabbed him by one leg. He was struggling helplessly in its grip and trying to punch at it, but could not even reach its head. Sebastian kicked out frantically and drove himself closer to the kelfer. He pulled back one arm and stabbed his index finger deep into one of its empty black eyes, feeling it sink to the knuckle in what felt like cold jelly. The kelfer's jaws snapped open, releasing Cornelius, and it swam off, twisting and thrashing in agony. Sebastian grabbed Cornelius and kicked back toward the surface, horribly aware that the little warrior's leg was torn open and releasing a thick cloud of blood. They came up together, gasping for breath. Cornelius's face was a white mask of pain.

"Is the leg off?" he asked through gritted teeth.

"No. But it's a deep wound," Sebastian told him.

He glanced around desperately, aware of more fins approaching from every direction.

"Make for the land," Cornelius advised him. "Maybe my blood will draw their attention away from you."

Sebastian shook his head stubbornly. "I'm not leaving you," he said. He threw an arm around his friend, aware that the nearest kelfers were cruising about, seeking an opening.

"You must!" snapped Cornelius. "There's no hope for you here. Get away, you fool! Escape while you can!"

"I know you wouldn't leave *me* in a fix like this," said Sebastian. He glanced down, aware of a shadow below him; an immense white shape that seemed to be rising up from the depths to claim them. He steeled himself for the impact and hoped that the end, when it came, would be quick.

Cornelius had not noticed anything. "It's my fault," he groaned. "I got us into this mess. If I hadn't bought that map, we'd be back in Keladon now, living like kings."

The shape was getting closer and Sebastian began to appreciate how huge it was. He caught a glimpse of a fishy body, dappled by sunlight.

"I don't regret anything," he said. "And whatever fate comes now, I go to it content that I have known great adventure."

Something fleshy pushed against Sebastian's legs and he closed his eyes, waiting for the teeth to tear into him.

"Farewell, old friend," he said quietly.

And then something grabbed his shoulders and pulled him backward. It was so unexpected, he cried out. An instant later, two pairs of hands were lifting him in over the side of a boat and he collapsed on the floor, gasping for breath. A familiar face was grinning down at him.

"That was a close one," said the Kid. He turned aside and helped his father lift Cornelius into the boat which, Sebastian could now see, was made from a hollowed-out log. Cornelius slumped down beside him and the two of them looked at each other and laughed incredulously.

"I don't believe it!" cried Sebastian. "We're alive!"

The makeshift boat shuddered as a heavy shape bumped against it, and Jack Donovan leaned over the side, wielding a homemade oar, and gave whatever it was a hearty whack.

"They keep on trying," he said, "but I made this boat good and strong." He glanced at Sebastian. "Well, had to pass the time somehow, didn't I? Thing was, I could never get up the courage to take it out into open water. Seemed like every time I thought about giving it a go, I'd see that big old kelfer cruising by the beach, looking for me, and I knew there was no boat I could make that would stand up to the likes of him."

"He's not around, is he?" whispered Sebastian.

"Not yet, young sir. But that's only a matter of time. No, I kept this boat way up the coast in a little bay, where only small creatures could get over the reef. Used it for fishing, mostly."

The Kid was examining Cornelius's injured leg. "You're losing a lot of blood," he said. "We've got to try and slow it down somehow." He shrugged off his jacket, then tore off a sleeve and tied it as tightly as he could above the injury, making Cornelius grimace with the pain.

"How's that?" asked the Kid.

"Better," grunted the Golmiran.

"But . . . I thought you two were going back to the *Sea Witch*," said Sebastian. "For a rest."

"That was the plan," said Donovan, "until we approached the beach and happened to see the *Marauder* waiting in a little inlet further along the coast. So we dropped back into the trees for a bit, and after a while we saw a landing party leave the *Marauder* and set off after you lot. Well, it wasn't too hard to work out what was happening. I could see the *Marauder* was listing really bad—only a matter of time before she went down. So it was clear that Trencherman needed another ship."

"And the only other one around was the *Sea Witch*,"

finished the Kid. "That was when Dad told me about his boat. We knew it was a long shot, but we had to give it a go."

"Trouble was, we needed to go all the way back up the coast to get it. Then we had to paddle it back down to the *Marauder.* Half killed ourselves doing it."

"We had this idea about trying to climb aboard her," said the Kid. "Grab a couple of weapons and take her captive before the main party got back. But they was already returning when we got closer, so we pulled into shore and decided to wait till dark. Only then the boat started moving along the coast and we could see what was going on—them making you walk the plank and everything. We came after you, but you was a good way out and we were half dead already."

"You did brilliantly," Cornelius told them. "But there's more work to be done. We must get back to the *Marauder.* My guess is they'll slow right down when they come up to the *Sea Witch.* If we can sneak up behind them, perhaps we can climb aboard and turn the tables on them."

Donovan looked doubtfully at the little warrior. "No offense, sir, but I doubt you'll have the strength to go climbing anywhere." He pointed to the gathering pool of red in the bottom of the boat. "You've lost an awful lot of blood."

"Nonsense," growled Cornelius. "You just get us there and we'll see what's to be done."

There was another abrupt thud as a kelfer's snout thudded against the ship's hull.

"Get away, you fiend!" snarled Donovan, and he thrust down with his oar, causing another great commotion in the water. "If only I'd had time to pick up some weapons! One of these beasts will have us over in a moment."

"Then let's not waste any more time," Sebastian urged him. He grabbed another oar, and he and Donovan began to row, thrusting the oars deep into the water. The boat moved slowly at first, but then, as they fell into a rhythm, it began to pick up speed. Far ahead of them, dwarfed by distance, the *Marauder* was moving briskly across the water, and beyond her they could just make out a tiny speck on the horizon that was undoubtedly the *Sea Witch*.

Sebastian put his head down, and he and Jack Donovan rowed with every ounce of strength they could summon, propelling the makeshift boat across the surface of the water.

CHAPTER 38

LAST HOPE

It seemed to take an eternity, and their arm muscles were screaming in protest by the time they'd narrowed the distance, but the *Marauder* gradually grew in size, until at last they were slipping in beneath the great towering stern of the ship; luckily nobody up there seemed to be keeping watch.

Donovan steered the boat expertly in the ship's wake and hung onto a wooden strut. Sebastian stood up and helped his friend to do likewise. He noted how pale Cornelius looked and how he was gritting his teeth against the pain in his injured leg.

"Perhaps you should wait here," he whispered.

Cornelius's eyes widened into a glare. "You are joking, I hope," he whispered back.

"We're coming too," said the Kid. He glanced sharply at his father, who stared at him for a moment and then nodded his agreement.

Sebastian shrugged and reached up to grasp the ornately decorated timbers of the stern. He pulled himself upward and began to climb. Cornelius followed as best he could, blood still seeping from the wound in his leg. The Kid came next, climbing with all the agility of a boobah, and Donovan brought up the rear, stepping off the boat and allowing it to drift away on the wake behind him. A moment after he'd let it go, a huge white snout suddenly lurched up out of the water and turned the boat over like a child's toy. Donovan stared down into the water in absolute hatred as a long white shape sank back into the depths.

Sebastian told himself that with their only means of escape abandoned, they really would have to make this work. He glanced doubtfully down at Cornelius, half expecting him to lose his grip at any moment and plunge back into the water. The Golmiran was still climbing gamely, but even if he made it up to the deck, he wasn't going to be at anything like his best if it came to a fight. Which meant that the others would have their work cut out.

It was hard enough just trying to climb up the stern. The trickiest bit came when he reached the windows of the captain's cabin, but a quick glance inside assured him that the room was empty and he was able to shuffle along sideways until he found more handholds and ropes to the side of the glass. As he moved past, he glimpsed two familiar-looking back-packs and a jeweled sword and scabbard lying on the captain's table. For a moment he considered smash-ing the glass and going in after the treasure but then he discounted the idea. The weight of a pack would only hinder him.

He glanced down a couple of times and saw that Cornelius was still following, but moving at a frac-tion of his usual speed. The little warrior looked up at him at one point, breathing heavily, his face as white as parchment. Sebastian began to worry that his friend had lost too much blood: he might just faint and fall into the water, where the blood seeping from his leg would soon lure kelfers. Behind him, the Kid was not even out of breath, but his father, thin and weakened as he was, was struggling to keep up.

At last Sebastian reached the rail along the ship's poop deck and was able to peer cautiously through the gap. What he saw gave him fresh hope. Trencherman and his entire crew were gathered in the forecastle, right at the other end of the ship, as it rode at anchor within hailing distance of the *Sea Witch*. Sebastian could see that Jenna was with them. Trencherman had an arm around her and was hold-ing a dagger to her throat. Sebastian fought down a powerful urge to rush straight over to her and directed his attention instead to Max, who was still lying bound and chained on the main deck.

He clambered quickly over the rail and then leaned back to reach a hand down to Cornelius. Not a moment too soon, for the little warrior looked to be on the point of collapse. Sebastian hauled him unceremoniously over the rails and onto the deck. Cornelius tried to get up, but Sebastian pushed him back down again.

"Stay here and rest," he said. "You can barely stand."

"I'm strong enough to carry a sword," protested Cornelius, "if I can only get my hands on one!"

"No. Leave this to us!"

"But . . ." Cornelius's eyelids fluttered and he sank back with a soft groan. It was as Sebastian had feared. He couldn't expect any help from his friend.

Now the Kid climbed over the rail and settled himself beside Cornelius's still form. He looked anxiously at the Golmiran and then leaned back to help his father over. Donovan crouched down, gasping for breath. He too looked pretty exhausted, Sebastian thought. A fine boarding party they made.

"You two stay with Cornelius for now," he told them.

"What are you going to do?" whispered the Kid.

"I'm going to try and even things up a bit," said Sebastian.

He turned away, assured himself that the attention of the crew was still fixed on the *Sea Witch* and then, on his hands and knees, crossed the poop deck, descended the short flight of steps and, pressing himself against the rail, crept toward Max. On the way there, he picked up a discarded carpenter's axe with a sharp blade. He froze for a moment when he heard Trencherman's strident tones bellowing at somebody, but the captain was simply hailing the *Sea Witch.*

"Crew of the *Sea Witch*! I have your captain as my prisoner. Throw down your weapons and raise your arms where I can see them. . . ."

Sebastian ignored this and continued on his way. As he neared the tethered buffalope, he heard an unfamiliar snuffling sound and realized with a sense of shock that Max was crying.

"Max, what's wrong?" he whispered.

"What's wrong? I'll tell you what's wrong!" grunted Max, his head turned away. "My master—the finest master a buffalope could have—is in the belly of a kelfer . . . and my best friend in the world, a plucky little Golmiran, is in there with him. And shortly I shall be ending my life as a meal for the scurviest bunch of sea dogs you have ever seen—"

"Max, it's all right, it's *me*," whispered Sebastian.

"You? Who's you?" Max turned his head and regarded Sebastian in silence for a while. Then he started snuffling again.

"What are you crying about now?" Sebastian asked him.

"Why wouldn't I cry? My own tortured mind has conjured a phantom to come and haunt me!"

"I'm not a phantom!" Sebastian glanced nervously toward the forecastle. "And keep your voice down! We don't want to lose the element of surprise." He laid a hand on Max's head. "See? I'm real. I managed to escape the kelfers with the help of the Kid and his father. And now—"

"Oh, master, it really is you!" Max's eyes widened in amazement.

"Yes, now shush! I'm going to need your help." Sebastian took the sharp-edged axe and began to saw at the ropes around Max's legs.

"But . . . where's Cornelius? Don't tell me that the kelfers ate him!"

"No, but they had a damned good try. He's lying at the stern unconscious. If anything happens to me, you must try and help him, do you understand?"

"Of course, master, of course . . ." The first strands of rope came apart and Max flexed his front legs with a sigh of relief. Sebastian looked toward the forecastle, where Trencherman was still shouting his demands; his crew's full attention seemed to be centered on the *Sea Witch*. Sebastian transferred his attention to the ropes around Max's back legs. After a few moments' furious sawing with the axe he had cut through those too.

Max clambered to his feet. "What about the chain?" he asked hopefully. "Did you find a key?"

"I'm afraid not," Sebastian told him.

"Well then . . . perhaps you could pick the lock?"

"I doubt it." Sebastian fixed Max with a disbelieving look. "Are you trying to tell me that the mighty Max is going to be rendered helpless by a mere length of chain around his neck?"

Max frowned. "It's not a mere chain," he protested. "It's solid metal."

Sebastian shrugged. "Metal or not, there was a time when it would have been no problem to you. Perhaps you're getting old—"

"Old? I'm not old!"

"Well, I tell you this, Max, with or without you, I'm about to attack that rabble up in the forecastle."

"You can't go up there alone!" cried Max. "They'll cut you to pieces!"

"Maybe they will, but I have to do it anyway—"

"Wait!" Max flexed his huge shoulders, lowered his head and began to walk backward, exerting a huge pressure on the chain. The thick timber rail to which it was fastened began to creak. Max continued to pull, his expression one of grim determination. Suddenly the timber snapped in two with a loud crack, and several members of the crew turned to see what had caused the sound. There was a long, terrible moment while Sebastian stared up at them and they stared down at him. There was no time to be wasted. He vaulted up onto Max's furry back and raised his axe aloft. "Let's go!" he yelled.

And Max leaped forward as though somebody had rammed a red-hot sword up his backside.

CHAPTER 39

THE SHOWDOWN

Max thundered across the main deck, his hooves drumming a furious rhythm on the weathered boards. He crossed its wide expanse in moments and then vaulted up the short flight of steps that led to the forecastle, each step creaking in protest and threatening to snap beneath his weight. Sebastian clung on for dear life.

He saw that the crew of the *Marauder* were all turning round now, their eyes wide with panic when they saw what was bearing down on them. Some turned to run, but there wasn't really anywhere to go. Max's huge horns crashed into the nearest and scattered them before him like ninepins. Meanwhile Sebastian flailed with the axe at anything that came within his range. Some crewmen, rather than face those formidable horns, opted to vault over the rails into the ocean below, while others just turned and fled blindly.

"Yes, run, you vermin!" roared Max delightedly. "Run like the stinking cowards you are! I'll grind you beneath my hooves!"

"Max, be careful!" yelled Sebastian. "Don't hit Jenna!"

Max realized just in time that Jenna and Trencherman were standing right in his path. He tried desperately to veer sideways, but his hooves lost their grip on the scrubbed deck. He began to slide like a great hairy toboggan.

"Oh poo!" he said. Sebastian saw Trencherman staring up at him open-mouthed as Max went whizzing past. He acted instinctively, throwing himself off Max's back, straight at the hated sea captain, and knocking him away from Jenna. He was only vaguely aware of Max, propelled by his own momentum, swinging sideways into a whole bunch of sailors and pushing them before him, before crashing into the rail of the forecastle. But then he and Trencherman were rolling over and over on the deck, and it was only when he had got free and clambered back to his feet that Sebastian noticed the big ragged break in the rails and realized that Max had gone over the side, taking half a dozen crewmen with him.

"Max!" he gasped. He took a step toward the broken rail, but then Trencherman recovered himself, drawing his sword as he did so. Sebastian threw a look in Jenna's direction, but she had snatched up a sword from a fallen man and was fighting with a couple of crewmen who had escaped Max's charge, while waving madly at the *Sea Witch*. Cries of delight echoed from her decks, and soon grappling irons began to fly across from the other ship to pull the two vessels closer together.

Trencherman scowled. He turned his attention back to Sebastian. "How the hell did you get back here?" he snarled.

"With a little help from my friends," said Sebastian. He spotted another fallen sword lying on the deck and started toward it, but Trencherman leaped forward to block his path.

"Oh no," he said. "I think you should stick with the weapon you have."

Sebastian looked down and realized that he was still holding the axe. Next to Trencherman's heavy cutlass, it looked pathetic.

"But . . . what about the laws of chivalry?" he asked.

"The hell with *them*!" snarled Trencherman. He lifted his sword, but then the *Marauder* gave a sudden lurch and tipped dramatically to one side. Water came swirling in over the starboard rail onto the main deck. Sebastian remembered Cornelius lying unconscious at the stern of the ship, but for now he could do nothing to help him.

"Give this up," he advised Trencherman. "Your ship's going down fast and you cannot hope to win."

"True enough," purred Trencherman. "But I can at least ensure that you don't live to enjoy your victory." And then he ran at Sebastian, swinging his sword in a series of wild slashes that obliged Sebastian to retreat, trying desperately to parry the blows with the little axe.

"Stand and fight, breed!" snarled Trencherman.

"The hell with *that!*" Sebastian told him. He looked around frantically and saw the Kid struggling to make his way across the main deck, which was already swamped with water. Back in the stern, Jack Donovan was still cradling the tiny figure of Cornelius, unable to leave him.

Realizing that he was on his own, at least for the moment, Sebastian ducked under Trencherman's next blow, threw the axe at him and then ran back to the foremast. Almost automatically his hands sought out the strategically placed metal rungs and he started to climb. He hated heights but he wanted to stay out of reach of that vicious sword and this seemed to offer his only refuge. Trencherman followed, cursing, occasionally reaching up to flail at Sebastian's heels with the sword, but never quite making contact, the razor-sharp blade hewing V-shaped wedges out of the mast.

"Come down here and fight!" roared Trencherman.

"No thank you," said Sebastian and kept right on going.

After what seemed an age he reached the sanctuary of the topsail lookout post and, climbing through the opening onto the small circular platform, he made a welcome discovery. Somebody had left a sword there, probably for an emergency such as this. He drew it from its scabbard and turned back to face Trencherman, who was just emerging through the opening.

"Sebastian!" The voice drifted up from below and he saw Jenna, standing at the base of the mast. She had finished off her two opponents, but now the forecastle and poop decks were filling with water. Some of Jenna's crew had swung across from the *Sea Witch* and were splashing through the rising water, finishing off what was left of the opposition. Sebastian saw the Kid among them, brandishing a sword and cutting down anyone who opposed him. Jenna moved to the base of the mast and began to climb but Sebastian waved her away and pointed toward the stern of the ship.

"Go and help Cornelius!" he bellowed. "Quickly, before we all go under!"

She nodded, turned back and moved toward the flooded main deck; but Sebastian did not have the luxury of watching her progress. Trencherman was approaching round the curved wooden lookout. He was studying the sword in Sebastian's hand with interest.

"You any good with that?" he murmured.

"This is the sword hand that brought down Septimus, the tyrant king of Keladon," said Sebastian haughtily. It wasn't entirely true but there was no reason to let Trencherman know that. "I met him in a high place just like this and I sent him tumbling to his doom. I don't see why you should be any different."

Trencherman was about to say something terse in reply, but he broke off as the *Marauder*, her stern now completely filled with water, started to tip backward, the weight bringing the bow up into the air and making the mast swing out of the vertical at a terrifying angle. Sebastian felt the floor of the lookout slip out from under his feet and he made a wild grab at the mast. Trencherman did likewise, and for a moment they hung there, too busy trying to hold on to worry about fighting. Sebastian got one leg up around the mast and pulled himself astride it, noticing that his opponent was doing exactly the same thing.

They were afforded a dizzying bird's-eye view of the chaos below. Sebastian saw a frantic melee of floundering, splashing people, desperately swimming away from the sinking vessel. He thought he caught sight of a huge hairy shape paddling toward the *Sea Witch*, surrounded by ominous-looking dorsal fins, but then the mast stopped moving and momentarily held its position.

Trencherman was the first to recover. He struggled to his feet until he was balancing on the steeply angled mast. Sebastian followed suit, knowing that he would be a sitting duck if he stayed as he was; but he was still in a crouching position when Trencherman struck, swinging the sword at his opponent's head. Sebastian only just got his own sword up in time, but even so, the impact nearly sent him tumbling from the mast.

He managed to struggle upright, and then Trencherman was coming at him again, his face a cold mask of hatred.

"You're dead meat," he growled.

"No, I'm Sebastian Darke—you must be thinking of somebody else!"

"Think you're funny?" snarled Trencherman.

"I have my moments! Did you hear the one about— Oof!"

Trencherman had unleashed a series of powerful blows. Sebastian parried them but quickly realized that he was no match for the experienced sea captain; and he began to retreat awkwardly along the mast, trying to keep his balance while staying out of range of that deadly sword. But Trencherman had the advantage of size and strength. He kept coming, lashing blow after blow against Sebastian's sword, forcing him to retreat.

"There's nowhere to go!" bellowed the captain.

Sebastian considered diving into the sea, but told himself that the fall would probably kill him just as effectively as Trencherman's sword, and he was horribly aware of a massive white shape moving in the water, getting closer all the time.

Then, without warning, the prow of the ship lurched downward as the hull stabilized before sinking beneath the waves, and the mast swung back to an upright position, pitching Sebastian straight into Trencherman. Together the two of them fell into the great sheet of canvas that was the foresail. As they started to slide down, Sebastian saw a length of trailing rope and he abandoned his sword and made a grab for it, abruptly halting his downward motion. But Trencherman, not to be denied, clutched onto Sebastian's legs with his left hand and hung there defiantly as the boiling waters rose higher and higher beneath him. Sebastian struggled to kick him free but he clung on, staring up gleefully, steadying his right arm to deliver the killing blow.

"Goodbye, breed," he sneered.

And then the huge kelfer came rearing up out of the water beneath them, its great jaws gaping and displaying row after row of jagged teeth. Sebastian saw the old scar stretching across the width of its white belly and he knew that this was Donovan's kelfer, the one that had nearly killed him on his arrival on the island. The jaws enclosed Trencherman like a fleshy purse, rising as high as his extended arm and closing with an audible crunch. For a long, terrible moment the kelfer hung there upon thin air . . . but finally gravity overcame it and it fell back into the raging waters, leaving Trencherman's upraised arm behind, the hand still clutching Sebastian's ankle.

"Oh, gross!" whispered Sebastian. He kicked his leg several times and the arm dropped into the sea.

The kelfer was gone and the water was rushing up around Sebastian and he was plunged into a roaring, bubbling world of madness, horribly aware that the wake of the sinking ship was dragging him inexorably down to the ocean floor. He remembered to let go of the rope and tried to struggle free of the sail, which seemed to have closed around him like a shroud. Eventually he found a way out of it and started swimming for his life, but he no longer knew which way was up and which way was down, and he was being bombarded by countless pieces of flotsam, which came spinning out of nowhere to collide with his struggling body.

His breath was almost gone, his chest was bursting and he could feel the undertow of the ship still pulling at him, seeking to take him into its chilly embrace.

And then suddenly, magically, his head broke water and he was gasping and staring up at the brilliant blue sky. He heard shouting, and turning round in the water, he saw the *Sea Witch* and the crew leaning over the side, yelling and beckoning him to swim to them. And he saw that Max was already being winched aboard, bellowing indignantly at his rescuers to be careful how they lifted him. A blinding realization came over him: he was alive, he had survived the sinking of the *Marauder* and all he had to do now was swim to safety.

He started doing exactly that, moving at a leisurely pace. But then the tone of the cries from the *Sea Witch* changed. Now they were yells of alarm. Sebastian glanced back over his shoulder and his blood seemed to turn to ice water in his veins. The big kelfer was following him at an incredible speed, its triangular fin slicing through the water. Not content with eating Captain Trencherman, it had come back for a lean and lanky second course.

Sebastian swam. He swam as he had never swum before, churning the water to foam with his arms, kicking out with his legs, horribly aware all the time of those savage jaws closing on his pumping heels. He thought of Jenna's father, who had lost both his legs, and he knew with a terrible certainty that he could not bear to live if such a thing were to happen to him. As he drew nearer to the *Sea Witch,* he could make out the crew, leaning over the side, urging him to hurry. Jenna had her bow and she was trying to take aim on the kelfer, but she wouldn't loose the arrow; and that told Sebastian that the kelfer was too close, that she was afraid of hitting the wrong target.

He knew in that moment that he was not going to make it; that he was going to die there in the water in full sight of his friends and the woman he loved. His arms were aching, his chest was ready to burst and he felt a terrible sadness enclose him, just as surely as the jaws of the kelfer would swallow him down.

He felt the advancing surge of water, smelled the kelfer's awful stench, and he steeled himself for the impact of those terrible teeth; but then something came between Sebastian and the glare of the sun. A figure was diving down from the rail of the *Sea Witch*; a small figure clutching a dagger in his teeth. For a moment Sebastian imagined that it must be Cornelius, recovered from his faint and leaping down to help his friend. But no, it wasn't Cornelius. It was the Kid.

An instant later he landed with a thud on the kelfer's striped back, and Sebastian turned in astonishment, just in time to see the Kid's right hand lifting the dagger and driving it down, down into the beast's black, vacant eye. There was an unearthly scream, the like of which Sebastian had never heard before. The kelfer's powerful tail thrashed the water as it went into its death agonies, the movement throwing the Kid aside like a child's toy. Then the creature was spiraling down into deeper water, a crimson cloud streaming from its stricken eye, and others of its kind, alerted by the taste of blood, were following it down, intent on feasting on its massive body.

"That was for my dad!" yelled the Kid, staring down at the diminishing shape in the depths. He turned in the water and grinned at Sebastian. "You OK?" he asked.

At first Sebastian couldn't find the words to tell him how he felt. Instead, he gave the Kid a fierce hug.

"All right, all right, there's no need to get all mushy," said the Kid, pushing him away.

"That was the bravest thing I ever saw," gasped Sebastian. "You . . . you saved my life."

"Yeah, I did, didn't I?" said the Kid. And he laughed at the realization that he had just done something incredibly heroic.

The two of them started to swim back to the *Sea Witch*. In moments they had reached the hull and the crew were lowering ropes to pull them to safety.

Sebastian had never been more grateful to climb aboard a ship. Jenna was waiting for him and they embraced while the crew roared their approval. Everyone wanted to shake the Kid's hand and tousle his hair, and then his father was there, hugging him and crying with delight at what he had done.

"You killed him, Beverly!" he cried. "You killed the beast that's haunted me all these years."

The Kid looked embarrassed. "Please don't call me Beverly," he hissed.

Sebastian and Jenna were still hugging each other as though their very lives depended on it.

"You can cut that out for a start," said a familiar voice; and there was Max, dripping wet and as cantankerous as ever. "It's a wonder I didn't kill myself crashing through that rail," he moaned. "Whose idea was that ridiculous charge, anyway? I could have drowned."

Sebastian laughed. "It was a funny time to go for a swim," he said. He looked anxiously at Jenna. "Cornelius?" he asked.

"Over here," she told him. She led him across the deck to where the little warrior lay covered in a blanket. His face was still unnaturally pale, but at least he was conscious and able to muster a weak smile.

Sebastian knelt beside him. "How are you?" he asked.

"Oh, I'll survive. As soon as the ship's surgeon is free, he's going to stitch up this leg. I daresay I'll be left with a limp, but it could have been a lot worse. For a moment, back there, I thought I'd lost the whole leg." Cornelius narrowed his eyes and fixed Sebastian with an admonishing look. "You're making a habit of going it alone," he said. "Or I'm making a habit of avoiding the action—one of the two. I'm told you fought like a hero."

Sebastian laughed at that. "I fought like a very

clumsy hero who had luck on his side," he said. "Not to mention a gigantic kelfer."

"You can thank Captain Donovan for getting you to the boat," Jenna told Cornelius. "That ship went down so fast at the end, it's a wonder you weren't lost along with everything. . . ." Her eyes widened in realization and she turned to stare at the spot where the *Marauder* had vanished, where now there was nothing more than a swirl in the water and a few motley pieces of wreckage bobbing forlornly in the waves. "The treasure!" she gasped. "I forgot all about it. It must have been somewhere aboard the *Marauder*!"

"Oh no." The words came to Sebastian's lips automatically, and yet he said them with no real trace of regret. After all, they had hung on to the most precious thing of all: their lives. He didn't bother to tell Jenna that he'd actually seen the packs lying on a table in the captain's cabin.

"Well, that's just typical, isn't it!" complained Max. "That just puts the ruddy cap on it! We go all that way, struggle through the worst odds, face the most terrible dangers . . . and for what? Our wonderful treasure ends up lying at the bottom of the sea."

Sebastian shrugged. "Well, Max, that's the way it goes. You win some, you lose some."

"Oh no, I'm not going to be reasonable about this. I was owed a share in that treasure and I earned it as much as any of you. Have you any idea how many fresh, ripe pommers I could have bought with that kind of money?"

"I'll buy you some pommers," said Sebastian. "As soon as we get back to land." He looked at Jenna. "Forget about the treasure," he advised her. "It's gone where we can never reach it. And besides, we know where there's plenty more, don't we?"

Cornelius moaned softly. "Grant me one favor," he murmured. "Let's wait a little while before we go looking again. To tell you the truth, I could do with a bit of a rest." He closed his eyes and slipped back into unconsciousness.

"Yes, go ahead, sleep," muttered Max. "I probably won't sleep for a month! All that lovely treasure, gone. It's enough to make you want to spit!" And he stomped off along the deck with a sour expression on his face, muttering angrily to himself.

Sebastian got to his feet, and he and Jenna walked to the ship's rail. She was still watching the spot where the *Marauder* had vanished, as if hoping against hope that the treasure would come floating to the surface again.

Sebastian put an arm around her shoulders. "What are you thinking about?" he asked her.

"I'm wondering how I'm going to explain to the crew that they're not getting paid for this trip," she said glumly. She turned and fixed him with a soulful look. "And I'm thinking that even if I'm not rich, I've still got my ship and my crew. . . ."

"And me," he prompted her. "Don't forget me."

She laughed. "How could I do that?" she said and she hugged him close. There was a long moment in which Sebastian found himself thinking that he had found exactly what he was looking for; that he would never need to go adventuring again.

Then Jenna stepped away from him and turned to shout to her crew. "All right, boys, let's rig those sails. We're heading home."

The crew ran to carry out her orders. Willing hands heaved on ropes, canvas flapped in the gathering breeze, and in a short while the sails were billowing full and the *Sea Witch* was gathering speed, leaving the scene of devastation behind.

It was a long journey back to Ramalat, but an uneventful one.

CHAPTER 40

THADDEUS PEEL

Sebastian stared across the tavern table at Jenna. He couldn't believe what she'd just told him.

"Two moons?" he said. "The trip's going to take two whole moons? You are joking, I hope."

She shook her head sadly. "No, I'm deadly serious. Sebastian, I really don't have any choice. My crew are patient men, but if they don't get paid soon, I'll have a mutiny on my hands."

They had been back in Ramalat a matter of days; time enough for them to get to know each other better; time enough for Cornelius to be able to limp around the place without too much trouble; and time enough for Max to eat his way through a massive number of pommers. So when Jenna had asked Sebastian to meet her at the Spyglass Inn, he had expected to laugh and drink a couple of tankards of ale and not much else. But she informed him straight-away of her plans. She had signed a contract to carry a cargo of cloth right round the coast to the southern shores of Mendip. The trip was a long one and she would be away for at least two moons. Fifty-four days. It seemed like a lifetime.

"It's not as though you didn't expect something like this," she reminded him. "We talked about it before, remember?"

"Well, yes, but I hardly expected it to be for so long."

She frowned. "I know it's a long trip, but it's a fairly easy one and it will pay good money. Two hundred gold crowns. I'll be able to give the crew all their back wages *and* have a healthy bit put by to tide us over. And . . . well, it's not as if you're bringing in any money, is it?"

He gave her a reproachful look. "That's not fair," he said. "You know I've been trying to find something."

"Maybe . . ." She glanced at him warily. "Maybe you could go back to your old jester's act. I'm sure you'd find the odd booking."

He shook his head. "There's no way I'll try that again. I already told you, I'm just not cut out to be a jester. No, my plan is to raise enough money to finance another trip to the treasure cave."

"Oh, Sebastian, I don't know—it nearly killed us all last time!"

"Yes, but this time we'd do it *right*. But we'd need to equip ourselves properly, and of course that takes money. Big money."

Jenna sighed. "It always comes down to that in the end," she observed. "I thought Cornelius was hatching some kind of scheme to raise the finance."

Sebastian shrugged. "Well, yes, he did say he wanted to introduce me to somebody. I'm supposed to meet up with him in a café later on. Only I'm not sure I'm in the mood now, you giving me that news and everything."

"Don't be such a baby!" She studied him for a moment. "I suppose . . . you could always come with me," she said.

But he knew from the sound of her voice that this really wasn't a serious option. He would only be in her way. And besides, he wasn't cut out to be a sailor. After his last trip across the sea he had pretty much decided to cross that off his to-do list.

"I don't think so," he said. "Sailing isn't for me. I've gone right off water after that close brush with the kelfers. It's just . . . well, how am I supposed to occupy myself while you're gone?"

"Oh, you'll think of something. Besides"—she fluttered her eyelashes at him—"I've heard that absence makes the heart grow fonder."

"Not possible, in my case." He reached out and placed a hand on hers. "When will you leave?"

She gave him a sheepish look. "In three days," she said.

"Oh . . . perfect." He scowled at her. "I suppose I should be grateful you've given me this much notice. It's a wonder I didn't wake up and find a note pinned to the door. *Gone south. Back in two moons.*"

She laughed and lifted her tankard. "Oh come on, don't be such a misery! The time will fly by, you'll see. And who knows, maybe we'll use whatever money is left from my trip to start our treasure-hunting fund."

He lifted his own tankard and drank dutifully, but the ale seemed to have lost its flavor and he found himself wondering how he was going to pass the time till she was home again.

He found Cornelius sitting at one of the tables of the outdoor café, opposite a prosperous-looking merchant in richly embroidered robes. Max, who had been assigned to help Cornelius get around while he was recovering from his wound, was tethered to a rail a short distance away from the two men. He was quite clearly eavesdropping on their conversation. Sebastian sidled up to the buffalope and murmured in his ear.

"What's it all about?" he asked.

"What's it *always* about?" grunted Max disapprovingly. "Pipe dreams and nonsense." He snorted. "Plus, of course, the prospect of some cash."

Sebastian thought about that. Maybe if he came up with enough gold, he could finance the trip to the treasure cave himself, and be waiting for Jenna with a fortune in gold and precious jewels. "Who's the stiff in the fancy robes?" he whispered.

Max made a face. "His name's Thaddeus Peel. A Berundian oil merchant. Aren't they always the ones with the fat wallets?"

Sebastian smothered a smile. Max had always had a dim view of Berundians. True, one *had* overcharged them for oil on the road to Keladon, but such a deep-seated dislike must have had more foundation than that. He told himself that he really must ask Max about that some time. But for the moment there were more pressing matters.

"Is he going to fund our expedition?" he asked Max.

"Don't think so. I gather he has an agenda of his own."

At that moment Cornelius glanced up and saw Sebastian. "Ah, here's the fellow I was telling you about!" he roared. "Sebastian, don't stand there skulking. Come over and meet Thaddeus!"

Sebastian gave Max a wary look, but he went oblig-ingly over and shook the fat, beringed fingers that the merchant held out to him.

"Mr. Darke," said Thaddeus in a soft but deep voice. "Captain Drummel has been singing your praises. He was just telling me how you beat that rascal Trencherman in bloody hand-to-hand combat."

"Was he now?" Sebastian took a seat at the table and Cornelius poured him a goblet of wine. "And did he tell you how lucky I was to survive?"

"Luck had nothing to do with it!" roared Cornelius, slapping Sebastian on the shoulder and nearly making him spill his wine. "He's too modest, Mr. Peel! You'll not find a more intrepid adventurer anywhere in Ramalat, I can assure you. Why, in these parts he's known as Sebastian Darke, Prince of Explorers! He'd be the perfect choice to lead your expedition."

"Expedition?" Sebastian brightened a little. "Then you *are* interested in our treasure hunt?"

Cornelius shook his head. "I told Thaddeus all about the treasure. And he admitted he might be prepared to fund us *another time*."

"Another time? But—"

"But for now he has a different quest in mind."

"Oh yes?" Sebastian looked at the merchant, puzzled and slightly annoyed. "What would that be?"

Thaddeus Peel smiled and leaned back in his chair. "Mr. Darke," he said, "what do you know of the jungles of Mendip?"

"I know they cover the whole of the Southlands," ventured Sebastian. "A green wilderness as far as the eye can see, even from the highest vantage point. I know that few men have ventured far beyond its edge. And I have heard people tell fanciful stories of how they are inhabited by monsters—"

"Monsters?" said Max, his voice full of dread. "W-what kind of monsters?"

Sebastian ignored him. "Others say that the jungles are cursed and there are many who would not dream of setting foot there."

"Oh, and a curse too. Lovely!" muttered Max.

Thaddeus Peel nodded. "And among all those stories, Mr. Darke, did you ever hear one about a mysterious lost city?"

Sebastian shook his head. "I can't say that I did," he admitted.

"Well, I have heard such stories, many times. Deep in the heart of the jungle, the legend says, lies a fabulous lost city belonging to a once-mighty empire, now fallen into ruin, but packed with treasures just waiting to be plundered. For some time now, the talk among the Brotherhood has been about the possibility of these stories being based on fact."

"The Brotherhood?" echoed Sebastian.

"Yes. It's a society of successful and influential merchants, of which I am a founding member." Thaddeus paused for a moment, looking at his beautifully manicured fingernails as though expecting his companions to congratulate him, but nobody said anything, so he continued. "We have discussed this matter in great detail and have decided that an expedition must be mounted to ascertain the truth and bring back proof of the city's existence."

"Hah!" said Max. "And where would you hope to find anybody stupid enough to go on such a trip?"

There was a long uncomfortable silence. Thaddeus glared at the buffalope, clearly affronted by his interruption. "Somebody should teach that impertinent beast to hold his tongue," he muttered sourly.

Sebastian shrugged. "I've been trying to do that for years," he said. "In the end I had to admit defeat. Bringing down a wicked king or an evil sea captain, that's one thing; persuading a cantankerous buffalope to accept his place in life is quite another."

Thaddeus tried to force a smile, but it was clear that his feathers had been ruffled. He cleared his throat and took a mouthful of wine before continuing.

"Yes . . . well . . . naturally, such an expedition would be fraught with danger, no matter how intrepid its leader. That is why I and my fellow merchants are offering a king's ransom for anyone willing to undertake the challenge. And an even more handsome bonus should they return with proof of the fabled city's existence."

"It would need to be a considerable amount to make me consider a journey like that," said Sebastian.

Thaddeus nodded. He took another sip of his wine,

leaving a couple of red crescents at the corners of his mouth. "What would you say to five hundred gold crowns?" he asked. "And another five for a success-ful conclusion?"

"Shadlog's teeth!" exclaimed Cornelius, then coughed self-consciously. "That, er . . . would seem an appropriate amount for a mission like that," he added. "Yes, in that general region."

"You are kidding, I hope!" said Max flatly. "To put all our lives at risk in a dank, stinking jungle, the pay-off should be at least ten thousand!"

Sebastian looked at him sharply. "Max," he said, "I don't think—"

"Ten thousand?" mused Thaddeus. "I don't think so. We might be persuaded to go to five thousand, but—"

"Six thousand," said Max. "But I don't know why we're even talking about it, because there's no way the young master would ever—" He broke off because he could see the dreamy look in Sebastian's eyes. "Oh no," he said. "Tell me you're not actually considering this!"

But Sebastian was thinking. He was thinking that with that kind of money in his purse, the trip back to Captain Callinestra's cave was assured; and that Jenna might never have to go away to sea again.

"Very well," said Thaddeus. "Let's say three thou-sand up front and another three on your successful return. But we would require some pretty compelling evidence that the city really exists."

"It's certainly a generous offer," conceded Cornelius. "But my friend and I will need to discuss it in detail. When would you require an answer?"

"I wouldn't wait around too long," said Thaddeus matter-of-factly. "There are plenty of other adventurers in this town who would doubtless take on the task for a lot less than you are asking. But . . . well, you come highly recommended, Mr. Darke, and I feel our best hope of success lies with you. I trust you will accept our offer." He drained the last of his wine and stood up. "I have business to attend to. I will give you until sundown tomorrow to decide. Then I shall look elsewhere." He nodded to Cornelius. "Captain Drummel," he said; and he turned and strode away, looking very full of himself.

"Typical Berundian," muttered Max disdainfully. "Thinks that money can cure any problem."

"You're quite the businessman yourself," Cornelius told him. "You just talked up our fee by five thousand crowns without raising an eyebrow."

Max shrugged. "Oh, it's not so difficult when you know how," he said. "You just have to let them know who's boss. Besides, I was just toying with him. I knew that after all the terrible hardships we've endured recently, we wouldn't even consider going anywhere near that rotten jungle . . . would we?"

Sebastian didn't answer the question, but instead directed one to Cornelius. "How long would an expedition like that take?"

Cornelius frowned. "Impossible to say," he replied. "There's no guarantee that we'd even find this lost city. Chances are, it's just a myth. But think of it this way. Even if we fail to find it, we'd still have three thousand gold crowns in our pockets, enough to finance our own trip."

"But . . . hang on a moment!" argued Max. "Are either of you up to it? Cornelius, you're still limping badly from that kelfer bite; and Sebastian, you very nearly ended up in the belly of one of those sea creatures. Goodness knows what kind of horrors might be lurking in that jungle."

Sebastian smiled at the buffalope. "And my reply to you is the same as ever," he said. "You don't have to come with us—you're free to stay here in a nice, warm stable and relax. After all, Max, you're not as young as you used to be—"

"Nonsense! I'm in my prime! And you know perfectly well that I'm not about to leave the two of you to run things. Why, without my help on that infernal ship you'd both have wound up as fish food!"

Sebastian and Cornelius exchanged smiles. Max had a very high opinion of his own worth, but they both knew that he was quite right. He had saved their skins on innumerable occasions, and to go on any expedition without him would have been unthinkable.

"So it looks as though you are in favor of the trip," observed Cornelius.

Sebastian nodded. "It would finance our return to the treasure cave. And besides, Jenna's going to be away for a couple of moons—I'll be at a loose end."

"So decorate the house," said Max. "Have a few lie-ins and the odd flagon of ale! Why must we be forever galloping round the known world, exhausting ourselves?"

"It's good for the soul," Sebastian assured him.

Cornelius grinned. "I'll go straight after Thaddeus and tell him we accept his proposition," he said. "May as well get the ball rolling." He clambered down from his chair and limped off in the direction that the oil merchant had taken. Sebastian and Max stared after him thoughtfully.

"Are you sure he's up to it?" muttered Max.

"Cornelius? Of course. He'd be up to it if he'd lost the whole leg!"

Max sighed. "And I suppose there's nothing I can do to talk you out of this?"

Sebastian shook his head. "Think of it this way," he said. "A large chunk of the treasure we lost was yours. If we can return and secure a portion of it for you, there's no reason why you should ever have to exhaust yourself again. Imagine, Max, a life of relaxation. All the fresh fruit you can eat and even the odd bucket of ale."

"Hmm." Max looked doubtful. "Excuse me, but my life just doesn't work out that way. At least, it hasn't so far. And I may remind you of this conversation when we're dying of heat in the middle of some stinking jungle swamp." He sighed again. "Now, come on," he said. "Since it looks like we've only a few days to rest our heels, you can take me to the Spyglass Inn and buy me that bucket of ale now!"

"Only if you promise not to sing," Sebastian warned him.

"The very idea!" Max looked positively affronted. "I'll have you know, I come from a very respectable family. I can assure you, they'd never have stood for any of that kind of behavior!"

"Is that so?" murmured Sebastian. He stood up, unhitched Max and led him back in the direction of the tavern. "So what happened the last time we were in there? That was just an oversight, was it?"

"I haven't the faintest idea what you're talking about," said Max haughtily. "Not the foggiest! Really, sometimes I think you make up these stories, just to vex me!"

EPILOGUE

"Well, I suppose this is goodbye," said Sebastian mournfully.

The *Sea Witch* was fully provisioned and ready to sail. The crew moved around the decks, making their last-minute adjustments with practiced ease. The sails flapped beneath a stiff breeze, eager to be tilted into the wind, to move the ship away from the dock and out into open water.

"I'll be back soon enough," Jenna assured him. "Besides, you'll be off on your own travels any time now."

"The day after tomorrow," admitted Sebastian. "Well, there's nothing to keep me here now, is there?" He glanced over the ship's rail toward the quayside, where he saw Cornelius and Max bickering about something. Bickering already and they hadn't even left Ramalat. Not for the first time, he asked himself if he had made a terrible mistake.

Other people were saying their goodbyes too. The Kid had signed on as cabin boy for the voyage, quite a step down from being captain of his own ship, but he was determined to prove himself a trustworthy seaman. He was over by the forecastle, bidding farewell to his father. Captain Jack Donovan was looking a lot healthier than he had back on that remote island. He had put on a bit of weight and his eyes had lost their hollow, sunken look.

His return to Ramalat had caused an uproar, and several days later he had hired one of his former friends to take him across to Lemora in search of his old adversaries Bones and Sully. After a short interval he had returned to Ramalat. Nobody knew for sure what had happened over there, but there hadn't been a sign of Bones and Sully since Donovan's visit and nobody cared about them enough to go looking for them. Since then, however, Donovan appeared to have turned over a new leaf. He was working in one of the local carpenter's shops, employing some of the skills he had picked up while marooned on the treasure island.

As Sebastian watched, the Kid and his father shook hands and strolled back toward the gangplank.

"Make sure he does everything he's told," Captain

Donovan told Jenna. "I want at least one of the family to have a respectable career."

"I'll watch out for him," Jenna promised.

"I'll bring you back a souvenir from the south coast," the Kid promised his father with a grin. "And you make sure you don't get into any trouble."

"I'm done with all that now," said Donovan. "From here on I'm going to walk along the right path." He bowed to Jenna and Sebastian, and then turned and left the ship. He nodded to Cornelius and Max as he walked by, but they were too busy arguing to even notice him.

"Well . . . ," said Jenna. "I suppose we really should weigh anchor now." She nodded to Lemuel, who in turn strode away to give orders to the other crewmen.

Sebastian nodded. He looked at her for a moment, wishing there was something else he could say, but he couldn't think of anything; so he took her in his arms and held her tightly. He had a sudden powerful feeling that he would never see her again and he wanted to tell her about it, but couldn't seem to find the right words.

"I think this is where you're supposed to kiss her," suggested the Kid gleefully.

Sebastian glared at him. "Don't you start!" he growled. "You've obviously been spending too much time with Max." But he *did* kiss her lightly on the lips and then, with a forced smile, he turned away and went quickly down the gangplank. He trudged across to Cornelius and Max, who were still arguing.

". . . and I say it's ridiculous, hiring a big heavy wagon like that," said Max. "We'll have to go along jungle trails and it will get bogged down."

"Who says we're taking it into the jungle?" retorted Cornelius. "No, we leave the wagon at the edge, hidden under the vegetation, and we continue on foot, carrying the equipment we need on pack animals—"

"Oh and I suppose you include me in that category, do you?"

"Well, naturally, I would have thought that you'd like to contribute to the expedition. Or perhaps you think you're—"

"You two," snapped Sebastian, in a voice harsh enough to silence both of them. "If you are going to bicker all the way through this expedition, I for one am not going. Do I make myself clear?"

They fell into a sullen silence and watched as the ship's huge anchors were winched from the sea bed. Powerful hands heaved on ropes and the sails began to billow as they filled with wind. The *Sea Witch* moved smoothly away from the quayside. Sebastian could see Jenna leaning on the rail. Beside her, the

Kid lifted a hand to wave. Sebastian waved back automatically.

"Isn't it strange how all your women keep leaving you?" said Max.

Sebastian looked at him. "What do you mean?" he said irritably. "*All* my women? I've only had two."

"Three if you count the witch," said Cornelius.

"You can't really include her," said Max, "because she changed into a big cat and died. But the other two, they both gave him the cold shoulder."

"I haven't had the cold shoulder!" protested Sebastian. "Princess Kerin had to sacrifice her feelings for the good of her people. And Jenna . . . well, she has a job to do, that's all. She'll be back in a couple of moons."

"Yes, but you have to wonder, don't you? One woman alone on a ship full of men for all that time. And some of the crew are very good-looking—"

"Max," said Sebastian quietly, "I'd like you to be quiet now. OK?"

"But I—"

"Shut up!"

Max made a discontented huffing sound, but he didn't say anything more. Sebastian stood there watching intently until the ship had dwindled to a tiny black dot on the horizon. Then he turned and walked away along the quay.

"Hey, wait for us!" yelled Cornelius. He hurried after Sebastian and fell into step beside him, still limping slightly. Max dropped into position on his other side.

"So . . . where to now?" he asked.

"To the jungles of Mendip," said Sebastian quietly. "And whatever fate awaits us there."

Philip Caveney has
written many novels
for adults. This is his
second book for young
adults. He lives in England.